Donated by
Women of Sugarmill Woods

A WRINKLE IN CRIME

A MAY LIST MYSTERY

A WRINKLE IN CRIME

T. DAWN RICHARD

FIVE STAR

An imprint of Thomson Gale, a part of The Thomson Corporation

THOMSON

GALE

Detroit • New York • San Francisco • New Haven, Conn. • Waterville, Maine • London

LIBRARY OF CONGRESS CATALOGING-IN-PUBLICATION DATA

Richard, T. Dawn.
  A wrinkle in crime : a May List mystery / T. Dawn Richard. — 1st ed.
     p. cm.
  ISBN-13: 978-1-59414-534-6 (alk. paper)
  ISBN-10: 1-59414-534-2 (alk. paper)
   1. Older women—Fiction. I. Title.
PS3618.I335W75 2007
  813'.6—dc22
                                                    2006034704

First Edition. First Printing: March 2007.

Published in 2007 in conjunction with Tekno Books and Ed Gorman.

Printed in the United States of America on permanent paper
10 9 8 7 6 5 4 3 2 1

To my husband, Glenn Richard, the first person I look for in a crowded room, a guy who makes a mean cup of coffee at six in the morning, a man with unwavering resolve and courage beyond measure.

ACKNOWLEDGMENTS

Thanks to all of my writer friends in the Northwest Writers Club: Ed Muzatko, Charlotte McCoy, Jeff Lewis, Mark Bessermin, and Gary Hotchkiss. Thanks to Lieutenant Chris Mozingo with the Altus, Oklahoma, Police Department and Corporal James Muzatko, with the Spokane, Washington, Police Department—two officers brave enough to take me along on their rounds and help me with critical details for my books. Thanks to Police Information Coordinator Dick Cottam for patiently answering questions about the Spokane Police Department, and to Dusty and Steve who own Dusty and Steve's Automotive Shop in Spokane, who got my car running and helped me with a bit of research. Thanks to Mannon Wallace, my brother, my friend, my first reader, and advisor on the technical details. To Greg Beeman who provided helpful information, and to Alja K. Collar, senior content project editor, Thomson Gale for Five Star Press. Many thanks to my editor, Alice Duncan; to Mary P. Smith, senior editor at Five Star Publishing; to the production and marketing team at Five Star Publishing; and to John Helfers, acquisitions editor at Tekno Books. Thanks as always to my family, for putting up with the late-night writing marathons, self-serve leftover dinners, and group brainstorming sessions. And thanks to the Airway Heights Friends of the Library—a warm and generous group brimming with talent, a curious nature, and a lively sense of humor.

CHAPTER ONE

The cell door slammed behind me, sounding like the clang of a metallic gavel attached to a long prison sentence.

"So. Whatcha in for, lady?" asked a skinny, half-dressed woman in the corner. She slid glazed eyes around to look me over and I could tell she held a standing reservation in the gray bar motel. The miniskirt, plunging neckline, and garish eye makeup said it all. The working ensemble of a gal in life's oldest profession.

"Murder," I responded with a convincing air of faked impudence, since it's important not to show fear when you're doing hard time. Actually, I was quaking in my socks, but that wouldn't do, so I balled my fists, turned to the prison bars, and gave them a hearty punch.

A loud *crack!* sounded when my knuckles hit steel.

"That musta hurt," said a second woman reclining on her bunk.

The pain shot right up to my elbow and I had to hold my breath for a few seconds before turning to face my new roommates. I answered weakly, "Not at all. Do it all the time."

"Then why ya eyes all red like you're gonna cry?" The first woman stepped away from her corner and sauntered over.

I pressed my back to the bars. "They're not red," I argued.

"Sure, they are. You on dope or something?"

"Yeah. That's it. I'm flying high. Wanta make something of it?"

The two women exchanged amused glances. "Really, lady, why ya in here? Forget to pay your taxes?"

"I told you. Murder." My tough demeanor was fading.

"I don't think so," the woman on the bunk said. "You look just like my granny and she couldn't kill time."

I crumpled, but maintained the lingo of the illicit. "Yeah, okay. So you made me. I didn't pop anyone, but I'm goin' down for the murder. Just my dumb luck. Wrong place—wrong time."

"So why don't you tell us your story? We got nothin' else to do in here." The woman on the bunk put her hands behind her head, stretching the buttons on her blouse.

"Well," I began, moving over to the bunk. I took a place beside my cellmate. "Gather around then, ladies, 'cuz I've got a story to tell. The trouble started when the police found a body in the trunk of my car."

The bunk lady sat up fast. "You had a body in your car?"

"Yeah. Bummer, huh?"

"Someone you know?"

"I'd met him briefly. And, well, actually the trouble started before the body showed up. Guess I'd better back up just a little."

CHAPTER TWO

The trouble really started after reading Gerty Knickers' obituary in the morning paper. I should have clucked my tongue, said a few "what a shame"s, and checked my pulse—just to be sure my own ticker was strong and steady—but of course I didn't. Instead, I stuck my nose into her business and it nearly got me killed. Some things don't go according to plan and that's usually okay. As for me, though, if I must be honest, most of my bright ideas turn into complete disasters.

My name is May Bell List. I'm sixty-seven years old, I've lost my purse again, and I'm a detective. The title isn't altogether official and I can't put it on a legal résumé but if life experience counts for anything, I should be getting my badge pretty soon.

I wasn't always this way, scrapping with perps and getting it on with reprobates—far from it. For years, my life had been one of social engagements, domestic tranquility, child rearing, charity work, and the occasional cruise or spa weekend where mud became therapeutic, and naps cost thousands. The life of a doctor's wife is full of opportunity and prosperity, and after years of thinking this was my lucky fortune, I found myself wondering where the years had gone, and why I was frittering away my time with the mundane when what I really wanted was excitement. Drama. Trauma. Danger and intrigue.

And why not? My daughter was grown and married, my doctor husband spent most of his time at the hospital, and somewhere along the way organizing aluminum drives for the limbless just didn't have the thrill it once had. I'd watched enough episodes of *Murder She Wrote* to know how to act and what to look for at a crime scene, and I was definitely good with people. I could spot a liar a mile away. I could do some good in this world with my keen senses and curious nature, and besides—a little police work would give me the research material I needed to write a mystery novel: my secret passion.

So now I'm flirting with the underworld, reading true-crime books like nobody's business (when I'm not vacuuming), and I'm recognizing malevolence around every corner. That's what happens when you know what you're doing. I am becoming brave and fearless. And because of my newly honed instincts when it comes to sniffing out crime, something about Mrs. Knickers' sudden demise made me sit up and take notice, because, although I didn't know her well at the time of her death, I had enough suspicions about what had happened to Gerty the night of her passing to question the obit's accompanying article, which said her husband had found her dead of a heart attack. Naturally, I didn't believe she'd been stricken with a common infarction. Oh, no! I was certain she'd been murdered, and I was going to prove it one way or another.

My conclusions were ignited by something she'd said two weeks earlier while I dined with Gerty and her two sisters—a comment she made that would give plenty of people motive for wanting to knock her off.

Like I said. I didn't know her well, but we did occasionally do lunch.

The morning I read the news of Mrs. Gerty's passing had started as a typical weekend. I was in my robe sipping coffee and eating toast at my breakfast table. Outside my kitchen window, what started as an overcast sky gave way to a slow, relentless drizzle. Wet trails ran down the panes of glass, reminding me that Ted needed to work on those gutters, and heeding the forecast, our paperboy had shoved the *Spokesman Review* into an orange plastic wrapper to keep it dry. Didn't much matter; it still had soggy edges. Autumn had officially come to call in the Northwest. Chilly, wet, and gray.

While the obituary didn't give many details, the third-page article about the town's public figure did. I patted the top of my head in search of reading glasses, couldn't find them there, so I squinted and read:

Local artist dead at the age of 78. Mr. Bernard Knickers, husband of the deceased, found his wife slumped over her drawing table Friday morning. She had a paint brush lodged in one nostril and was apparently painting a portrait when she died of natural causes. According to Mr. Knickers, his wife had a history of coronary disease . . .

Coronary disease? This was certainly news to me. I recalled our lunch and the subsequent visit to an art exhibit where Gerty had bounced and bubbled, enthusiastically showing off her featured paintings, explaining the colors and shades with gusto. She'd been spry, effervescent, and vibrant. She'd even told me about her plans to compete in the next Spokane Bloomsday 12K run. She'd taken up biking. She did yoga. Her complexion was dewy; her cheeks blushed a charming pink. No telltale blue tinge around the lips, no shortness of breath, no indication at all she was ailing. Who'd have known she'd soon be cleaning her last brush? Fascinating.

My attention turned once again to the article. More details, a lot of mumbo jumbo about how Mrs. Knickers had a quirky habit of painting late into the evening, sometimes all night even, and how she was well respected in the local community, something about her work, her admirable involvement with a regional environmentalist group called FETA (Folks for the

Ethical Treatment of Animals), the Humane Society, the South Side Soup Kitchen, Habitat for Humanity, and the usual blah, blah, blah.

"Got the sports section there?" Ted, my husband of more years than I care to count, ambled his long skinny legs into the kitchen wearing green silk boxers and pink fluffy slippers. His heels went well beyond the backs of my favorite house shoes and he didn't seem to mind that he was squashing them.

Ted caught my disapproving eyes staring at his feet.

"Couldn't find my own," he said without apology.

Curtly, I replied, "I think I can help you there. I soaked them in bleach and now they're in the washer. On rinse, I do believe." I placed the newspaper on the table and stabbed at the butter.

Ted looked crestfallen. "May, those are expensive, Italian leather slippers."

"They were," I said, and slathered my toast.

"I guess they're beyond saving now."

"Really?" I put on my innocent face. "Don't consider it a total loss, Ted. Trixie can wear them on her tiny little paws after I leave them in the dryer a couple of hours." I glanced over at my cat. She curled her lip at me in a wicked, conspiratorial smile.

Ted frowned.

"Oh, stop moping, sourpuss. They're under the bed where they always are," I said, wishing I had thrown them in with the socks. "Just a word of caution, Ted—I've decided to start putting loaded mousetraps in the toes of my fuzzies from now on. Maybe that will help keep your big feet out of them. Look there. You've smashed them all down now. I'm sure they're ruined."

Ted shuffled across the kitchen floor, not bothering to kick off my slippers despite the tongue-lashing. He leaned into the refrigerator and came out with a pint of cottage cheese.

"What are you eating?" I asked. "It's Saturday, Ted—you

always have pancakes on Saturday. I've whipped up the batter—it's there for you on the counter."

"Thanks, but I'm gonna skip it. Starting my new fitness program today—Maybe Baby." Ted found the spoons and scooped white glop into his mouth. It was pretty disgusting but I admired his enthusiasm. "Going for a quick jog around the block after breakfast, and then I think I'll do some work around the house. Maybe replace some shingles. Don't know yet, just need to keep moving."

I waved him away and went back to my paper. Fitness program at our age? What's the point? A circular fell from the center of the paper to the floor. I let it lie, not wanting to strain an abdominal muscle. I bit my toast.

"Here's the sports section," I said around a mouthful, and handed it to Ted, who accepted it gratefully. He was marching in place, inspiring the flaccid muscles on his chest to jiggle up and down like a wave, and he looked over the sports page while trying to lick the inner sides of the cottage cheese carton.

"Oh, by the way," Ted said, "some police officer called while you were in the shower."

I stopped chewing. My nerves began to jitter. I turned cold, wondering if the Spokane Police Department had caught me doing twenty-eight in the school zone. How could they have known?

"He said your paperwork has been approved. You're scheduled for three o'clock today."

"Oh." I breathed a sigh of relief and swallowed the ball of toast. "That's good. The paperwork has gone through." I sipped coffee, feeling my nervous system return to a manageable hum. I'd momentarily forgotten the news of my dead friend in the wake of envisioned cavity searches and incarceration. The prospect had given me quite a scare.

"Paperwork for what?" Ted stopped marching and plopped

down into one of the kitchen chairs. He stuck his spoon in the cottage cheese and plunked the plastic container on the table, after which he shook out the sports page like it was an event. There were a few little white curds stuck to his gray chest hairs but he didn't mind. I leaned over and brushed them away with my toast crust.

"I applied for a ride-along program," I explained. "Don't you remember I told you? You never listen. Anyway, it's one of those community service things where civilians get to be a cop for a day. Doesn't it sound thrilling?"

Ted looked at me over the top of his reading glasses in that way he had. *May Bell's off her rocker again.* I think he was getting used to my unusual activities in the detective world, but he still felt the need to act sensibly, just to believe that one of us in the marriage was sane.

"If it makes you embarrassed, you just tell your friends I'm collecting data for my mystery novel."

"Who says I'm embarrassed?" Ted raised his eyebrows. "I'm just afraid one of these days you're going to get hurt running around pretending you're a cop."

"Oh, don't worry about me." I put on my confident face. "I think they'll teach me how to use their guns or something just in case." I tore the Gerty story from the rest of the paper, folded it, and shoved it in my robe pocket.

"Just in case what?"

"Who knows? And guess what else, Ted." I leaned over the table on my elbows, unable to hide my excitement. "I'm working on some high-speed chase stuff. You know, what if the police officer is down and I have to take the wheel or something?"

"So, you've finally gotten the Camaro up past fifty?"

I let the sarcasm slide. Of course I hadn't pushed the old Camaro up past fifty. What did he think I was—mad?

"It's all simulated, Ted. I bought one of those computer game things. You know, where I use a happy stick and race around the track and avoid pitfalls and obstacles. It's very realistic and I'm getting the hang of it."

"Oh, yeah. That works." Ted snickered. "Do me a favor, May. Learn how to use the police radio. Then if an officer is down like you say, phone a friend. On second thought, wear your emergency-alert necklace. 'Help, I'm shot and I can't get up!' "

"You go ahead, Ted. Make fun." I stood and gathered my plate, complete with cottage cheese toast crust. I dropped the whole mess into the sink with a lot of noise. Ted wasn't paying attention, so I picked up the plate and dropped it in again. Since it broke into three pieces this time, Ted took notice.

"It would do you some good to enroll in a few self-defense courses yourself, you know. These are dangerous times, Ted, dangerous times. You never can tell what horrors might be lurking around the corner." I shook my finger at him.

"You've been watching *Forensic Files* again, haven't you?" Ted scooped the last of his cottage cheese and shoveled it into his cynical yap.

"At least I won't end up like her. I reached into my pocket and snatched out the story of Gerty. I stepped over to my husband and waved the page under Ted's nose. "Gerty Knickers is dead. She's been murdered."

"Is that what it says?" Ted tracked my hand, made some air grabs, and finally got hold of the paper. He crumpled it, but not too badly, gave it a glance, and handed it back.

"Of course that's not what it says here. A heart attack, they say. Inevitable considering her condition, they say." I thumped the paper with the back of my hand.

"But naturally, you think there's foul play involved." Ted stroked his neck and stared at the ceiling.

"You just keep it up, mister. When I crack this case we'll see who's laughing." I bent down and snatched my slippers off of his feet. "And from now on, wear your own darn clothes."

I stuffed the article back into my pocket and left the kitchen in a huff, while Ted called after me.

"You mean I can't borrow your brassieres anymore?"

Ted was snorting. I guess he thought he was a funny guy. I quickly moved out of earshot before he did anything to make me say something I'd regret. I had a busy day ahead of me, and I simply couldn't be bothered with nonsense.

While dressing for the day, I planned my schedule. First, I would pay a visit to Inez and Bertha Peach. They were the younger siblings of Mrs. Gerty and a little on the rugged side, if you get my drift. If I had to guess, they were in their late sixties, never married, professional gals.

The sisters owned the Poochie Hooch, a pet-grooming facility west of Spokane in a town called Hunker Hills, where I took Trixie for her flea dips and cat baths. As a new resident to Spokane, and not knowing all the avenues and dark alleys or their questionable reputations, I'd found the Poochie Hooch while perusing the yellow pages. Hunker Hills was inhabited by the more "colorful" citizens of Spokane County. Not shackled by social pomp, they scratched out a living through hard work and grit, and when warranted and the beer was flowing, settled disputes with fists or hunting rifles. If I'd known what types of people lived in that section of the city, I would have been nervous venturing there, but after forming a business relationship it wouldn't have been polite to cut and run. Besides, through our business dealings, Bertha and Inez had become my friends; they'd taken a liking to me for some reason, their personalities were delightful, and so I was often invited to accompany them on their weekly lunches with Gerty.

Gerty was nothing like her sisters. By all appearances she was successful, thriving in a tenuous vocation, and had carved out a lucrative career as an artist. She wore the right clothes, knew what fork to use for her salads, oozed grace and sophistication, and spoke impeccable English. Away from the admiring crowds, however, she used a tone of derision and contempt when speaking to Inez and Bertha—they were a disappointment to her. If I had never seen them together I would have liked Gerty, but despite her cordiality to strangers, she could be cruel to her own family. I mustered polite conversation, but at the end of the day, I was much more comfortable hanging out with Bertha and Inez, even with all their rough edges and bad grammar.

Gerty's death would have been quite a shock to the Peach sisters, and it would be my charitable duty to offer them some consoling. After tending to them, I would be cop for a day. I just hoped I wouldn't have to perform any high-speed chases. I'd lied to Ted. Actually, I hadn't done too well on the game track, but he didn't need to know that, did he?

The day was getting away from me and I had to get over to the Poochie Hooch. The Peach sisters were waiting. And . . . maybe once I got there, I could do a little snooping into this Gerty business.

CHAPTER THREE

After makeup, I selected a pair of comfortable slacks, a blouse, a string of pearls with matching earrings, and some athletic shoes (in case I had to chase down a perp or something). My mood was greatly improved. I'd cooled off enough that I decided I would smooch my husband goodbye. He'd be on his own for the day, and I felt bad about leaving him unassisted to his exercise program but I just couldn't be his athletic supporter today. This was his day off, Saturday, no rounds at the hospital unless Mrs. Kimble decided to deliver her twins early, so he might get lonely with me gone.

I headed back into the kitchen, where I'd left the good doctor with a full pot of coffee. I had my lips pursed, ready to give Ted the kiss-off, when I got the shock of my life. It was nothing, though, compared to the shock Ted was taking as he stood beside the microwave. It was a horrible sight, and not one I'll soon forget. Ted had been serious about working on the house, and he'd apparently decided the counter outlets needed to be rewired.

A cord ran up the length of his waist, and Ted was taking on maximum voltage. His eyes were rolled back in his head; he jerked like a rag doll, and flapped his hands at his sides. His feet stomped up and down. Ghastly.

I did the only thing I could think of at the time. There was a broom handy, and I took charge of the situation. I had to get Ted away from the electric currents ravaging his helpless flailing body, and I had to do it fast. Already my CPR training was coming to mind. No doubt I'd need that when I got him free and onto the floor. Was that two breaths, three compressions? Or should I start with a Heimlich?

With a yowl of bravado I leapt forward and thwacked Ted with that broom. The act went against every bit of wifely instinct I had, but I knew it was for his own good. I just closed my eyes and beat him like a piñata at a San Antonio birthday party. Whack! Whack! Swing, whack! It had to be done.

I must . . . thwack! . . . save . . . thwack! . . . my . . . thwack! . . . husband! It was a horrible thing. I'm not too strong, but I smacked at him for all I was worth. I just couldn't watch, but I hoped my thrusts and jabs were doing some good.

"May, what am I now, your urban legend?" Ted grabbed at the broom and tossed it aside.

I opened my eyes.

Ted pulled his iPod earbuds out and glared at me. The little wires hung around his neck and there was quite a bit of broom straw sticking out of his hair.

I realized my error. He never had been a very good dancer— should have recognized the spastic two-step. I felt my face grow hot, but turned on my heels to hide my embarrassment.

"That will teach you never to wear my slippers again." I marched out, mortified at what I'd done, but I think I covered my mistake pretty well. He had it coming, after all.

It was raining hard when I jogged from the house to my car. I covered my head with my purse hoping the rain would let up a bit, because although it was October, the weather around Spokane could turn in a minute and that would mean snow and ice. I couldn't be hindered by that when there was so much investigating to do.

I turned the key in the ignition, thumbed on the wipers, and checked my face in the rearview mirror. Pink lipstick that hadn't yet settled into the little lines spreading like rivulets around my mouth, heavy mascara, dab of rouge, and a new hairdo—sort of a swoop-up-and-back thing, quite attractive if I do say so myself, and the color wasn't too bad. After a professional fashion disaster, I'd taken to doing the color myself. A golden blond, because, you know, I'm worth it and all.

Once on the road I relaxed a bit and wound my way down the hill, mindful of the traffic and one-way streets. While Ted and I loved our new place in Washington, I'd never felt quite at home living in the South Hill neighborhood. Oh, it was beautiful, upscale and handy; our neighbors were generally nice (with the exception of the guy across the street named Mr. Fitz, a real busybody); but lately I was trying to talk my husband into relocating to a place north of town, a little bedroom community called Harvest, a place I'd learned about when riding with Bertha and Inez to pick up Gerty for our lunch. She'd lived there for years before going DOA. In the fall, it was overrun with bright-eyed locals and tourists encouraged to pick their own apples, sample some hot cider, run wild through the corn mazes. Besides being green, pristine, and peaceful, it was full of my kind of people: creative, goofy, talkative, and inspiring.

I imagined a cozy log cabin on a wooded hill there, with a vegetable garden and a coop full of chickens. I had all the house-building magazines, but Ted was less than enthusiastic.

"We're comfortable here, May Bell. Why do you want to go rock the boat?"

Ho hum. Something had to give. Restlessness is what you call it, boredom, frustration, plain old tedium. I needed drama in my life. High drama.

I thought of Gerty. Dead Gerty. Was she dead because she'd been a flirty Gerty? Dirty Gerty? Too talkative perhaps. Wordy Gerty? Maybe the reports were right. Maybe she'd just keeled over because of a faulty ticker. I hated to think that way; a good solid murder was much more alluring.

Suddenly I had an inspiration. I grabbed my cell phone and punched some numbers. It was difficult to talk and drive at the same time so I slowed the car to accommodate the added hand-to-eye coordination requirement. A black Toyota behind me tried to pass, nearly hit an oncoming Jeep, swerved behind me again, and honked loudly. I waved and stuck the phone between my cheek and shoulder. Ted answered after two rings.

"Hullo?"

"Ted. I need a favor."

"Whazzat?"

"Get the SPD on the phone and tell them I want to change my assignment. I want to do my ride-along with someone from the Harvest Police Department."

"SPD?"

"Spokane Police Department. They have my paperwork. I'm sure it won't be difficult for them to arrange. Call me back."

I slapped the phone closed and dropped it onto the seat beside me. Just as the Toyota started to pass again I stepped on the gas. The driver honked again but fell back.

This was perfect. Perfect! My plan was twofold. First, if I could get in with the Harvest cops, learn about their operation, and establish myself in the community, maybe I could convince Ted to move there. And second, this was Gerty's town. Someone from that area would have to know the morbid details about her death. I was a genius.

I looked both ways and readied myself. When all was clear, I pulled out onto the highway. There were plenty of lanes for everyone, but apparently everyone wanted mine. Driving in Spokane was practically an art form and not for anyone with a nervous bladder. I sat up straight in my seat and put my hands at ten and two. Elbows out, I leaned forward and sped down the road.

The obnoxious Toyota driver blared his horn at me one last time as he attempted another pass. I turned to wave and noticed he was pointing his finger at me, stabbing it really, like he was poking holes in a balloon, as he rumbled over the bumps along the shoulder. His head was bouncing in a staccato fashion. Sheesh. I hadn't wandered that far over into his lane. I jerked back, held my car steady, and stomped on the gas. Ha! That'll show Ted. The speedometer needle hovered around forty. The Toyota whipped around on my left, still riding the shoulder, pointed a finger at me again, and pulled away just to insult me. A van passed me on the right and sprayed rain spittle over the side of my car.

I was making good time, but the Poochie Hooch was still about fifteen miles away. The weather was nasty and it was no time to be careless on the road. Remembering my turn signal for at least a good thirty seconds beforehand, I moved into the middle lane heading in a westerly direction. Despite my driving precautions, a monstrous grill suddenly filled my rearview mirror. Through the gray sheets of rain I saw the semi truck bearing down fast. I pushed the gas pedal, urging my Camaro up a notch. The truck wasn't slowing. In fact, it looked as if it would climb right onto the trunk of my car. Willing myself to stay calm, I gripped the wheel tightly and looked rapidly from left to right, searching out an escape route. Nothing. Both lanes to either side of me were full, and I was at the mercy of the crack maniac on my tail. More speed. I needed to put the hammer down.

There was something ominous about that truck. It stayed with me mile after mile, and even started blinking his lights and blaring his horn. What did he want? A couple of times I even caught a glance at the driver—a ferocious hairy-faced man, glowering and motioning to me. Crack maniacs everywhere. Just as the truck started to swing around me, probably to get in a position where he could ram my Camaro and force me off the road, I noticed an exit sign on my right. This was my chance.

No time for the signal, I cranked the wheel hard, shot across two lanes, and hit the exit ramp doing forty-five. Colors of blue and green and mauve swirled around me with a lot of honking and screeching, but I was clear. I struggled to maintain control, failed, and whipped and swerved like a rogue fire hose after misjudging the ramp's angle and curve. I slid sideways through a parking lot, dodged several cars, screamed wildly, went airborne over a speed bump and helplessly skidded across the wet pavement toward a McDonald's restaurant. After doing a complete 360, I shuddered to a stop in front of the order microphone. Trembling, I slowly rolled down my window.

"Hi," came the perky voice. "Welcome to McDonald's. May I take your order please?"

My chin quivered when I replied, "How did you know my name?"

"Excuse me, ma'am?"

"My name? How did you know it?"

"Are you going to order, or what?"

"My name is May. You said May, can I take your order? How did you know that was my name?" The adrenaline rush had pushed me into a paranoid frenzy. I was ready to get out and wrench that darn metal box off its moorings. There was a whole lot of spooky stuff going on.

"Ma'am, I said *may* I take your order please? Now you wanta super size or what?"

"Excuse me? How rude! I might be larger than your average woman, but you can hardly call me super size." I was shouting at the box now, still quaking from my narrow brush with death.

A loud sigh came through the box, followed by a lengthy

pause. Then, "Can I interest you in a cup of coffee perhaps?"

I cleared my throat and smoothed down my collar. "Yes. Yes, that would be rather nice. A latte would be good." Rain smacked me in the face. My up-do was quickly turning into a flat-do.

"I'm sorry, we don't have lattes. Just plain old coffee." The voice sounded weary.

"Fine. Not too hot. Just put some cream in it, okay?" I craned around the steering wheel, rubbed my sleeve over the inside of the fogged windshield, and looked for a face to connect with the voice but all I saw was the side of a window. I took deep, cleansing breaths for relaxation, closed my eyes, and felt the raindrops poke at my neck.

"May?"

There it was again! Someone was calling my name! I jerked upright and looked around me.

"Er, May, ma'am, you have to drive forward. We have your coffee ready."

I worked the clutch and gas with my gelatinous legs and pulled forward cautiously. When I got to the window, three pimply-faced girls filled the space and giggled as I took the coffee.

"You have a holder for that?" the voice I recognized asked.

"This is a '67 Camaro. They didn't come with holders back then. I'll just put it between my legs."

"No!" the girls chorused. "We'll find you a holder."

While I waited, my nerves calmed considerably. I was quite proud of the scald scare I'd given the gawkers.

One of the girls stayed behind, leaning on a little shelf just inside the window. She chewed open-mouthed on a huge piece of green gum. She blew a bubble and then sucked it back in.

"Just thought you might want to know," the girl said, "your coat is hanging out the side of your door."

Oh my. She was right. The hem of my nice wool coat was

slammed in the door, all brown and wet when I pulled it in. That truck driver probably thought he was doing his good deed for the day. My hem would have been flapping like a white flag all the way down the highway, but how could I have known that? He didn't have to scare a poor old woman half to death to point this out, did he?

I took the coffee, gave each of the girls a dollar tip, and continued on my way, safely and calmly, toward the Poochie Hooch. I wasn't expecting Bertha and Inez to be at their place of business so soon after their sister's demise, but they had a home number on their shop door, one I could write in my notebook, a number I could dial to get them on the phone in order to offer up my sympathies. I'll have to admit, my desire to talk with the sisters wasn't completely altruistic. I was increasingly curious about Gerty—why she died, and who might be involved—and yes, I probably could have found their home number in the phone book but that would have interfered with an opportunity to snoop at the Hooch.

My phone rang.

"Hello?"

Ted was on the line. "It's all set. It took some doing, but you're scheduled to ride with an Officer Murphy. He'll meet you at the Harvest precinct."

"At three o'clock?"

"Yeah. By the way, they wanted to know why you requested the switch."

"What did you tell them?"

"That you couldn't find your way to the Spokane Police Department."

"Oh, Ted. They'll think I'm an idiot."

"No they won't. I took care of that. I just said you had a hint of dementia. They were very understanding."

"Thanks." I growled.

"No probs, Baby Cakes!"

"Gotta go, Ted." I folded up the phone and slid it into my coat pocket.

A glance at my watch told me there was plenty of time before my shift at the police station. No need to hurry. The rain accompanied me as I rumbled down Highway 90 past some pastures and fields, and soon I entered the tiny strip town of Hunker Hills. Just a little while longer and I'd be at the Hooch.

Once in the tiny town I slowed, and noticed on my right a disheveled-looking man ambling down an ill-kept sidewalk pulling a Radio Flyer wagon behind him. His head was tucked under a stained hood in a vain attempt to avoid a total soakage from the pattering rain. A woman I imagined to be his wife was in the wagon. She had a plastic bag on her head and her legs hung over the sides. I waved at them both and the man nodded politely. His wife waved her legs.

I drove on.

Being mindful of the speed limits, I stayed between the white lines and passed a discount movie store, a Taco Bell, a couple of bars, and a motel painted in the most awful-looking purple I'd ever seen. I slammed on my brakes once when some ruffian kids on scooters threatened to dart out into traffic ahead of me. Unfortunately I couldn't avoid mashing a possum I didn't see until I thumped over it with both right tires. That gave me a cringe and a shudder, but what could I do? Veer off and take out a few Crips or Bloods?

I drove on.

Adjacent to the Hunker one-street business district rested a community of trailer homes, piles of abandoned rusted vehicles, stained mattresses, and discarded tires. This was where Inez and Bertha had set up shop.

When I pulled in front of the Poochie Hooch I was surprised to see their *You bet, We're Open!* sign hanging in the door. Maybe they'd hired temporary help while going through the mourning phase.

The Hooch was a rundown trailer house, not so different from ones inhabited by many of the Hunker residents, although it had been transformed into a pseudo-professional structure. Nailed to the building an enterprising sort had erected a sign with the store's name scrawled over it in thick letters from a can of red spray paint: *THE POOCHIE HOOCH!* The insides of the windows were wallpapered with weathered and faded advertisements, price lists, and a proud announcement that said, *Yuh huh! We do cats and small rodents too!*

The parking area was small, a dirt patch cordoned off by railroad ties, and there was no grass at all in the lawn, just some large rocks, a leafless tree, a stained fire hydrant, and a tenant-less birdhouse.

The rain mixed with snow as I walked the short distance from my car to the front door. Just as I feared. We'd have three inches of the white stuff by midnight. I turned the handle and let myself in.

And that's when all hell broke loose.

Chapter Four

My presence in the Poochie Hooch was announced by a legion of barking, frenzied dogs, all trying to out-yap one another. Along a wall to my left were wire cages housing psychotic animals hurling themselves at me. And lucky for me, those cages were sturdy. The racket rattled the walls and caused me to drop my purse. The din was accompanied by a consuming stench of doggie doo, flea-dip solutions, and pup shampoos. It was always this way when I paid my visits, but that's just not something you get used to easily.

There was no one at the counter, and after recovering my purse, I stood waiting for a helper to come from the rear of the trailer. The door leading into the grooming and clipping area was an old Santa Fe–style blanket hanging from a wooden rod. There was some loud cursing from the back and the sound of buzzing. Someone in there was getting a pretty good shave. I could be patient.

On the paneled walls of the Hooch, Bertha or Inez had taped snapshots of their victims. Lucky, Prince, Lars, and Harold looked uncomfortable and embarrassed in their photos, especially the ones with bows clipped to their ears. Trixie was up there too, but she just looked furious.

Out of the corner of my eye, I saw a weathered hand reach out through the door and the blanket was forcefully swatted aside. Bertha poked her hair out, saw me standing there, and hollered out, "I'll be with you in a minute, May!" Then there was a lot of growling, some more cursing, and Bertha ducked back into the melee.

Hmmm. That's funny, I thought. Why in the world would Bertha be there with her dead sister still aboveground? There was bound to be a good explanation for that. Still, I found it interesting and quickly dug around in my purse for my notebook.

Sisters of deceased doing business as usual, I wrote. More data for my mystery novels. I hadn't actually written one yet; I was still in the research mode. And, as anyone knows, that could take a long time. Maybe years.

Bertha stuck her head out from behind the blanket door again and explained the commotion. "Sorry, May, a mean bitch back here is giving me some trouble."

Inez showed her head over her sister's shoulder.

"I am not!" she said with a huge buck-toothed smile. The two looked at each other, screeched with laughter, and disappeared again.

Of course Bertha was referring to a dog, and not her sister, but it took me a minute to figure that one out. More barking, growling, and cursing, and soon things got reasonably quiet. It sounded like the sisters had exhausted the raging beast. They sauntered into the waiting area and into my waiting hug.

"So what brings you to these parts?" Bertha snapped off some yellow rubber gloves and shoved them into her apron pockets.

"Yes! It's so good to see you. Wait a minute, May, are those new pearls?" Inez reached out and fingered my necklace with a look of longing on her face.

I glanced at Bertha and then to Inez, looking for some sign that they were troubled, depressed, or saddened by the loss of Gerty, but they acted as if it was just another dog-duty day. This knocked me off balance, I'll have to admit. Here I was prepared to soothe and comfort, while they smiled brightly and even inquired about Trixie. No, I hadn't brought Trixie in for a bath, I said, now hesitant to bring up the question of Gerty's death. Maybe they were deep in the throes of denial. Would they collapse in a heap of realization if I mentioned their loss? I had to be clever.

"Oh, these old things?" I touched my pearls. "I've had them for years. So, what's new?" I asked innocently, knowing good and well what was new, but they were acting awfully strange. Surely they would begin to cry now. I wondered whether or not I had enough tissues in my purse.

"Got a brand new litter of Cresteds, wanta see?"

Deep throes.

I kept my sneaky eyes on the sisters as they herded me along toward the back of the trailer. I didn't pull out my notebook; a good detective can remember details. I worked over everything I saw and had a pretty good mental list before we got to the rug-door. All of these things about the Hooch, along with details about the sisters, I'd noticed on previous visits, but it's not a bad idea to go over them at least one more time.

Bertha's face was bright and shiny. She had chapped-red cheeks, bleached yellow Brillo-pad hair, and lumberjack arms. Despite the fact that she was probably closing in on seventy years old, and should have been shriveling, her stocky form looked as if she could haul a load of bricks without so much as a grunt. Short and stout. I doubted if she was much taller than five-four, but every inch was put to good use. Her fingernails were ground down to nubs, from years of hard work. Her arms were covered in a fine layer of dark hair.

Her sister Inez, a few years younger, was skeletal. Her unfortunate features had been dredged from the silty bottom of the gene pool. She stood a good six inches taller than her sister; I gauged her height to be around five feet, ten inches, or more.

Her teeth looked like a picket fence shoved up from underneath, protruding from her top lip on a horizontal plane. Her hair was black with the exception of a white stripe that started on her left eyebrow, cut a swatch of pale pigment up her forehead, continued on through her back-combed bangs, and trailed down the hair on her neck. Her eyes bulged like they were being shoved outward by brain pressure, and her ears stuck out. Her chin was too long, and it sported a large mole (complete with two hairs) just below the lip line. Her only redeeming feature was a dainty, pointed nose, which supported a large pair of blue-framed glasses. The glasses, however, sat low. I imagined if she had pressed them higher, those bug eyes would have given them a pupil wash. Her bony shoulders poked spikes under a ragged T-shirt, long arms protruded from gapping sleeves. The little feature of the mole was something I'd avoided paying close attention to before, but now it was worthy of notice. You just never know when something might be important.

I passed through the blanket to the business side of the Hooch and cringed. The smell was worse here (if that were at all possible) and my sinuses did a mercy lock just before I was sent into a faint on the floor. The sisters didn't seem to notice at all. The dogs erupted again and the noise was incredible.

"See? Look at these little darlings!" Bertha lumbered over to a cage.

"Oh? Are these the Cresteds?" I peered inside, and reached for the little door handle.

Bertha shouted, "Shut it!"

I jerked my hand away like I'd been scorched.

"Not you, May. She's talking to the dogs." Inez burst into laughter, amused by my reflex.

"Oh."

The dogs took the order as a challenge and raised the noise level.

"Now. Aren't these just the most adorable things you ever seen?" Bertha reached her beefy arm into the cage and pulled out three little hairless balls.

"Oh, my gosh. Do they have thyroid problems or something?" Maybe they had meant to say "crusties." Sometimes the gals got words wrong.

Bertha and Inez looked at one another and exploded in another round of screeching laughter.

"Oh, May, these are Chinese Cresteds. They're hairless dogs. See?"

Inez pulled out mama dog and held its pointy nose next to her moley chin. That was the ugliest-looking thing I'd ever seen. (The dog, not her mole, but that was pretty ugly too). Horrible it was, really, with a tuft of white hair on its head, huge upright ears, and some hair on its feet and tail. Hmmm. Sort of looked like Inez. Everything else on the dog was naked. Its skin was a blotchy pink with big black freckles. I shuddered to think people actually went for that look intentionally.

"You want me to put you down for one after they're weaned?" Bertha shoved the little doggies back in their pen.

Not on your life. "Sure," I said, already working out some way to wheedle out of that commitment if and when the time actually came.

"These babies go for an easy seven hundred, but for you, May Bell, we'll knock off two hundred bucks. How's that?"

"Wonderful!" I started to sweat. Next they'd have me signing my life away for a bald dog that belonged in a freak show. But wait. I had a way to turn the conversation around to something that just might take their mind off of a quick five hundred dollars.

"Why don't we talk about it in the waiting room?" I backed toward the blanket door and pushed my way through, finally ready to question the sisters about poor Gerty. "I think I heard someone at the door," I added. Not likely, since the yapping had numbed my eardrums, but what the heck. It might work. Anything to get away from that reek. Another minute back there and my jewelry would start to melt.

"Sure, honey," Bertha shouted, and then to her sister who was just inches away, she screamed out, "Inez, let's go out front!"

"Okay, Bertha!" Inez shouted back. Both sisters broke up into hilarious laughter again.

So curious.

Of course the front was empty—there had been no one at the door, but at least we had a little bit more room to talk.

"Your hair looks so nice, May." Inez pushed at her glasses and clasped her hands by her flat bosom. She looked as if she wanted to touch my up-do. "Do you think I could get mine to do that?"

"Oh, I think with some gel or bobby pins we could wind it into a nice French roll or something, Inez. It wouldn't take much."

The poor woman was always finding nice things to say about my hair, or clothes, or jewelry. She had such a sweet nature it made me feel sad that there was probably very little we could do for her despite all the lotions and sprays and pastes on the market these days.

"Remember that blouse you were wearing last week? It was so pretty. And guess what? I found one just like it at the Salvation Army! Look!" Inez slipped out of her apron, and darn if she wasn't wearing the very blouse I'd donated! Now, though, it was stained and smudged with something brown.

I smiled weakly. "Yes! It looks just like mine!"

"So, May," Bertha said. "Why's it that you're here without Trixie? You can call for an appointment, you know."

I cleared my throat and coughed loudly a few times, just stalling and wondering if I should go for the direct approach, or wind my way around through the back door of the dead-sister topic. Bertha quickly scooped out a throat lozenge and thrust it into my hand. I stared at the little yellow disk, all sticky and covered in dog hair.

"Better not let those coughs get any worse, hon."

"Thanks," I said softly; made as if I were putting the cough drop in my mouth; and palmed it.

Inez tiptoed over to the window and peered through. "It's snowin' Bertha," she stated.

"Guess it's not likely to let up for Gerty's funeral." Bertha said it casually, in a tone she might use after hearing they'd cancelled *Seinfeld*.

Not likely to let up for Gerty's funeral. Just like that.

A good segue doesn't come along every day, but here was a good one and I wasn't about to let it get away.

"Her death must be very hard for you." I placed my hand on Bertha's forearm, glanced down, and noticed I was stroking a Tweetie Bird tattoo. Eeek. I patted Tweetie's beak and pulled away, hoping it looked like a natural retraction and not a recoil. "I read her obituary this morning. What a shame, and so sudden too."

Bertha and Inez looked at each other like they had before, with that lock-eyed, private-message look, and then, much to my astonishment, they started crowing again. Big open-mouthed guffaws.

"You think we're sad Gerty's dead?" Bertha wiped her eyes, rubbed her lower back, and shook her head. "She was the biggest pain in my fat behind next to these darned hemorrhoids. May, you ever have screaming hemorrhoids? I'm here to tell you, the only way to take the itch away is . . ."

"Good grief, Bertha, I don't think we need a medical report," Inez butted in. "Do we, May? Get her started and the next thing you know she'll be talking about her kidney stones. She keeps 'em in a little bottle with—"

I held up a hand and blinked rapidly, looking from Bertha to Inez. Hemorrhoids and kidney stones? What about Gerty? "I thought you were close to your sister," I said.

Bertha snorted. "Because we did lunch once a week?" She scratched her back pocket.

"But you were always so nice to her. You're not even a little sad that she's gone?" I was stunned. At least some fake bereavement would have been appropriate, but then I remembered, things were different in this part of town. I had to remember that.

"You're a pretty smart cookie, May Bell. I thought you'd have noticed." Inez pushed at her glasses. One finger in the middle. They slid down again immediately.

Noticed what? Oh my. I needed to work harder at my powers of perception. But there was the thing Gerty had said while we were dining. At least that hadn't escaped my attention. And of course if you counted the sarcasm Gerty dripped while speaking to her sisters, there was some obvious tension there, but I never thought the girls were bothered by it. Apparently I'd been wrong.

I lifted my chin. "Well, I did notice something when we were eating together. Something quite out of the ordinary."

Bertha and Inez locked eyes again. This time the laughter didn't follow.

Before I had a chance to tell them what had caused me to suspect Gerty had died under suspicious circumstances, Bertha jerked her head toward the door. Inez answered the silent command by walking over on her stork legs. After a quick glance through the cloudy glass, she swung the *You bet, we're open!* sign to the *Scat! We're closed!* sign, and stood tapping her toe. The boats on her feet would come in handy if there was a fast melt outside.

37

"Don't say anything here. Let's move on over to our trailer," Bertha said.

Inez took a hairy coat from a hook and shrugged into it.

Bertha slipped out of her apron, tossed it in a corner, and said, "We've got a little time before our next appointment. There's something you should know about our dear departed sister. There's gonna be talk, so you might as well hear it from us first. Besides, these hemorrhoids need a treatment, and I'm starvin'."

CHAPTER FIVE

Behind Bertha and in front of Inez, I traipsed through lazy, feathery snow, stepping from one flat stone to another, a makeshift walkway between the Hooch and the sisters' single-wide, a place they shared mere yards from the noise and stench of the boarding and grooming facility.

It was my first foray into the home of Bertha and Inez, and once the door was slammed behind me the urge to turn and run was something hard to quell. It was obviously a place not often touched by a mop or dust rag. On the other hand, I couldn't help but feel welcome and at ease, having been deposed of the usual constraints of social pomp. I've complied with the unspoken expectations as doctor's wife for years and found most of the people I know have coronaries if their carpet fibers aren't all leaning in the same direction; heaven help anyone who forgets to wipe down the guest sink if they find it necessary to visit the loo. Once, while attending a party at a urologist's house, I spilled red wine on his white ottoman. I've never been invited back.

I stood near a hairy couch and watched the sisters as they bustled. No talk yet; that would come in good time. For now, it was the feedin' hour at the Peach residence.

Bertha squatted in front of an old-model refrigerator and tossed produce at Inez, who caught and placed tomatoes, cucumbers, and a head of lettuce on a cutting board in the middle of a cluttered counter by an olive green sink. Inez grabbed a knife and hacked at the vegetables.

"We'll start with a salad," Bertha said. "Then, oh, let's see what else we have in here." The woman was on forage like I'd never seen before. She made her way up the fridge's shelves, fingered, and then dismissed mystery meals in Tupperware, pulled open the freezer door, and hauled out four cardboard packages of Lean Cuisine. She stacked and balanced them on one broad arm and shouldered the door closed.

"Here, May, just pop these in the microwave while I wash my hands. It says nine minutes each but our oven runs hot, so just shove 'em in and hit the button for four minutes. That should do."

I had to dance around the slicing Inez to get to the microwave. It was a big brown seventies model sitting on a crooked wooden table across from the sink and refrigerator. There wasn't much room in that mobile home, and what room it did have was cluttered by a treasure trove of white elephant paraphernalia and garage sale treasures. Trinket heaven. That explained the inch or so of dirt and dog hair that had settled over everything. So much stuff would have been nearly impossible to dust around, and after all, these were working girls with very little free time. I was looking hard for ways to excuse the mess.

Even in the place I'd call a living room, the hairy couch was barely visible under a mountain range of laundry (some of the clothes I noticed were my Salvation Army discards). The carpet was green shag—I think, but it was hard to tell—and there were piles of magazines stacked in every corner. A swamp cooler was wedged in a window, turned off, but dripping water steadily. An orange rust stain ran down the wall. The windows were shrouded, thank goodness; I didn't want to know if there were dead flies on the ledges.

"Run out back and grab us some Slim Fast!" Bertha shouted at Inez while the robust woman pulled a long knife from her "miscellaneous" drawer and took over Inez' job. Bertha whacked at the head of lettuce holding the knife handle with both hands. Her forearm muscles flexed. Inez hustled out to the back porch and retrieved a six-pack of diet shakes.

I ripped at the Cuisine boxes and had the frozen meals bubbling in no time. Bertha hadn't lied. The oven ran hot and the plastic plates were withered when I pulled them out with the aid of some folded towels.

"May, you're still in your coat!" Inez scolded. "Let me take that for you. Is this vicuna?" She tugged at my collar and I couldn't resist without looking rude, so I dropped the meals on the counter, shrugged out of my expensive wool, and allowed the woman to drape it over the dog couch. It would require at least five or six sticky tapes from my lint roller to get it looking presentable again, but after my door-slam mess it would need a deep clean anyway, so I let it go.

The lunch was coming together, but as I stood by the sink rinsing out forks (they only had five, and none had yet made it to the dishwasher), I felt a warm fuzzy thing scurry over my insteps.

My reaction was immediate and dramatic. I threw my arms back, letting one fork go, which lodged its tines into a withered philodendron trunk behind me, and shrieked like a banshee. Somehow, with the strength of the panic-stricken, I vaulted upwards and landed atop the counter, with one knee in the sink. I was on my way to the top of the refrigerator when Bertha looped an arm around my waist and held me firm.

"It's just Horace, May, our ferret!" Inez explained and scooped up the creature.

Bertha hauled me back down.

"Poor baby," Inez said, and at first I thought she was talking about me, but then I realized she was referring to her ratty friend. "You scared him half to death, May. Look."

Inez thrust the beast toward my face, compelling me to put my fingers up in the shape of a cross. The sisters looked at each other and cackled.

"Better put you in the back, buddy, May Bell just ain't ready for you yet."

I said a silent prayer of thanks while Inez sped off toward what I imagined was the sleeping quarters with her bubonic bundle. The gangly sister chattered as she left, telling me how Horace was always stealing their socks and it wasn't good for him to be running loose anyway. How silly. I'd always thought it was the washing machine taking my socks.

As I watched Inez disappear into her bedroom, I wondered about my irrational terror. My heart was still thudding away and at that moment I gave myself a good mental head swat. How in the world could I be cop for a day if I suffered palpitations at the sight of a friendly ferret? Well, if truth be told, I'd rather look down the barrel of a loaded gun any day, and having come out of this trauma intact, my resolve was solidified. I could handle anything. I was a rock. Later I'd be icing down my swollen sink knee, but it was a small price to pay to test my nerve.

As we sat around a Formica-topped, aluminum-legged table for an early lunch, I watched the sisters carefully. There were no signs that their lives had changed for the worse since Gerty's death; in fact they couldn't be more jovial. Bertha polished off four cans of Slim Fast and two Lean Cuisines before coming up for air. Inez picked at her salad and motioned continuously for me to "Eat, eat, May. Don't be shy now," but I just couldn't muster an appetite after watching a poodle hair float down and land on top of my croutons. Besides, although the outer edge of my dinner was burned, the inner portion was frozen solid. I shoved my plate away mumbling something about having had a large breakfast.

I leaned my wrists against the sticky edge of the table and steepled my fingers.

"May, your nails look lovely!" Inez said, freeing a bit of lettuce. It dropped from her mouth onto her plate. "Acrylics?"

"Thank you, Inez. Yes, I had them done yesterday."

"The color is stunning. Such a bright red, and they're not chipping or anything. Look at her nails, Bertha! Maybe I can get mine done some time?"

"Phooey," Bertha said and took a swig of her Slim Fast. "Wouldn't last through one wash. Forget it."

Inez pouted. She scrunched her face and her glasses shifted up higher on the bridge of her nose.

"But they do look nice, May," Bertha added.

"That's sweet of you to say," I said, wanting badly to get off the topic of my acrylics. What had happened to Gerty? And what was the big secret the girls were keeping from me?

"So," I said casually after taking a deep, fortifying breath. "Is Gerty's funeral soon?" There. It was out. The topic I'd been dying to get to, but I said it casually, maybe even a bit sadly, careful not to sound too excited about her death. Most people don't know about my detective status or that I live on the edge, always on the job, and the last thing I wanted to do was tip off the sisters that I thought there was something mighty suspicious about Gerty's death. It hadn't escaped my keen observation that these gals were pretty tough and maybe even capable of something heinous. I never rule out anyone at the beginning of a murder investigation, without good cause and a thorough shakedown.

"Huh?" Inez looked at me curiously and I blushed—a result of my guilty conscience. Sometimes I get a little carried away when I'm on a case.

"When is Gerty's funeral?" I asked again, this time with

genuine interest. There was a death in the family and here I was acting inappropriately. A little compassion was in order.

"Who cares?" Bertha waved her bent fork (the one I'd played darts with) over her head, and looked at me with a grease-stained face. "Good riddance, I say. And by the way, what was it you noticed?"

The girls looked at each other for a brief second. The secret signal didn't get past me, though; they were feeling me out to see what I knew. I played innocent.

"You're not even the least bit upset?" Why were these two acting so dispassionate in the wake of a, well, a wake? It just wasn't natural. I got this funny feeling that we were doing a dance. Bertha had asked about my observation at the luncheon. Very curious. They wanted to get me talking about what I knew before offering anything on their end. Okay, I'd parry forth and watch their moves.

Bertha stabbed something orange and plopped it on her tongue. She kept her eyes trained on her food as if she were expecting it to get away from her. "You said you noticed something the last time we had lunch with Gerty," she said.

"Yes, yes I did. Something very strange."

The sisters were exchanging glances again, adding to my confusion. I was perplexed and just didn't have the stomach for any more for these games. I burst out with, "Did something happen after our lunch? Did she say something to make you angry with her?" It seemed a ludicrous question. My impression of Hatfields and McCoys was that blood stuck together no matter what insults or blows were thrown within the DNA circle. Beating each other to a pulp was okay in the family sphere, but catch an interloper stepping over the line, and he was in for a swift and unified kin pummel. Maybe I'd been wrong.

Bertha looked at me briefly, then again at her sister with those protruding eyes. Inez sucked on her large teeth. "We've been mad at her for years. She knew it, too. Gerty didn't like what we do. She was, what would you say, Bertha, different?"

"Pain in the hind parts is what she was." Bertha balled up her lunch trash and made two points into the waste can.

"What do you mean?" I showed calm, but inwardly I was squirming. This was getting good.

"Like I said before. There's gonna be talk. You ever heard of something called FETA?" Inez scooped up a glop of salad dressing with her napkin.

"I've heard of it. Something about the treatment of animals? It was mentioned in the article I read in this morning's paper. Here. I've got it right here." I pulled the article from my purse, where I'd stashed it after changing out of my robe that morning. I handed it to Bertha, who glanced at it and handed it back.

"Yeah," she said. "Gert got herself involved with that group and all sorts of other things when her artsy-fartsy career took off. Tree-huggin' liberal's what she was. She saved whales, cried about the ozone hole, mopped oil off of ducks—" Bertha was interrupted by a giggling Inez, who added, "Yeah, got those birds all nice and clean with dishwashing soap. There was a news camera crew filming the release and everything, and guess what happened? Just guess."

Bertha was snickering.

I shook my head.

"Gerty tossed them birds into the air. Everybody was clapping, and hooting, blowing those little paper horns, you know, the ones that curl out and back, and cheering. And then guess what happened? Just guess?"

I shrugged my shoulders.

"The birds flew right into the path of a low-flying Cessna. I ain't lyin', May. Took the birds out and brought the plane down. Sparks were everywhere. Nearly started a forest fire. Now ain't that the perfect thing to show on America's Funniest Home Videos?"

The sisters hooted.

"That's so sad." I frowned, not finding their joke at all amusing.

Bertha got serious. "You know we love animals, May—it ain't that we don't care. But she was tryin' to put us out of business, don't ya know. And that whole thing about those ducks, with her acting all charitable and everything, made a huge point. She was trying to be the big hero, and instead, she did more harm than good. Just like what she was going to do to us."

Ah. So that was it. Gerty was shutting down the Hooch.

Inez blew her nose on a napkin and shoved the mess under her plate. "She said we were being inhuman, that our business was nothing but a puppy mill, and that we were breeding dogs bald, which of course we are, but she said it gives the pups poor self-esteem. All that just didn't cut the mustard in her book."

Yes, it seemed like an ugly problem. Despite their affable public appearances, the sisters' tide of ill will must have run very, very deep.

"I didn't get the impression you were having problems when we had lunch together, in fact, you all acted very civilly to one another."

"You know the old saying, May." Inez wagged her mismatched eyebrows. "Keep your friends close . . . but your enemies closer."

I'd heard that somewhere. Who said it? Patton? Maybe it was Martha Stewart.

Bertha said, "Ah, we was just hoping if we acted friendly and all, she'd drop the whole thing. She'd already turned our neighbors against us, and to top it off, she was taking us to court next week. To court! I'm guessing what you saw at lunch was the papers she kept shoving at us. Accusing us with all kinds of stuff and maybe, we thought, we could charm our way back into her good graces. I mean, without the Hooch, Inez and me'd be out on the street."

I imagined Bertha scooting down the Hunker Hills sidewalk dragging Inez along in a Radio Flyer.

"Yes, I did see the legal papers. I didn't want to ask, but it did seem rather odd." I was lying now, and I'd pay penance later, because I hadn't noticed any legal forms, but from what I was learning it would have been bad timing to reveal what I'd really seen and heard at our luncheon. It hadn't escaped my attention that a woman was dead, and the two with the most to gain by her demise were within fork distance.

"So, this accident of Gerty's wasn't exactly bad news." I slipped the word "accident" in purposely. The word "motive" was blinking through my mind like a neon sign in Vegas, but I remained calm. Even Ted would have been proud of my brazen courage.

Bertha shook her fist. "She was getting the law involved! She'd filed all the paperwork to get our business shut down and bestarch our good names."

I thought Bertha probably meant "besmirch," but language had a way of morphing in the Hunker district, so I gave the woman props for trying.

Inez plucked at the white streak in her eyebrow. When she spoke there was a hint of dismay in her voice. "She always was the favorite one, ever since I can remember. Best toys when we was kids, new clothes, piano lessons—Mom and Dad gave her whatever she wanted. It was like me and Bertha was indivisible!"

Bertha nodded her agreement and put her hand on Inez' arm. I placed my hand on Bertha's Tweetie Bird.

Inez whispered, "This was for the best, really."

"For the best," Bertha echoed.

"For the best," I said.

What was I saying? My gosh. The poor woman was dead! And let's not forget the little thing that caused me to believe she'd been murdered. That one sentence, said almost as a joke while we cut through our calamari, should have kept me on my guard, but here I was stroking the Tweetie to keep the mood passive. Considering these two women might be capable of something swift and permanent, it was probably the best thing to do after all, so I stroked once more before asking, "Bertha, how was Gerty doing with her art—you know, before she died? Was it selling well?"

To the more astute, this question would have leapt out as a complete shift from the current topic of conversation. No segue here. I just had to count on the gals' distracted mood to ignore the leap and get me the information I needed.

Inez answered for her sister. "She was doin' all right. Not great, but she had an art show that did pretty well last month, and that other one we went to was pretty good. I heard someone say she was up and coming, whatever that meant."

"Yes, she mentioned her art show at lunch. She sounded quite pleased," I agreed, but didn't mention what she'd said afterwards. The thing that made me sit up and take notice at my breakfast table while reading her obituary. The reason I wasn't so sure her death was an accident. After talking about how her paintings were finally starting to sell, she leaned over to me and said, "This junk will be worth a whole lot more after I die. You know how it is, May, artist dies and the prices go right off the charts. It's one of life's cruel little secrets that nobody tells you about when you're sucking on your pacifier. Considering I've been doing this half my life with little to show for it, mine will probably sell for millions. Wouldn't that just bite the big one?"

Or maybe, just maybe, Gerty my dear, that's why you bit the big one. Not wanting to jump to conclusions, I pushed for more notebook fodder. My little black spiral pad was sitting patiently in my purse, just waiting to be filled with critical details. It would have to wait. I just prayed my memory would hold up long enough for me to get it down later.

"Will Gerty have other family at the funeral?" And who else might want to get their hands on Gerty's paintings?

"I guess her husband will be there." Inez started shoving stuff off the table, into the trashcan. Fur balls flew.

"What about your parents? Her kids? Friends, business associates?" I smiled innocently. Just gathering data.

Bertha said, "No kids. Mom and Dad are both in a nursing home gumming their tapioca, trying to remember what state they're in or what their names are. I don't expect to see them there."

Mentally I scratched off two potential perps. "And I don't know who she worked with."

"Phillip Bottox," Inez said, her eyes twinkling.

Bertha said, "Oh, yeah. You're right, Inez, Phillip Bottox. Bottox the dish, and I don't mind sayin' he can eat crackers in my bed anytime."

I screwed my mouth into another smile. "So what happens with all of her art now?"

"Don't know, don't care," Bertha said, tying up the white trash bag. She slid open the back door and plopped it on the porch. "Oh crap," she said in a low growl.

"What is it?" Inez was immediately at her elbow. "Geez. Lock the doors, Bertha. Don't let her in."

"Who?" I jumped to my feet, looking for my purse, regretting that I'd put off buying that set of nunchucks I'd seen at the sporting goods store. Now where the heck was my purse? I had a good fat set of keys in there that might work as a weapon. The girls were definitely giving me the jumpies.

"It's Jolene Ward. She's coming around front, and she don't look happy. Gonna give us hell again, I suppose, and she's got her whole brood with her this time."

The canine alert unit in the nearby Hooch erupted in howls and barks, yelps, and a whole host of other noises I can't really describe. The noise rattled the windowpanes, even at that distance. The banging on the side of the sister's trailer home was slightly louder and definitely more threatening.

"Bertha! Inez! Getcher lazy buns out here! I've got something to say to both of you and I mean business this time!"

CHAPTER SIX

Inez hurried to the front door window and peeked through. "She's at it again, Bertha. Don't open the door."

Bertha sighed, rolled her eyes, stepped around her sister, and opened the door.

Inez slapped herself on the forehead.

A young super-sized woman stood on the wooden porch. She wore a stretchy tube top around double-D breasts, showing a lot of skin with nothing covering her shoulders, even though the snow was coming down steadily. In the yard, close to the steps, three children ran in circles and a couple of others hugged the woman's legs. The children's faces were smeared with orange stains from what I deduced to be Spaghettios or Cheetos. A little boy plucked at hardened boogers in his nose, then stuck them in his pocket.

"I'm calling the cops this time," Jolene said. "I've warned you before and now I'm doin' it!" Jolene's stomach bulged and quivered over the top of her tight faded jean shorts. She pointed a smoldering cigarette at Bertha. "You know Stanley works nights. He can't sleep with all that racket going on over there, and it stinks to high heavens, besides." Jolene stuck her cigarette in the corner of her mouth and hefted a toddler onto her broad hip.

"Is Stanley her husband?" I whispered to Inez.

Bertha stepped out onto the porch to confront her neighbor.

Inez whispered back to me. "She's been trying to reel him in

for years. I think that one over there is his, but I'm not sure."
Inez pointed to a little girl with stiff braids. "He lives in the
green-and-white trailer back there, but he spends his share of
time at Jolene's. She's keepin' her hopes up."

Things heated up on the porch, while Inez and I kept a safe
but protective distance just inside the door behind Bertha.
Jolene flicked her cigarette away, handed the toddler off to the
little braid girl, blew out a stream of smoke, put her hands on
her hips, and stuck her chest out. Her face was inches from an
unfazed Bertha. Jolene gestured and railed about the noise, the
stench, and Stanley's need to sleep, without getting anything
like an apology or even an acknowledgement from my Tweetie
friend.

"Yeah, yeah, yeah," Bertha said. "Whatever." She held up her
palm. "Why don't you just talk to the hand?"

Jolene's face was practically purple. Then as the woman's
anger and frustration mounted, she began something I imagined
to be either a primitive fighting ritual or a replication of mating
peacocks. She wagged her head and shoulders side to side, then
shimmied down, bent her legs, and moved up again, down, and
up.

Bertha, egging Jolene on, copied her, mocked her, and carried on move for move. Up, down, shimmy, shimmy. The women
leaned in close, nose to nose, yelled at each other, and waved
their arms around.

"You just . . ." Jolene said.

"I just what?"

"Well, I'm gonna . . ."

"Yeah? You gonna what?"

"It's just . . ."

"Just? Just? Okay, honey, bring it on." Bertha pushed up her
sleeves. Tweetie danced.

They continued their repartee, saying nothing really, a bunch of truncated threats from both sides, all the while doing the funny head wag, shoulder shimmy dance.

Jolene ended it all with a raised fist. I was ready to jump in if it came to blows, but Inez held me back.

Snap, snap, snap. Jolene made a Z in the air to signal she was done talking. She spun around and stomped down the stairs while shouting back over her shoulder.

"My boyfriend can't get no sleep! Those stupid dogs bark night and day. He's already talked to your sister about this and she's going to shut you down. In fact"—Jolene tossed her black-root, bleached-orange hair back off her forehead—"I'm going home and I'm gonna call her myself. You'd better start packin', witch." Jolene stomped off, hauling her litter behind her.

Inez looked at Bertha and they hooted. Then they doubled over with laughter.

Bertha called after Jolene's bouncing buns. "You go on ahead, honey, you just go and talk to my sister about shutting us down. Now get your Daisy May shorts and your lard, swingin' no-tone behind out of here!" Bertha threw the door closed with a metallic slam.

The sisters screeched with laughter and leaned on each other for support while I stared.

After helping finish a minimal cleaning of the kitchen I decided it was time to leave. The girls had more dogs to shave and more bald pooches to coddle, and I had some questions for Mr. Stanley Boy—but of course I didn't tell them that.

We said goodbye at my car, and I watched Bertha and Inez make their way back into the Hooch. Quickly I turned the ignition key and backed out of the parking lot. I checked the time. A couple of hours before cop duty. Plenty of time for a friendly interrogation. I swung around as if I were going back to the highway; but instead, I found a dirt alley road spotted with dented, metal trashcans. This must be the sanitary service route. I had made note of the green-and-white trailer the sisters and Jolene pointed to when talking about Stanley. I parked behind his trailer and jogged up to the door.

With heart thudding, and thanking the stars I'd found my purse (it would serve as a weapon if necessary), I stood for a minute before rapping on Stanley's door. Timid tap. No response.

I knocked more loudly, trying to imagine the kind of guy who would be shacking up with the likes of Jolene. I envisioned a Bubba-type. Cowboy boots and Schlitz tremors.

The trailer remained stone quiet, but there was a pickup parked in the driveway so I was pretty sure he hadn't made a beer run.

I banged on the door.

A roar came from inside the trailer.

"Go away, Jolene! You done wore me out last night and I gotta sleep."

"Mr. Bubba? I mean, sir, it's not Jolene. It's May List." Yikes. This was not going well. What would I say if he opened the door?

More growling from inside and my question was about to be answered.

"Just a minute. I've gotta get some pants on."

I was sure happy about that. It wasn't hard to hear Stanley at all. The walls of these trailers must be paper-thin. No wonder he was having trouble sleeping. And, just as Jolene had said, the reek of Hooch hovered around even more pungently by Stanley's front door. It smelled like a combination of cat urine, doo-doo, and rotten eggs. Must be the wind direction or something.

"Yeah?" The door opened a crack and I saw the puffy eyes of a barrel-chested man. He was shirtless and hadn't bothered to do his button fly all the way up. Boxers pooched out above his waistband and disappeared under his inflated belly.

"Sir, I'm from FETA. Heard you had some complaints about the grooming service over there?" I yanked my purse open, then closed, for effect, jerked my head toward the Hooch, and waited.

Stanley squinted his bloodshot eyes at me, probably not believing a word I'd said, but then again, why else would I be standing in front of his door?

"It's under control." Stanley scowled, looked me up and down, and then glanced around. Probably looking for my backup. "Have a good day."

Before the door closed, I stuck my foot out, and nearly got it slammed into the size of a Vienna sausage, but it kept the door open.

"I'd like to just ask you a couple of questions if you don't mind."

Stanley opened the door a little bit wider than before, but not much.

"Listen, lady. I said I got it under control. I've talked to a couple of people and they're gonna take care of it. Now look. I work nights and you're cuttin' into my sleep."

"Oh? Where do you work? The hospital? My husband works at the hospital, spends many a night over there. Maybe you know him." I wanted to butter him up with some preemptive questions before the strike. Just being friendly.

"No, I don't think so. I work out at the Air Force base." He gave me a look as if to say, *Like it's any of your business.*

The snow kept coming down, making me wonder why I wasn't invited inside, not that I'd have gone, but Stanley was clearly annoyed at the intrusion. This guy wasn't the talkative type. More like the action type, by the looks of the Jolene's many kids. It hadn't skipped my observations that the toddler had her father's eyes—shifty.

"Oh? Are you a pilot?"

"Listen, lady, I'm a tech sergeant. I work for a living."

"What do you do?"

"Aircraft maintenance. It's a hard job, and something you shouldn't do if you're not thinking clearly. You understand what I'm saying? Now can I please get back to sleep?"

"Oh, my. How impressive! And I can see you do take your job very seriously and you're quite proud of what you do. Do you have a nickname? Like, 'Stan the Man'?"

Stanley rolled his eyes and flicked a dead spider off the doorjamb. "Give me a break," he said.

"No problem, sir, just one more thing and then I'll go. Did you by any chance have an opportunity to talk with one of our representatives, a, Mrs. . . ." I pretended to search my memory, checked my purse again, lifted my notebook, and flipped through a couple of blank pages. "A Mrs. Gerty Knickers?"

"Yeah, I talked to her. That's the dog ladies' sister." Stanley scratched a hairy chest.

"I take it she hasn't been too supportive of the operation." I jerked my head toward the Hooch again.

"You ain't heard the news?" Stanley yawned.

I put on my innocent face.

"She's dead, lady." Stanley rubbed his nose and yawned again. "I was hoping Gerty'd get the place shut down, but I guess that's all down the crapper now."

"Oh, my." I flipped through more blank pages. "I've been out of town. That's very unfortunate. Unfortunate, indeed!"

"Yeah, well, what ya gonna do?" Stanley played with the curly hairs on his chest, back, forth, back forth, round and round.

"Very bad news. When did you speak with her last?"

"Oh, I don't know. A couple a weeks ago maybe? I went by her place to complain about the noise and the smell again. She said she'd been getting the paperwork together. For court and stuff. Come on, lady, I really got to get some sleep."

"I'm sorry to bother you. Thanks so much."

That was as much information as I was going to get out of Mr. Hairy Chest. He started to close the door again, then paused and pulled it open one more time.

"Lady. How long did you say you'd worked with FETA?"

"Oh, about five years in this area, ten in Idaho before moving here." I was doing the tap dance, thinking on my feet and coming off pretty believable from what I could guess by Stanley's expression.

Stanley sucked in his cheeks and narrowed his eyes at me. "So. Are you going to get that place shut down? You and FETA or whatever?"

"We're certainly trying, sir. With Gerty gone, though, it will take some time. Just be patient."

And away I went.

Back in my car I puzzled over the situation at the trailer park. Stanley knew Gerty was dead, but Jolene apparently hadn't yet heard the news. Maybe their relationship didn't leave a lot of time for small talk. I would have been very surprised if Jolene read anything more than the *Inland Tattler*. The only reason I knew about Gerty's death was because of my interest in current events, and of course, the latest obituaries. Not a very significant issue that Jolene was clueless, but then again, I didn't imagine Stanley was perusing the obituaries either. He said it had been two weeks since he last saw Gerty, so how did he know she was dead? More questions for my notebook. I drove out to the road and after making my way through most of the Hunker business district I pulled off into the parking lot of a hardware store, where I could scribble without distractions. The place obviously doubled as the local feed and grain station too. There was farm equipment and grain bags piled under a lean-to by the front of the establishment.

With my car in neutral and my foot pressing the brake, I left it running while I jotted down some of my observations. There were plenty of people coming and going at the Hunker Hardware, but most of them paid no attention to me. Just as well; I needed to think. There was a crazed killer on the loose and it was up to me to run him, or her, down.

I sat up in my seat and gazed through the windshield. What was happening to me? When did I start seeing murderers and suspicious activities around every corner and in everyday situations? At my age, it was quite natural for friends and acquaintances to pass away for any number of reasons. Yes, I had been bored lately, and yes, solving a case or two in the past had given me a cheap thrill, and yes, I really wanted to believe I was developing that uncanny sense cops have for feeling a thing or two out of place when everything looked normal to the untrained eye. What did I know about Gerty that would cause me alarm? Was it really the conversation we'd had about her art being worth a lot of money after she died? Well, there was no way of knowing that kind of thing for sure. Her sisters clearly benefited from her death. They would remain employed for a while longer, but they hardly acted suspicious or secretive about their feelings for her. If they'd spooked her into a heart attack I was quite certain they wouldn't be so quick to say how happy they were that she was dead.

Ted's voice played through my mind. *Crazy like a fox, May.*

What about Stanley Boy? He seemed pretty chummy with Gerty before her death, and maybe that had made Jolene crazed with jealousy. She looked the type. She could have done something to knock off the old lady, but Jolene didn't even know Gerty was dead.

Or did she?

I made a mental note to go back and question Jolene later. She might have been putting on a pretty good show back at the trailer.

A man with a load of pigs drove past me, a little too close, and I was distracted for a minute. Then I was back to work, head down.

I sifted through the list of suspects, jotted them down, and then considered the husband, always the first suspect, and Gerty's business partner, the guy who Bertha said could eat crackers in her bed—whatever that meant.

Hold on, May Bell. Gerty died of a heart attack. That's what it said in the paper. Not a garrote to the throat, not a drowning in her bathtub, not a knife to the temple, no sign of a struggle, no forced entry, no bloody skin under the nails. She'd just keeled over onto her drawing table.

Splat and done.

A thunderous knock on my car window startled me so badly I snorted.

"Where do you want this hay, lady?" A man with a dolly stacked with alfalfa bales glared in through the glass. I quickly rolled down my window.

"I didn't order any hay. I'm sorry, just taking a break here."

"I was told to bring this hay around. I can tie it to your roof if you want." The man was sizing up my convertible, eyeing the ragtop. He pulled a section of baling wire out from his back pocket and started twisting it around his hands.

I screamed, slammed the clutch, and threw my Camaro into reverse. I was back on the road spitting gravel before he had a chance to wrap the murderous ligature around my little old crepe neck.

It was happening. I was turning into one of those old ladies who had become so bored with her own existence that I was beginning to invent terrible events just to believe there was drama and excitement around the bend—a reason to get up in the morning.

My heart was beginning to calm as I thought of an old man I

used to visit in the nursing home with my church choir. He could usually be found under his bed hiding from "commies." Every day he would fight imaginary Nazis, rising victorious from under the bedsprings brandishing a urinal sword and bedpan shield. I had to get control of myself lest I end up like that. It was time to stop this insane paranoia about killers and murderous plots.

But then what? I suppose I could go back to my activities as the good doctor's wife, put away my computer high-speed chase programs, and plan a nice dinner for the upper crust. How boring. No, I'd do my own snooping, and if nothing came of it, at least I'd feel I'd done something more than knit, clean, and paste more pages into my scrapbook.

I looked at my watch. It was a stroke of genius to change my ride-along to Harvest. It was close enough to Spokane to be in the county, but smaller than the big conglomerate SPD, which was both intimidating and confusing. Starting out simple was better. Later, when the time was right and my skills were perfected, I'd move on up to an assignment with the big boys.

While the SPD was impressive, complete with a bomb squad, dog unit, SWAT team, etc., etc., etc.—all of the makings of a first-class crime unit—for now I was content to stick with something I could handle. Homeboys. Small town. To sweeten the deal, it was in the town I loved, with apple orchards and forested slopes. Perfect for my little log cabin and writing room. Plenty of beauty and inspiration to help me get my first mystery novel started. I considered it the perfect blend of serenity and simple crime, enough to keep me busy. Now if I could only convince Ted.

Who was I kidding? I'd switched from the Spokane ride-along to Harvest because that's where Gerty had lived . . . and died.

A glance at my watch told me I'd have to kill about an hour

since my cop duties wouldn't start for a little while, and that meant I didn't have any good reason to avoid the grocery store. One of my least favorite chores. Oh well, suck it up, May. I wouldn't exactly be able to do the full shopping spree, since what I bought would have to sit in my trunk for the full shift, but my pantry had been sorely neglected. Ted didn't complain much, but after I'd caught him joyfully caressing a package of Top Ramen he'd found in the bottom of our napkin drawer, it was the least I could do.

I left the Hunker Hills district, didn't run over any suicidal varmints on my way out, and pushed the car up to fifty. My confidence was building, which was good, since I'd be going through Spokane city traffic before turning north toward Harvest. I merged without any problems, and after driving along the highway until I was close to the city center, I exited and pulled into the first grocery store I found. Oh darn. This was a big one, unfamiliar, and that would mean I'd have to learn the aisle layout in a hurry. All the more reason to keep the shopping to a bare minimum. Grab what would hold us over, and get the heck out.

The snow was wet, melting when it hit the pavement. I didn't like the looks of that. If the temperature suddenly dropped, we'd be in for some black ice. No problem, I thought. What Ted didn't know was that although I hadn't done so well on my first driving program, I'd found a new one that was more my speed and while he was at work last week, I'd spent all day practicing. If I could master Crazy Taxi, I could manage anything.

Bring it on.

It took five minutes to find a parking place, and in the end I had to settle for one a mile from the front door. Well, not exactly, but it felt like that after the hike, which left my shoes soaked and squishy. The front of the grocery store was replete with shelves of Halloween candy, and I was proud of my self-control. I didn't even look twice at the bags of Snickers.

Of course the grocery carts were stuck. I jerked and shook the lot, making a lot of noise, but they stubbornly clung together. I was just about to curse them apart when a kindly young boy came along and dislodged one for me. I thanked him, embarrassed because my face was sweating and my breath was coming out in gasps; then off I sped as if I knew what I was doing. Two steps toward the produce aisle and I noticed one of the wheels on my basket was locked in place. I didn't dare go back and try for a replacement after the last scene, so I muscled it along. The stuck wheel rubbed stubbornly across the linoleum; the other wheels wobbled and shuddered. I was determined to keep things moving. Eventually, that darn wheel had to give.

First—juice. Got it. Next—spaghetti. Tossed it in. Canned vegetables, soups, cat food, Tide, Windex. No problem. I was making good time, but I needed to hurry. It wouldn't be good for me to be late for my first day as a police officer. At the far end of the store I found a lovely bakery section where I parked my troublesome cart. It could just sit there while I perused the bagels and croissants.

It took a little longer than I anticipated to sort through the baked goods. Finally I'd loaded my arms. Donuts, bread, hamburger buns. I threw them over the rim of the basket. One more stop, at the deli section for cheese. It would be fine in the chilly car. Thankfully, the shopping cart wheel had bounced loose and rolled freely. I careened around corners, coming up on two wheels and slid to a stop near the deli counter, where I ordered a pound of provolone, and threw it on top of the apples. Before making my way to checkout, I reached for my purse.

I reached for my purse.

I reached, no purse.

Now I was sweating. My purse was gone! Someone must have stolen my purse while I'd neglected the basket by the baked goods. Oh my gosh. This was very, very bad. And not only had the miscreant stolen my purse, but he'd played a cruel prank on me, adding things to my basket I didn't need. Apples, lettuce, leechies, cabbage, all sorts of things. And to boot, they'd taken my cat food.

Now I'm a pretty smart woman and it didn't take too long for me to realize I'd accidentally grabbed someone else's grocery cart. Easy enough mistake. But if you think I'm woman enough to admit my error, you're wrong.

I had to think fast. I grabbed the stolen basket and crept along the aisles, furtively looking for any sign that someone had noticed my dastardly deed. I made it halfway down the cereal aisle, creeping, creeping.

So far so good.

I'd get to my own basket, make the exchange, and dash for checkout.

Then. As I passed in front of the dried cereals, a loud shriek and a whole lot of commotion caused the pleasant voice over the intercom announcing "ground round at bargain prices" to halt in mid-sentence. Some woman not far away was shouting out words that were foreign to me, but I knew what had caused the hysteria.

I'd been found out.

I shoved the basket aside, grabbed up a box of Raisin Bran, and held it in front of my face, because, much to my horror, the chatter had rounded the corner and a ball of fury was coming toward me. I froze there behind my box of cereal, with sweat coursing over my trembling body. A trickle ran between my breasts, and tiny drops of perspiration popped out along my hairline and across my upper lip. The temperature in the store shot up a good twenty degrees.

A small Asian lady strode past me keeping up a running verbal tirade. Flanking her, a young clerk walked quickly to keep up. He consoled, assuring her that he'd find the basket and persecute the one who'd done the hideous crime. The two passed by, paying me no mind. I shoved the bran under my arm like a football, wrapped one hand around the misappropriated cart handle, and the race was on. I swung around in the opposite direction and pumped my thighs.

My only comforting thought was that I knew where my basket was, and she didn't have a clue about where to find hers. Time was on my side.

I careened around shoppers, passed the ground rounds, and on impulse snatched a few beef packages and tossed them in. The box of bran fell to the floor when I did that, but there was no opportunity to retrieve it. By the time I reached the path in front of frozen pizzas, I was flying. I'd run two steps, then lean over the handle, and ride the basket for a good three feet, then I'd run another two steps, run, ride, run, ride. Finally. I could see the croissants. I slid to a halt and jumped from the basket. My groceries were just where I'd left them. One more step and I'd have my purse—and I'd be in the clear.

"Mrs. List. How good to see you. I didn't know you shopped on this side of town."

Oh, dear. It was the pastor of my church, and just my luck that I'd pick the grocery store two blocks from his house. Should have thought about that.

Turning slowly while the heat notched up another ten degrees, I pasted on a broad smile and impulsively stuck out my hand. He shook it vigorously, almost dislocating my shoulder.

"Just picking up a few things, it is very nice to see you, pastor." I reached behind me for my purse but caught air.

"Did I see you're on the schedule to sing a solo tomorrow?" The pastor's feet were planted. That usually meant he was in the mood to chat. I could hear the distraught Asian woman making her way through the aisles. One more turn and she'd be back where she started—the scene of the crime.

I'd be fingered for sure.

"Tomorrow? Oh yes, certainly, yes, that would be fine." I was blabbing and a twitch started under my left eye. I needed to get out of there. How would it look if I were tackled by a furious little flailing woman with a bad case of grocery rage? A sweat trickle ran down my right cheek. When the pastor turned, curious about the commotion and undoubtedly hoping someone might need some pastoral counseling, I quickly jerked my head to the side and flicked off the sweat drop.

My pastor turned back to me and studied my face. He was a nice, easy-going man, but very astute, and it didn't escape his beady little eyes that something wasn't right.

"Mrs. List, are you feeling okay? You look a little flushed."

"I'm always flushed," I said in a hurry. "It's an allergic reaction to vinegar."

"Really? Interesting. I've never noticed it before."

"Oh, yes. I ate some olives and they always do this to me."

"That is very strange. Well, then I don't think these will do you any good."

To my astonishment, my pastor reached into my stolen basket and pawed through the produce. He picked up a jar of dill pickles and held them aloft.

He really shouldn't have done that.

"There! There!" The little woman was so beside herself she couldn't think in English. Only one word came from her mouth—"There!"—while she gesticulated wildly, and thumped the poor clerk on the shoulder.

What followed was what one reporter called a vicious veggie mob. Every concerned citizen in the store converged on the scene, while I slipped away. I left my poor pastor, looking stunned and confused as the clerk patted him down, the victim kicked him in the shins, and three little old ladies beat him with fresh zucchini.

I couldn't see how he'd hold me responsible, but just in case, I planned to be at the Wednesday night business meeting to vote for his pay raise.

In the interest of self-preservation I'd abandoned my groceries, but at least I had my purse. On my way out of the store I heard a voice over the loudspeaker demanding that the thief who'd stolen a cart out of baked goods should 'fess up.

Sorry, Ted, Top Ramen for dinner tonight.

CHAPTER SEVEN

So I was in my car again, huddled in my dog-hairy, street-stained coat steering through the wispy snow, when I thought I'd better just get to the police station in Harvest. I wanted to forget the grocery store incident and decided that while I waited for my shift to begin, maybe I could make friends with some of the officers there and finesse them for information about Gerty. I was certain someone would have investigated her death, even if they concluded it was a natural occurrence. There would have been reports, fingerprints, photos—all kinds of data I could dig through.

I would soon find out how wrong I was, and maybe I should have just left things at that. Maybe I should have been satisfied with the simple explanation about Gerty's demise. My curiosity had gotten me into some pretty tight fixes before, but nothing compared with what I would soon stumble upon, simply because I couldn't admit my prime years were behind me.

Heck. If truth be told, I was counting on my bunions, wrinkles, and liver spots to cover the fact that, deep down, I was a cunning detective, and a bear when it came to sniffing out evidence. I figured the officers would be kind to a grandma-type. Helpful and gentle. Maybe they would even carelessly leak information about the "crime scene," thinking I couldn't hear or wouldn't understand the jargon. And of course they wouldn't have the slightest idea of the disturbance I'd caused at the Super Save. I was just a helpless old lady with a withered brain and puffy ankles. No danger of me treading on sensitive evidence, no worry that I would point out their mishandling of a murder case. Since I was quite certain the police investigation had ended before the whole story was told, it was up to me to align the puzzle pieces and slide them into place. Knowing I had my work cut out for me, my knees started getting a little wobbly. That happens when I'm nervous.

To bolster my confidence, I fingered my life-alert necklace as I stood for a minute in front of the police station. Finally under control, I smoothed my tattered coat down as best I could, pushed at my drooping hair, and shouldered my way through the front door. I walked up to a desk with my chin held high.

The outer reception area was empty, with the exception of a uniformed man behind a tall desk who slowly lifted his eyes from a stack of papers and gave me the once over. By the pallor of his complexion, I didn't imagine he was doing many outdoor foot pursuits these days. Probably stuck back there because of bad behavior. We all have our off days, and a kind word can do wonders. I thought I'd just cheer him up a bit before getting down to business.

I walked up to the desk and gently placed my fingertips on the wood. "I've heard good things about you." I smiled sweetly.

The man cocked an eyebrow. "Oh?"

"You're the best at what you do, aren't you?" I didn't know exactly what it was that the man did, but the broad, overarching compliment usually worked like a charm in these situations. I waited for the appreciative smile. It didn't come.

"Lady, do you want to file a report or are you taking up collections for AARP or what?"

How rude! I was trying to be nice, and here was this guy skipping all kinds of formalities. He hadn't even introduced himself. I saw a name plate on the desk, though: one Sherman Post.

I stuck out my hand. "Hi, Sherman. I'm May List. SPD should have given you a heads-up. I'm riding with Officer Murphy today."

The man ignored my hand and I couldn't exactly blame him for that. While smoothing my coat I'd picked up a lot of dog hair. It looked like I was wearing a fuzzy glove. And that throat lozenge had got stuck to my hand as well and dropped off onto Sherman's desk. I felt a blush coming on, retracted my reach, and stuck my fist in my pocket.

"So. Murphy gets the honors today, does he?" The desk sergeant licked a thumb and dug through a file folder. "May List you say?"

I nodded. "Ride-along program."

"What a treat."

"Isn't it though? I'm so excited about this. I've been waiting for . . ." I trailed off when I realized the guy was being sarcastic. He sat there looking at me with a bored, conciliatory expression and I thought about giving him a two-finger jab in those eyes of his, but I refrained. Probably wouldn't look good on my performance report, if there was one.

After a loud sigh, which fluttered his mustache, the desk sergeant pointed to a row of chairs. "Take a seat. Mike's in roll call right now. I'll let him know you're here when it's done."

I tapped the desk, smiled again, and left Mr. Rude. I found a chair, sat, crossed my legs, pumped my foot, and waited.

Pedestrian traffic was steady through the reception area, and although I'd never met Officer Murphy, as I waited to meet him my imagination said he'd probably be an older guy, heavyset, with hardware hanging from around a pudgy waist. It was some kind of composite I'd developed from watching *Cops* on TV. Never mind that most of the uniforms throwing curious glances my way were very fit and tough looking, I was really hoping to have someone slightly disabled if I were to be of any help. I desperately wanted to practice some of my self-taught police procedures, and it would be especially wonderful if my chaperone wore orthotics and walked with a limp. Better yet if he had a speech impediment. More time for me on the radio.

While I thought of these things, I noticed an odd sound coming from my purse. Maybe it was my imagination. I strained to hear. No, there it was again—a scrabbling, scratching noise coming from inside my large handbag. I looked around, hoping I wasn't the only one who heard it; but although people came and went, mostly from a locked door off to the left side of the desk sergeant, nobody pointed or yelled or anything.

Slowly, carefully, I pulled my purse up onto my lap. My heart was thudding hard. In addition to the strange noise I'd heard, I now saw the leather sides of my purse thump as if someone was tapping a message to me from the very bowels of my personal things. The room spun and dipped around me. Certain that God himself was giving me a sign, punishing me for giving my pastor a vegetable clobber, would have seemed ridiculous before, but there it was again, the thud and thump, the scratch and scrape, and I couldn't imagine what would do that right there in my own purse if it weren't for . . . Gerty!

Gerty. Giving me a sign from the Beyond. Now I'm not the sort to buy into these kinds of things, but there was a lot of spooky stuff happening around me these days. Afraid of appearing daft and demented, I said nothing. If Gerty was calling me from the Other Side, I was the only one to answer her pleas. I was the chosen one.

I heard the rush of blood pulsing through my ears. The fabric under my arms was moist and I felt tears pool in my eyes. There was nothing else to do but take a look.

"Gerty?" I whispered. "I'm here, Gerty, I'm listening." With two fingers I reached for the little brass clasp thingy on my purse. I turned the thingy, squinted my eyes, and lifted my purse flap.

It was like popping a can of soda after a good shake. The Peach sisters' gray ferret launched itself at me in a full frontal attack and hooked its little claws into the front of my coat. It hung there. By the look in his eyes (terror and confusion), I could tell he was about to take refuge in my hair. It might have been the look of horrified surprise on my face, but for whatever reason, he suddenly changed his trajectory, scampered down the length of my arm, and wasted no time darting through my open sleeve hole. He then wriggled past my elbow on his way to my chest. He was up to my armpit and moving fast when I found my voice.

The scream that came from my mouth caused the desk sergeant to spew coffee in a long, brown arc. I catapulted to my feet. I flailed. I dashed around in circles, waved both arms wildly, screamed some more, grabbed both of my breasts, and wrestled myself to the floor.

More screaming. I could feel the furry beast bucking and scrambling inside of my coat, most certainly looking for something soft to grab with his sharp little teeth. I flipped over onto my back and spun myself like a break-dancer on acid, and beat my chest with both fists. The ferret was dodging fast and I kept missing. Twisting around, I got to my knees and finally had the presence of mind to grasp the lapels of my coat and rip it wide. Buttons flew, because I'd accidentally popped open my blouse as well. My full-figure support bra was exposed for the entire world to see.

Out shot the beast. Just a galloping blur of hair across the wood floor. I think he ended up under the sergeant's desk, but I'm not sure on that point. I could only hope.

"Lose a contact lens?"

A pair of boots appeared under my nose. I followed the black leather to the ankles, ran my gaze up the legs, and craned my neck around so I could see who was asking.

A police officer bent over, offered his hand, and helped me to my feet. I grunted quite a bit, held onto my busted blouse, resisted the temptation to rub my knees, mostly because I didn't have a free hand, but also because I had to make a quick recovery and I had to act brave. I was feeling like my duties as "officer for a day" were teetering on an early dismissal.

I noticed Murphy's nametag. How in the world was I going to explain what just happened? To make matters worse, I'd been assigned to an incredibly handsome young man, complete with blond flattop, rippling muscles, broad shoulders, and steel thighs. (Okay, so maybe I filled in some of the details.) The smell of testosterone and aftershave hovered around him and, of course, this threw me off balance quite a bit. If I'd been forty years younger, Ted would have been in serious trouble.

"Hi, sir, thanks for the help. I'm your ride-along." I tried to pop to attention, even thought about whipping out a smart salute, but my joints had locked, and I managed only to creak to a bent squat. Of course I didn't let my discomfort show. A couple of short jerks and I got my spine straightened out. Good as new.

As I pulled my shirt together, an older, clearly irritated police officer walked past us, propelling a young woman who looked as if she could use a bath and three weeks of sleep.

She leaned toward me and asked, "Where you get your dope, honey?" She was roughly hauled away.

Smiling weakly at Murphy, I said, "I can explain."

"It's okay," he said. "Guess I should have warned you we've got a little rat problem." He winked at me. "They're everywhere, but I sure don't want to be here when your friend crawls up Sherman's pant leg. They scare the crap out of him." Murphy slid his eyes over to the desk sergeant. "One rodent in the crotch and you'll see the fastest striptease of your life. Wouldn't want that to happen. I've heard he's got some, well, physical deficiencies that we might not want to witness."

I cleared my throat. "I see." I felt a flush creep up my neck. I really wanted to fit in, so I added my two cents' worth. "No big deal?"

Officer Murphy laughed a deep, spontaneous chortle and I felt a hot flush light up my face. Egad. I was always so proper, and my comment was definitely in the ballpark of lewd and lascivious. I think there's a law against that.

"Let's get you checked in and I'll show you around."

He started off, but I couldn't move. I had no buttons on my blouse, remember, so I held onto it with both hands, thinking with great disappointment that I'd just blown my chance at real detective work. I'd have to go home, and explain it all to Ted. I'd be the talk of the choir. Darn.

Murphy was a quick study. He put his arm around my shoulders and nodded toward a door. "I think we can find you something to wear."

I was very grateful. I wiggled my fingers at the desk sergeant, who was dabbing at the coffee on his desk, and followed Murphy, my spirits high once again.

After slipping into a large blue sweatshirt with the words Harvest Police Department across the front in white letters, I felt much better.

First stop. Murphy ushered me into a little room where he explained fingerprint and photograph procedures. I'd settled down quite a bit after my scare with the afterlife, and concentrated on his every word.

The handsome officer took my fingers and pressed them onto an inkpad. "You roll them like this," he said, and transferred my prints onto a card with little boxes on it, one for each finger.

"Now you've done it." I told him.

"It's okay, we have soap and water in the sink over there; it rinses off pretty easily."

Murphy had misunderstood. "What I mean is, now I'm on file and if I hotwire a car you'll know who did it."

Another hearty laugh, and I was quite proud of myself. He was warming up. Soon enough, I'd have the Gerty files in hand.

While I rinsed at the sink, the older officer I'd seen before walked into the room. He gripped the arm of a scruffy-looking guy who was weaving and hollering "False arrest! False arrest!" A blast of beer-stink fouled the air. I could smell it from where I stood.

"Good to see you, Frank," Murphy said. "It's been, what, three weeks? Isn't that a record for you?" He turned to his comrade. "So tell me, Paul, where did you find him this time, in the ladies' john?"

"He was at the mall. Peeking under the women's dressing room doors at Penney's." Paul shook the guy's sleeve.

Beer Breath stumbled and said, "Jus' wanted to find out where that pretty gal got her shoes. No crime in that, right, lady?" He tried to focus on me with eyes so red they looked like they were bleeding.

"As a matter of fact, I got these at Penney's," I chirped, and lifted my left foot.

Paul looked at Murphy.

I drew my head down close to my shoulders. "Or maybe it was Sears. Now that I think about it, it was definitely Sears." Instead of looking more of a fool than I already did, I grabbed up a couple of paper towels and patted at my hands.

"We've got his prints on file. Just snap a couple of shots, will ya? Sherman's out there throwing a fit about the paperwork."

"Well, we don't want to keep the man waiting do we?" Murphy grabbed Frank, moved him in front of the camera, and signaled me over. Oh goodie. I would get a chance to see how this all worked.

As Murphy positioned the guy, who kept trying to sit on the floor, I examined the camera. It was positioned on top of a sturdy tripod. Very sophisticated-looking machine. There was a silver button near the top of the tripod and I ran my finger over it. I pushed it, just to see what the thing was.

Much to my surprise, the camera shot toward the ceiling and came to a lurching halt at the end of a long silver pipe.

"What did I do?" I yelled, my hands nervously fluttering around my mouth.

"It's okay," Murphy said. Poor guy, he had the patience of Job. "It's spring loaded. Makes it easier to move around. I think, just as a precaution here, that you might not want to touch anything else just yet. You know, until you get fully acquainted with everything."

Tears were once again burning at the rims of my eyes. Things weren't really going as well as I'd hoped. Just in case Ted asked, though, there were some details about the evening that wouldn't be mentioned.

Loud noises and the sound of breaking furniture came from the reception area. I looked to Murphy in question.

He frowned. That could only mean one thing. Something bad was happening out front.

"The glamour shots will have to wait, big boy." Murphy hustled Beer Breath over to one of the chairs and whipped out a pair of cuffs. He slapped them over a hairy wrist and had his prisoner shackled to the chair's arm, quick as a whistle. "Take a nap and I'll be right back."

"Okay," I said.

"Not you, just, . . . well, wait here."

Officer Murphy raced out of the room. I heard the sound of breaking glass and some colorful language that I certainly would never repeat in polite company.

I sat beside the shoe peeper. He craned around to get close to my face, which made me very uncomfortable, and his breath curled my eyelashes, but since his hands were tied I could give him a kung fu grip if need be. That might get me some points.

On second thought, there might be something else I could do.

"You're getting your picture taken in a few minutes," I said.

The guy's eyes crossed slightly, then came back to center while he examined my mouth. Maybe that meant he'd gone beer deaf and he was reading my lips.

"I've noticed you have a few blemishes that certainly wouldn't look good in a photo."

More than that—I'd noticed huge red veins criss-crossing over his swollen bluish nose and his pores were large enough to park dippin' dots into quite easily. The man's jaw and eyelids drooped simultaneously. I was losing him.

"Here. I can help you out. Just sit up now. Sit up. Here. Sit up for crying out loud."

Beer Breath had slumped plum over and tried to rest his head in my lap. I jabbed with my fingertips at the top of his head. Since Murphy was still occupied—and from the sound of it, every other cop in the precinct was, too—I was on my own.

"Now that's better. Just sit up like that and let me work my magic. I used to sell Mary Kay and always keep some samples around, just in case."

Just in case? Well this was certainly a first, but God bless Mary Kay, she was always there when you needed her. Well, she was until she died, but never mind that. Her quality products live on, a large variety of which were in my handbag.

With a scoop, I had samples in my hands. I assessed Beer Breath's skin tone and texture, concluded he was on the oily side, lifted some foundation swabs up to his chin, and after making my decision, I went to work.

When Murphy walked in, our criminal was almost prepared for the photo shoot.

"Not yet," I said. "I just need to back comb this a little more and I'll be finished."

Murphy slid to a screeching halt in the middle of the room. A funny strangled sound came out of his mouth, but I couldn't take the time to look at him; I was behind Mr. Beer, yanking the long thin strands of his hair, twisting them into a nice bun. A couple of bobby pins, and it was in place.

"There! What do you think?"

When I looked up at Murphy I knew I was in trouble. His jaw had dropped so far I could count the number of fillings in his lower teeth.

Murphy was such a nice young man that he didn't punish me for the makeover. I admit I'd gotten a little carried away, and maybe Frank had come off looking like Tammy Fae Baker, but that lip color was perfect!

While I waited as the camera flashed, I had time to take a few notes. I was gathering evidence in police procedures, remember, so I paid close attention. I made a special memo to myself about what Murphy had said: Mary Kay was illegal in the booking room. I should have known that.

Paul came in after the pictures were done, looking like he'd got caught in a paper shredder. His clothes were hanging from his body in tatters and the beginning of a good-sized goose egg was purpling and swelling over one eye.

"That woman is gonna be the death of me." He shook his head and accepted Beer Breath.

"Your grandma giving you fits again?" Murphy looked concerned.

"It took four of us to pin 'er down this time."

"I know. But don't you think putting a sleeper hold on her

was just a tad bit over the top?" Murphy gently put his hand on Paul's shoulder.

"She kicked me in the 'nads!"

Paul put a finger to his lips and slid his eyes toward me. I pretended not to notice, careful not to show my sinking disappointment. Darn. I'd missed a good takedown. I wondered who Paul's grandma was, wondered if we'd played bingo together once or twice, but I didn't get the chance to find out.

Paul hustled Beer Breath Frank away, and after checking a few things with the desk sergeant, Officer Murphy signaled for me to follow. He led me out the back way, down a hall, and through a door. We passed the lockup, used, he said, to hold miscreants until they were released or sent on up to the big house, depending on the severity of their crimes. There was only one perp behind bars when we went by: Frank, who sat on the floor and admired my shoes. Another door took us into the garage and eventually out to the police station parking lot. Our car was waiting. My cop shift had officially begun.

CHAPTER EIGHT

I followed Officer Murphy to a parking lot filled with identical cars, white with Harvest Police Department painted in green letters across their sides. I was feeling pretty important. Expecting to take my place in the back of Murphy's car, I stood by the rear door, but when my escort pulled open the front passenger-side door, I played muscle tug-o'-war with my lips trying to hide my smile. This was getting better by the minute.

A brief orientation by Murphy taught me a few of the particulars. He showed me how the radio operated, but with all the buttons and funny sounds and complicated doodads, and because, as Ted likes to remind me, I'm a bit technologically challenged, I nodded a lot without understanding and figured I'd read up on it later. Murphy pointed out something mounted between the sun visors and explained it was a video camera. This was used to record subjects during a stop, and I imagined was a good manager to keep the cops honest too. I learned the car was called a cruiser, and between our seats was a shotgun. That perked up my interest, since I'd already noticed Murphy kept a gun holstered on his firm thigh. Maybe the extra gun was for me.

"And what's this for?" I started to touch a lever on a black, plastic box, but when Officer Murphy looked panicked and made a false lunge, I thought better and put my hands in my lap.

"This?" Murphy flipped a switch.

Imagine every cell in your body bursting at warp speed. Good thing I still have pretty good bladder control, because the button he'd toggled was the siren.

"Sorry, ma'am, didn't know your earrings would fly out when I did that." He quickly quelled the noise. "I'll help you find 'em when our shift is done. I hope you don't wear hearing aids too." The poor guy was as white as rice.

"Don't you worry about them." I waved him away. "And I don't wear hearing aids, but thank you." But I just might need them after that assault. Should have been prepared for that.

"So where do we go now?"

Murphy pulled out of the parking lot. "Mostly I drive around, look for anything out of place."

"Drug busts, prostitutes, that kind of thing?"

"Well, we have a few prostitutes this side of town, but mostly it's kids getting into trouble or your out-of-control family argument."

"Darn. I wanted to meet a prostitute," I said. "Maybe I could be a decoy and we could arrest some johns."

"Hmmm. Maybe."

I don't know if Officer Murphy took my decoy idea seriously, but I wanted him to know I could talk the talk. Already I was thinking Jolene could probably lend me some of her shorts and tube tops. Get some cheek leak going. I'd seen some pretty good stings on *Cops* and with some heavy mascara I might be able to pull it off. Not my tube top, of course—unless it was for a really good cause.

"We see a fair amount of drug activity." Murphy switched on the windshield wipers. Snow had become heavy and floated in his line of vision. "Unfortunately, it tends to lead to a lot of the other crimes that happen around here. It's not just a local problem. It's everywhere."

We drove along and I noticed everybody was following the

speed limit and using their blinkers, and not because of the weather conditions. A few people waved at us, and I returned the gesture. When I saw a woman trying to cross the street without the aid of a crosswalk, I scowled and pointed a reprimanding finger at her as we passed. She quickly stepped back onto the curb. The law is a powerful thing.

Maybe I should have opted to ride along with someone from the big city of Spokane after all. There certainly would have been more action than what we were getting. After about thirty minutes of driving down this street and up that one without any gunplay, I decided it was time for me to make good use of this opportunity.

"I had a friend once," I started, ready to introduce the matter of Gerty.

"Really? Just one? That's sad."

"No, no, I mean, I had a friend who died recently."

"That's even worse. Your only friend, gone."

"Oh, I have lots of friends, this one just happens to be dead."

"I hope you're not keeping her in your guest room." Murphy looked at me out of the corner of his eye.

"Is there a law against that?"

"Not if you don't tell anyone." He grinned.

"You'd certainly be the first to know. But seriously, you probably heard about my friend, as a matter of fact. Her name is Gerty Knickers. She was found dead in her home. I'm sure you have people who investigate that sort of thing."

"When?"

"All the time. Or maybe you just investigate the suspicious deaths."

"No. I mean, when did she die?"

"Yesterday, I think." I was trying to remember what the article had said. "It could have been two days ago. How long does it take to write obituaries?"

"Probably an hour or two."

"Okay, smarty pants, how long does it take to get an obituary in the paper after a death?"

"I have no idea. Did your friend die of natural causes?"

I wanted to say, *It was murder I tell ya, murder! And your department screwed things up big time!* But I didn't. It wouldn't have been good to alienate the officer when I really needed him to help me with this case.

"Officer Murphy," I said.

"Please. Call me Mike."

"Okay, Mike, from what I know, she died of a heart attack. She was working late and her husband found her the next morning. She was a painter. It looked like she just keeled over."

"Are you sure? She might have fallen from the scaffolding."

"Huh?"

"Or, if she was stripping the siding she could have gotten a lung full of asbestos. It's still in a lot of old insulation. That'll kill ya quick as snot."

"I'm afraid I didn't make myself clear. She was an artist. She didn't paint houses or anything like that. For Pete's sake, she was seventy-eight years old if she was a day!"

"Well, my father retiled our whole basement when he was sixty-nine. Right after that he had a heart attack. I kept telling him he was too old for that sort of thing, always trying to act like one of the kids . . ."

Murphy must have remembered whom he was talking to because he was suddenly silent. Actually, I took it as a compliment. Maybe I looked younger than I really was, and that was the reason for his careless remark. I pushed at the back of my hair and reached for my lip gloss. I had to dig around for my purse because the evening had crept up on us and I couldn't see a thing in the shadows by my feet.

"If it looked like your friend died from a heart attack, but it was questionable, there probably would have been an autopsy, but I haven't heard anything about an investigation. Sometimes these things are quite obvious."

"Maybe, but what if—and I'm just gathering info here—what if someone had a reason for her to be dead?" I rubbed my lips together and examined them in my little mirror light.

"If her death looked suspicious, then there would be some questions. Usually the detectives start with the ones closest to the victim, and work their way out. You know, check the in-laws before the outlaws. Was she married?"

"I think so. Yeah, I remember hearing something about him." I also remembered Gerty saying, "My paintings will probably be worth a fortune after I'm dead, May Bell." And the words of Betty and Inez came to mind: "She was getting ready to shut us down! We'd have been out on the streets!" Not to mention her art dealer and other disgruntled FETA infractionators. I don't know if that's a real word, but it's an ample description nevertheless. I wondered, too, if there were people out there with a lot of her artwork, needing quick cash, and not above shoving a paintbrush up her nose.

"By the way, where did she live?"

I felt my heart sink. I didn't remember where Gerty lived, exactly. I'd only been to her house once. "Does that make a difference?"

"Of course. If she lived in Spokane, her death would have been handled by the SPD. But I have to tell you, an elderly lady dying of a heart attack doesn't usually give the detectives much cause for alarm. They have a hard enough time keeping up with serial murders."

"We have those here?"

"Oh, yeah."

I sat up straighter. Serial killers in the Northwest. Who'da thunk it?

"No, she died here in Harvest. I know that much, but I can't remember her exact address."

"Hmmm." Murphy seemed to be searching his memory. "It was probably when I was off shift. Did someone call the police, or the ambulance?"

I groaned. "I don't know." I should have asked Bertha and Inez. I had come to a dead end. "What usually happens when somebody dies?"

"Well, most people call nine-one-one. Then the dispatcher calls for an ambulance and the police. If the person is dead when the ambulance driver gets there, the medical people won't move the body. They'll let the responding police officers look at the scene, talk to people who might have been in the house at the time of death. They'll check any meds the decedent was on, ask about any prior medical conditions, that sort of thing. If someone was in the house and it just looks like a natural death, they call the medical examiner, ask the family what funeral home the body should go to, and that's it."

"So they don't order an autopsy or anything?"

"Probably not, if there's nothing suspicious about the death."

Hmmm. I sat quietly. So Gerty was probably just hauled away without so much as a proper investigation.

Murphy turned on his blinker. "What do you say we stop for coffee? Looks like it's going to be a pretty quiet night. Sorry, May."

"That's okay," I said, but couldn't hide my disappointment. This wasn't at all like *Forensic Files* or *LAPD Blues* or whatever, just a lot of driving, and I had yet to gather any worthwhile information about Gerty's death. This was looking less and less like a murder every minute. If the cops didn't see anything out of place—and they would have asked questions if there hadn't been any heart medication lying around—then my ideas were just the product of an active imagination.

Murphy pulled into a parking space in front of a convenience store.

"Sit tight, Mrs. List, I'll get the coffee and you can wait in here." Officer Murphy was such a gentleman. I thanked him and said I like a lot of cream.

The guy behind the counter must have known Mike, because he waved and smiled at him when he entered the store. I watched them through the large, bright windows. Mike chatted for a minute with the guy, and then walked toward the back where I knew the coffeepots were simmering. I had to admit, the guy was one handsome fella. His uniform fit like it was tailored, and all the hardware hanging around his belt just added to the vision of masculinity. Wasn't I the lucky girl?

Mike had left his cruiser running, so I was warm and toasty, but I could tell the temperature had dropped outside. A couple coming out of the store breathed plumes of vapor breath and they were bundled up. Even the short trot from the front door to their cars left their shoulders sprinkled with white flakes. They drove off, and shortly after, two guys parked beside me in an old Ford pickup. Both guys jumped out. Under the falling snow they paused to talk before going into the store. They were bundled in long black trench coats, ski masks, and gloves.

It wasn't that cold out.

While Mike was in the back filling up our portable Styrofoam cups with sippy lids, the two guys approached the counter. They didn't have a thing in their hands to buy. One leaned across the counter. The cashier stepped back guardedly.

Oh my gosh! It must be a holdup! How brazen! Right in front of a police car, they were holding up the store, and if I didn't do something they were going to get away with it. This night wouldn't be a total waste. Not if I had anything to do with it. Officer Murphy and I would get our collar if I had to do it myself.

I was so nervous I couldn't think. What should I do? Which button was the radio? Which one was the siren? Was the camera on? Should I honk the horn? No, that would alert the robbers. Oh, Mike, what's taking you so long? Was he taking a bathroom break? Probably. Or perhaps he was taking a little special care with the coffees. Maybe it was my fault. I shouldn't have asked for the extra cream.

Then I was hit with a horrible thought.

If these guys were so cavalier about holding up a store right in front of a police cruiser, then they weren't afraid of being seen. They were prepared to shoot it out. I knew that. They always shoot it out. Take no hostages. Leave no witnesses. They weren't afraid of getting caught, because first they were going to kill Mike as soon as he came around the rack of cheese puffs and Eskimo pies. Then they were going to shoot out the surveillance cameras, and after that—they'd come for me.

The robbers were getting impatient. The cashier was having a hard time with the register. He looked flustered and banged on it while glancing around. I prayed nobody else would drive up right then. No telling what would happen if the robbers were interrupted. I had to act, and I had to act fast. I didn't want this to turn into a hostage situation.

Careful not to draw attention to myself, I climbed awkwardly from the passenger side over behind the wheel. Remember there was a fully loaded shotgun between the two, and I was thankful the barrel was pointed down and forward.

Forget the radio, forget the other toggles and switches, I didn't know what was what, so I quickly formulated a plan.

With trembling knees, I quietly backed the car away from the store and moved it around to the dark side of the convenience store, while close enough to see through the front windows. I wanted them to think Mike had just driven away. I was breathing hard, praying and hoping Mike would stay put. If he surprised them . . . I shook off the terrible vision. I knew what I had to do.

I'd wait out the robbers and chase them down when they made their getaway. Good thing I'd bought that computer car chase program. I was about to put my skills to good use.

I didn't hear any gunshots. Mike was taking his time and didn't make an appearance. No chance to feel relieved, though, because when the two young men dashed through the front door and jumped into their truck, I grabbed the gearshift, thumbed on the cruiser's headlights—at least I found those okay—and the chase was on.

CHAPTER NINE

The smell of exhaust and burning rubber filled my nostrils.

Romping on the gas in my haste merely caused my back tires to spin for a few seconds until they caught, and when they did, I zoomed forward heading straight for the gas pumps. Cranking the wheel hard, just like I'd learned in my lessons, I avoided slamming fender-first into the pumps but couldn't avoid careening off the refuse cans placed inappropriately in my path. They bounced and scattered sippy lids, napkins, and crumpled bags across the parking lot.

I squinted; afraid for a minute I'd lost the truck in the falling snow. There! Red taillights turned left onto the road. The truck was moving fast. So fast, in fact, that by the time I got the cruiser behind it, there were two cars between us.

Mike was back at that convenience store, by now wondering where his car was and worrying about me, but I was sure that after talking to the traumatized cashier, he would understand. He'd be making calls to his officer buddies, telling them about the holdup, telling them they should be on the lookout for two thugs followed by his police cruiser. Maybe he'd even alert the whole of Spokane County—the sheriff's department, highway patrol, all units.

I just needed to keep the crooks in sight long enough for backup, but with the precarious road conditions, people were driving cautiously and the truck was pulling away.

No time to be timid, May Bell.

Elbows out, I cranked the wheel, swerved around the first car and whipped back into my lane. I was actually panting after that daring move. This adrenaline rush thing wasn't quite as invigorating as I'd hoped. More like an electric shock to the spleen.

The truck took a hard right heading in the direction of downtown Spokane. I followed. Where was my backup? The truck was gaining speed again, moving out farther ahead, so I pushed the accelerator down harder. Instead of pulling off onto one of the business roads, the truck looped around and headed east toward Idaho.

My jaws ached, my teeth chattered, my hands trembled, but there was no help in sight. Maybe the two had done something to Mike back at the store and he couldn't call for help. Maybe I was all alone! Oh my gosh, what should I do? I just couldn't let them get across state lines. I heard a low moan and realized it was coming from my throat.

Calm, May Bell, calm. Figure out the radio. Flip some switches, get the bubble lights turning, sound the sirens, and make a citizen's arrest on these two!

It was so dark and slick on the roads that it took everything in my power to handle the car with my left hand while pushing, pulling, thumbing, jabbing, and toggling switches and knobs with my right. Without realizing it, I was a mere car length away from our perpetrators when I hit the right button and the hyper-warble sounded on the police cruiser. Simultaneously, the lights began to rotate. This time I didn't have any earrings to lose, but my dental work shifted slightly.

Apparently I'd done something noteworthy, because the truck slowed. But still, it didn't stop. I reached out my hand and felt around. In the process I hit the siren knob and turned it off. Just as well, I could finally hear myself think. I found a cold, hard knobby thing, which I determined to be the radio. Wish

I'd listened more carefully when Mike explained how to use it, but it didn't make a difference at this point; raising it to my lips I shouted into it the first thing that came to mind. I needed to alert the dispatcher immediately.

"Civilian at the wheel! Civilian at the wheel!"

Amazingly, the truck moved out again, this time full-throttle.

"I don't know how to use this thing!" I cried into the radio. "What should I do?"

The truck left the highway and darted toward an underpass. I had no choice but to follow. We bumped over railroad tracks, we both caught air, we both bottomed out, sparks were flying, lights were spinning, and my stomach was in a permanent panic-spasm. Soon we would be in the industrial district of town, away from civilization, and that thought didn't sit well with me at all. There was another convenience store up ahead, and that's where I decided I'd take these two guys out.

Still, I tried numerous times to raise someone on the radio.

"I have no badge! I'm all alone! I'm totally untrained for this!"

Nothing at all. Not even a squawk from the radio to make me feel at ease. The guys in the truck weren't intimidated in the least by the cop car behind them.

My mood turned from fear to anger. Here I was, representing the law, and these two guys were thumbing their noses at me. In my computer course there was a little maneuver I'd practiced over and over. It was called a fishtail. I think the police call it something else, like a PIT maneuver, but it was all the same.

Hunkered over the steering wheel, I tromped on the gas. With pinched lips and flexed thighs, I braced for the impact.

All it takes is a well-placed nudge on the rear quarter panel and an evading car will go out of control, spin around, and be incapacitated.

This is how it's supposed to work.

For some reason, I misjudged, punched the back of the truck with my car, and got its big trailer hitch stuck through the grill of Murphy's cruiser. A large white airbag billowed out, struck me squarely in the face, and quickly shriveled. I shook my head and blinked back the tears pooling in my eyes.

There was a lot of screeching as I pumped the brakes in an attempt to disengage. Plenty of smoke, more burning rubber, and a lot of swerving on the wet streets while I continued to scream into the radio.

"Civilian at the wheel! Approaching convenience store! Defenseless old woman! A little help here!"

I was scared and full of fury, but the truck driver was in a rage. Since there was no controlling my own car, I hunkered down, waiting for the shots to start flying. I was certain the two thugs had high-powered rifles now trained out their back window.

But wait. I had a high-powered shotgun of my own between the front seats. What was I thinking? I clawed at the deflated airbag, moved it aside, and in the process hit the hyper-warble siren button to on again. I reached for the shotgun.

The truck driver rocked his vehicle left and right, struggling to shake its cop-car tail, but it was no use. We were locked up tighter than Fort Knox.

Out my window, I caught sight of the convenience store as we flew past. Darn! Soon we would be away from town in a dark and deserted area, and that was bad. I needed to bring this fight to an end really fast, or I was toast.

One thing I did remember during my orientation with Murphy was his instruction about the shotgun. There was a little key on the key ring for the locking device holding down the bulky weapon. Since I wasn't driving anymore anyway, there was no need to keep the car running. I slammed the brakes again, and this time we went into a complete spin. Fighting centrifugal force, I shoved the car into neutral and shut off the engine. More screeching and burned rubber. Even as the lights twirled and the sirens blared, I was thinking clearly as only one in this type of situation can do. I found the little key and unlocked the shotgun.

We weren't going too fast at this point; I could actually make out the winking neon sign of a bar a quarter mile down the road. I had just enough time.

Somehow I got my window down and hung out of it with the butt of the shotgun planted firmly against my left shoulder. I rested the gun barrel on the outside mirror. It was impossible to see the tires from this angle. I needed to get the truck moving left so I could get a bead on his back tire. With my free hand I cranked the steering wheel of the cruiser and nudged the truck off to the left. Perfect! I had a clear shot and took aim. If you must know, I had my eyes closed quite a bit of the time this was all happening, but what the heck. Whatever works.

With the first shot I got lucky and blew out the truck's left front tire. I think I might have fractured my clavicle and I knew I would definitely need some cotton in my left ear after that, but the truck shuddered to a stop in a grassy field beside the bar. Smoke billowed from under the hood of the cruiser, giving me enough coverage to dart out the door and around to the back of the car.

Using the car as a shield I peeked around and shouted. "Get out with your hands up!"

I transferred the weapon to my business hand and kept the shotgun trained on the men in the truck. Something went "pop" under the cruiser and a foul-smelling liquid gushed out onto the ground.

"Get out now, and don't try any funny business!"
Nothing.

Oh for Pete's sake. They couldn't hear a thing with the siren going. I ran in a low crouch back to the car and found the right knob. The siren went off but I kept the lights going. Blue, red, round and round. I peered out again and shouted with every ounce of energy I had left.

"I said, get out with your hands up!" To make my point I pumped my gun like I'd seen Arnold do in *T-2* and shot off another round. I blew away the truck's left door handle. That got their attention.

Two men tumbled from the truck, their eyes wide, hands high in the air.

"Don't shoot! Please, lady, don't shoot! We ain't armed!"

Likely story. "Get on the ground." I forced my voice down to a low growl.

They complied without a whimper.

The excitement had caught the attention of the bar patrons. Weavers and craners staggered right into the crime scene. I waved my gun around and ordered them back. From a distance I heard sirens approaching. I breathed a sigh of relief. Murphy was okay. He'd called for help. I was saved.

When a police car rolled onto the scene I imagined how surprised the officer would be to see me standing there with the situation under control, my foot firmly planted on the neck of the bigger perp, the gun pointed at the head of the other dude.

Paul jumped out of the car, and he had Officer Murphy with him.

"I got 'em for ya, Mikey!" I sang out, nodding my head toward the two guys on the ground.

"She sho' did!" A very drunk man from the bar chuckled and pushed at his cowboy hat.

"Get back." Murphy shooed the bar crowd away.

"Yes," I cheerfully echoed. "Get back everyone, nothing to see here."

Mike didn't look as proud as I thought he would. In fact, he looked downright nauseated. He was a sickly shade of gray and his eyes had lost their sparkle.

"Hey, you! Here they are. I got 'em for ya." I searched his face for some sign that I'd done the right thing. "They would have gotten away. Sorry I took the car, but it seemed like the right thing to do under the circumstances. I'm really glad they didn't hurt you."

Paul was hauling up the two men, who were very cooperative. After all that racing and screeching, I was quite surprised to see they were as docile as all this.

"They knocked off the convenience store," I explained to the crowd, still gawking around us.

"Ohhhh," they all said in drunken unison. They weren't too impressed and trundled back to their liquor.

"May, can I talk with you a minute?" Mike whispered into my ear and took my elbow.

"Sure, bud, no prob." I hefted the shotgun onto my shoulder and walked off to the side. Two more police cars pulled up and the officers got out to chat with Paul. I wondered what they were talking about.

"May, what gave you the idea these guys robbed the convenience store?"

My stomach twisted into knots.

"They didn't?"

Mike slowly shook his head.

"But they had ski masks, and they didn't buy anything, and the cashier looked really nervous."

"And that's why you chased them down, blasted them with my shotgun, and destroyed a perfectly good police car?"

"But . . . but, I was sure they were up to no good!" I could feel a big lump in my throat, and the thought of a prison uniform flashed through my mind. What had I done?

"And they resisted arrest! Doesn't that count for anything? I had my siren and flashers going and they just kept going!"

Mike just frowned while he looked at my face.

"I suppose you'll be wanting this." I handed over the shotgun.

"Mike!" Paul signaled for Officer Murphy. The other officers were chatting amongst themselves.

I followed, feeling miserable. The two guys stood by their truck, ski masks pushed up on their heads. They didn't look as traumatized as before; in fact, they looked downright relaxed.

"Apparently, these guys stopped in to see their buddy at the convenience store before driving up to Mount Spokane. They have a little cabin up near there, and they were going to do some skiing tomorrow."

Murphy shined his flashlight into the back of the truck. Sure enough. Nice skis, new boots, I thought. Shoot. Another collar gone bad.

Murphy gave me one of those "boy are you in trouble" looks.

"Sorry for the scare, guys." Paul patted the big skier on his shoulder.

The guy shrugged off the apology. "Could happen to anyone," he said. "If you don't mind, though, we'd like to get on our way. It's late and we don't want to get caught in the snow."

They're in an awfully big hurry, I thought. And you're going to leave with a flat tire? I wondered why they weren't screaming about that. They even waved off help in changing it.

The smaller skier laughed loudly and told a rude joke while he pushed at the cruiser's fender with little effect at dislodging it from the trailer hitch. His partner reached for a spare, hefted it from the back and rolled it toward the disintegrated tire.

"You guys can go on now—we'll take care of this. But thanks, anyway." He giggled a high nervous chirp.

And you're just a bit too cheery.

Oh no, May, don't start thinking wicked thoughts again.

You're already bum deep in doo-doo. Still, I couldn't help but wonder, skiing in October?

A few of the other officers jumped in to help get the cars disconnected. Murphy crawled onto the truck's bumper and started bouncing it. That got the vehicles unhooked. I noticed then that I'd done some damage. The bumper on the truck had been cracked.

That's strange; the black bumper was fractured and splintered. I thought those things were metal, but this one looked plastic, like a hollow tube. I walked over to the truck and bent down.

"Mike? What's this?" I shoved my finger through the crack and a trickle of white powder spilled out onto the ground.

Four officers whipped their guns from their holsters at the same time and went into a crouch, all screaming, "Get on the ground! Get on the ground!"

I hit the dirt.

Mike hollered, "Not you, May, get up!" In a frenzy, Mike leapt from the bumper, reached out, and grabbed the back of my coat. Those muscles I'd imagined were real. With a powerful jerk, he had me behind him. The other police officers scurried to take cover behind open car doors.

"Get on the ground!" Again all of the officers were shouting commands, but not at me, thank goodness; they were pointing their guns at the two guys from the truck.

I tried to see what was going on, but Mike kept pushing my head back.

"Get down!" What a strong voice coming from Mikey. He got those guys down on the ground, had his cuffs out, and with the aid of his fellow officers, had the two all bound up before he explained.

"Well, hit me with a brick." Paul laughed and reached out to pump my hand.

What had just happened? I looked at Mike.

"Come here, May." Mike took my arm and led me back to the truck. The whole place was lit up with swirling lights and some strobes.

He pushed his finger into the crack in the bumper. A tatter of plastic poked out and along with it more white powder. Murphy dropped some of the powder into a plastic pouch and shook it. A line of pink on top of a line of blue liquid came into focus. He held it up for me to see. "Do you know what this is?"

"Baby powder?" I asked weakly.

"Cocaine. Lots of cocaine. I think we just made one of the biggest busts this year. If my guess is right, this whole bumper is hollow and filled with it. These guys aren't going skiing; they were probably on their way up to Bonners Ferry and over the Canadian border. I don't know how you knew, but you just caught yourself some bad guys."

I heard the two men on the ground cursing at me, but they could have called me anything at that point; it wouldn't have taken away the relief I felt at not having to spend time in the gray bar motel.

"Maybe the guy at the convenience store was their contact." I was all serious.

"Could be." Mike smiled broadly. "Could very well be."

"And that's probably why they ran from me when I was after them. They didn't even act scared or anything." Still serious.

"Possibly, but I think I have another idea about that."

"Oh? What?"

Murphy got into his police car and asked me to take my seat on the passenger side. What I learned next was about as embarrassing as it gets. At least up to that point in my life.

CHAPTER TEN

"When I came outside and noticed you and my police car were gone, you can probably imagine how shocked I was," Mike said.

I nodded innocently.

"But I thought, surely if you had taken the car you would have a really good reason, and you'd use the radio like I'd shown you."

I felt a flush make its way up my neck. "I didn't really know how to use it."

As if to hammer home the point, the radio squawked out nonsense. Murphy put his mouth to it and mumbled something I didn't understand. Then he turned to me.

"But you tried, right?"

"I was just so nervous. I kept calling on it. I tried to get help. I said 'civilian at the wheel!' I said, 'I'm not trained for this! What should I do?' All the things that I thought would get someone's attention, but nobody helped!"

Officer Murphy put his tongue on his upper teeth and pulled his lip down. I'd seen Ted do that when he was trying really hard not to laugh at me.

"What?" I asked.

Murphy pointed to the little black plastic knobby thing I'd been talking into. There was another nearly identical one on the left. They were both tethered to the black box by a plastic coil. "Do you see this?"

"Yes."

Murphy picked up the thing on the left. "This is the radio," he said. Then he picked up the other one on the right. "And this is the PA."

"I was talking on the PA, wasn't I?"

"Yes, you were."

"And everything I said, those guys could hear."

"Yes, they could."

I pursed my lips. "Well, now I guess I know why they didn't stop."

"Rookie mistake." Murphy's eyes were twinkling again.

The evening was nearly over. All that excitement, a good bust, and the beginnings of frostbite got me a real cup of coffee at the Harvest Inn, a charming country home turned B & B in Harvest's city center. With a bookstore and coffee shop in its lobby, the inn was a popular place—warm, cozy, and bustling when we entered. The sound of an espresso machine hissed a greeting, and the smell of coffee beans sent me right up to heaven. There was even a rugged stone fireplace with a crackling fire in one corner.

Murphy clocked out for his "lunch" hour and walked me in. He escorted me to the counter, where I placed an order. That was probably the best latte I'd ever had in my life. I got the vente and bought Mike a regular house blend. We found a little round table near the fire and settled in.

While I sucked through two skinny straws, I decided this would be my last chance at digging up some information on Gerty.

I let Mike blow on his coffee in silence for a few minutes before asking my first question.

"Will you have a lot of paperwork to fill out this evening after our bust?"

"Always paperwork. It's just part of the glamour of police work."

"I guess there's a lot of paperwork when there's a murder too, huh?" Sip, sip.

Mike didn't flinch. Blow, blow.

By now I don't think anything I did would surprise him. Questions about murder were just innocent things.

"Tons of paperwork."

Mike nodded his head at three young, well-dressed ladies as they stood up from a couch near a back wall. He locked eyes with one of the girls, and as the trio passed us on their way out, she stopped.

"How've ya been Mike?" she purred. Lifting a finger, she trailed it down the back of his neck and then bent around, took his jaw in her manicured hand, and gave him a lingering kiss on the mouth. Lots of tongue.

Mike gently pushed her away and cleared his throat. "I'm working, Sheila."

"Yes, Sheila, Officer Murphy is working. Move along." I waved my hand at her.

Sheila snickered. "Your taste in women sure has changed, babe. When did you start dating my grandma?"

The sorority sisters snorted.

Without missing a beat, Mike answered, "Right after I dropped you off at preschool."

Sheila's cheeks colored and then she narrowed her eyes and addressed me in a snotty little voice. "So, lady. Has he let you handle his, uh, gun yet?"

I bristled. "My dear, not only have I handled his gun"—I winked at Mike—"but it's huge, nearly blew off my shoulder, and I have the bruises to prove it. And by the way, I'm wearing his shirt."

When I looked at Mike he was sitting lower in his chair.

Sheila flipped her hair and stomped away.

When they were gone I whispered loudly, "Prostitutes?"

"Not her. That was my sister."

For a minute I was struck dumb. Then, I dismissed the admission. I wasn't there to judge. There was certainly a reasonable explanation.

"Kidding, May. She's an ex-girlfriend."

"And good riddance, I should say. You're too good for her."

"That's what my mom says."

"Smart woman. Now. About your homicide paperwork." I was determined to pursue the line of questioning. "Do you keep all of that information at the station?"

"It depends." Mike lifted a napkin off the table and wiped at his mouth. "Where the murder was committed, of course, and whether or not it's an ongoing investigation or if it's a closed case."

I sucked some more and did some thinking.

"Do you handle all of the cases in Spokane County?"

"I'd be a pretty busy guy if I did."

"Are there that many killers out there?" I was aghast, but the thought of so much to do was enticing.

"Actually, I don't handle any of the Spokane cases. We're a separate jurisdiction here in Harvest. Spokane proper has its own investigation team. The SPD doesn't get involved unless we ask. However, since the SPD has better resources and more experience in a lot of things, when the smaller stations hit a dead end they might call on the city for help."

"Dead end?" I asked.

"You could say that."

"When it's not cut and dried," I said, nodding.

"Oh, I think we had one of those a few years ago, as I remember—it was the husband. Used a meat cleaver, or maybe it was an ax. Cut up his wife and—" Murphy stopped suddenly, checking my reaction, but I was getting used to his jokes.

"You're sick."

"Gallows humor." Mike scratched his chin.

"It's nice to know a Good Humor man, but I need a favor," I said.

Mike raised his eyebrows.

"I'd really like to know more about what killed my friend Gerty. What was the cause of death? What did the autopsy say, if there was one? You know, how was it listed, who found the body, how was it reported, that sort of thing." Sip, sip.

"Well, you can do that yourself, May. Autopsy reports are available to the public."

"Really! I didn't know that!" How wonderful! Sip, sip.

"You just have to fill out the right forms. If, and I say if, there was an autopsy."

"Just like that. I thought there was always an autopsy."

"Not necessarily, and probably not if it looked like natural causes."

"But what if her death is being investigated?"

"Now, that would be different. I'll tell you what." Murphy leaned forward. "If you really want to know more about this, I'll ask a few questions and see what I can find out." He leaned back. "But I'm not promising anything."

"Oh, no. Nothing that would get us in trouble."

Mike blinked rapidly, no doubt reliving what had happened just before our coffee break.

He shook his head to clear the vision. "Right."

I glanced around, leaned over the table, and lowered my voice. "Can you get hold of the lab reports, too?"

"The toxicology reports?"

"Yeah. Those. I mean, if there were any."

"First, I guess we'll have to find out where she died, in whose jurisdiction, and who would have that report. You know, the police might not have even gone to her home if her husband drove her to the hospital."

I hadn't thought of that. "It would be pretty creepy if she was already dead, don't you think?"

"Some people just do crazy things."

"But if her husband called nine-one-one the police would have shown up, right?"

"Right."

"And there would be some paperwork."

"Right."

"And if they did some blood tests or something, we'd be able to know."

"It should be on the autopsy report, I think. I'm not sure. I'll check it out."

"That would be really nice." I patted Mike's hand.

I stopped short of telling him about my suspicions. Actually, there wasn't much I had to go on except my suspicions, but the reports would help me decide if this was a case worth investigating.

I certainly hoped it was.

My first day on the police beat ended with some of the paperwork Murphy had mentioned, but otherwise uneventfully. I left the station after he promised again to find out what he could about Gerty Knickers. Like a gentleman, he walked me to my car and waited as I backed out of the parking lot.

The drive home seemed to take forever. When I pulled into my driveway, I was moving on sheer will. Every joint in my body groaned and creaked. The weather hadn't improved; the air was crisp and cold and the sky was falling. There was a fine white snow blanket covering my front lawn. My neighbor, Mr. Fitz, peeked through his curtains. Nosy.

The minute my key was in the lock, Ted opened the door,

kissed me on the cheek, and asked, "So, how'd it go?"

I took his kiss, answered it with one of my own, and said, "It was all right. You'll probably read about it in tomorrow's paper."

"That's nice." Ted took my coat. "You want some coffee? I put on decaf."

"Ted." I looked at his feet. "You're wearing my slippers again."

"No, I'm not."

"What do you call those?" I pointed at my pink fluffies.

"Got you a new pair today. These are mine, now."

"Don't go outside with those on. Mr. Fitz will report you to the medical board."

"I had to get you some new ones. Trixie spoiled mine."

"You two need to call a truce," I said, and looked over at the couch where Trixie was sprawled in the glow of a reading lamp. She raised her head and grinned.

Ted didn't tell me how my cat had spoiled his slippers and I didn't ask. That detail was best left alone. My new fluffies were nice. After changing into my pajamas I slid my feet into them, careful to be ready if I felt something warm and squishy.

It was after midnight when I caught up with Ted in the kitchen. He looked tired, but like the good husband, he'd waited up for me. It would be a few minutes until I could settle down after all of the excitement. I mentally sorted through the events of the evening, expecting Ted to be curious, and thought there wasn't much I could share without him pulling out some twist ties and binding me to my bed on house arrest. I tested his professional knowledge instead.

"Ted." I took my seat at the table and slurped at my decaf. I quickly talked about my visit to the Poochie Hooch, left out the bit about my undercover interrogation with Jolene's boyfriend, skimmed through a few police work details, said that I'd been given my new shirt as a reward, and then asked,

"Do you think Gerty had an autopsy after she died?"

"Are you still obsessing about your dead friend?"

"Obsessing? Are you saying I'm obsessing? Like I'm nutty, or I have some kind of mental disorder? Obsessing, huh? That's a pretty strong word. I'd call it more professional curiosity."

"What kind of profession?"

I sat up straight in my chair and puffed out my chest. "I'll have you know I got my first collar tonight."

Ted rubbed his swollen eyes and dragged his hands down his face, catching his lower lip before heaving a big sigh. "They let you write a traffic ticket?"

I stood abruptly and walked my coffee to the sink.

"I'm just bustin' your chops, May. Come on. Tell me what you want to know about autopsies. I have a couple of seconds before I drop face-down onto the table."

"No, never mind. We'll talk about it tomorrow."

Let the guy give me one more smarty-pants remark and I was going for the broom. He just didn't understand.

Ted shuffled off, and after rinsing my cup and applying a little ice to my swollen sink knee, I headed for the bathroom to scrub my teeth. One look in the mirror and I wished I'd just gone off to bed unchecked. My hair was flat against my head, one strand hanging over on the wrong side, and my mascara was pooled under my lower lids. Mary Kay would have needed a whole team of specialists to get me looking presentable again. It didn't matter really, unless Mr. Fitz was peeking through the bathroom window—and I wouldn't be surprised if he were—I was heading to bed, so I slathered on a white mask of cold cream, and wiped off the makeup that hadn't already slid off onto my new police shirt. In the mirror I proudly read the backwards letters spelling out *Harvest Police Department*. You can imagine my surprise, however, when I took it off and hung it over the bathtub ledge. On the reverse side of the shirt, in large, white letters, it said *INMATE*.

Feeling my way through the bedroom with the aid of some moonlight, I found my bed after three pieces of furniture connected with my thighs. Ted was already snoring.

I could hardly wait to slide my bruised flesh between those cool sheets. This was going to be one glorious night of sleep. But what was this? A big fat ball of fur was down by my feet under the covers. Trixie.

"Move it," I whispered.

I stretched out, teetering on the edge of the bed. Careful not to disturb Ted, I folded the covers back to allow Trixie an exit. Trixie hissed.

"Don't even start with me." I pushed my feet against Trixie, sort of like peddling a bike, trying to get her angry enough to leave the bed. Instead, she wrapped me up in a ball of claws and a mouth of teeth. I bucked and writhed, kicking like an idiot, and accidentally shot out one leg from under the covers, which launched Trixie across the room. Poor thing. She landed just fine on a pile of laundry, and knowing when she'd been bested, she sulked off down the stairs to find something she could shred. Probably my new linen drapes.

I began to drift away, replaying all of the things that had happened in the last twenty-four hours, but suddenly jerked awake. How could I have been so stupid? I was going about this Gerty business all wrong. A huge piece of evidence was there for the taking and I'd almost missed it. I needed to find out a little more about Gerty's medical history.

I could hardly wait to start a new day of investigation. Tomorrow would prove to me something one way or the other. And if my suspicions were right, the police were going to have some serious explaining to do.

CHAPTER ELEVEN

The next morning I awoke to the sound of Ted singing in the shower. The tune, slightly off-key, was, "If I Were a Carpenter."

What was he doing up so early? It was Sunday. Oh darn! It was Sunday. The investigation would have to be shelved until after church. I ticked off all of the ailments in my little treasure chest of hypochondriac's excuses for missing church and couldn't find anything convincing. Where was a convenient Munchausen's syndrome when you needed one? I should have planned ahead and worked up a good cough the night before. Sometimes it doesn't pay to be married to a doctor. He'd spot a fake bleeding ulcer in a flash, and a bogus stroke would get me a one-way ticket to Spokane General.

I stumbled to my closet and plucked a dress from the hangers. If I hurried, I could get my things together and make a phone call before Ted finished. Hose, shoes, girdle, bra, panties, all flew from drawers and landed on my bed.

I raced to the kitchen and grabbed first the phone and then a business card stuck to my refrigerator by a little magnet. The magnet clattered to the floor. I scooped it up. Darn. No home phone number there. I'd forgotten. What was it? What was it? Aha! I remembered the number as it was written on the outside of the Hooch.

The buttons on the phone kept dodging my fingers. Hurry, May, hurry!

"Hello?" The voice on the line sounded sleepy.

"Bertha?"

"No. Want me to get her?"

Before I could respond there was shuffling on the phone and another sleepy voice came on.

"Yeah?"

"Bertha? This is May."

"Oh, yeah? Well how ya doin', May?"

"Listen. I don't really have time to explain, but I need you and Inez to come to church with me this morning."

"We already went."

I felt my heart drop. "Oh, really? Early service?"

"No, Easter. Last year."

"Can you manage church this morning?"

"I don't know, honey, me and Inez ain't much for religion. We worship in our own way."

"There's something I have to ask you about Gerty. It can't wait until after church, because if my hunch is right, we've got to move immediately on this."

"I guess we can throw something on. What is this about?"

"There's really no time to explain. I'll let you know when I see you. Meet me in the lobby of the Hills Baptist Church. It's on Second and Cherry. Can you do that?"

"All right. You've got me curious now. What time?"

The clock over the stove said we had an hour.

"Can you be there by nine?"

"No problemo, hon." I heard Bertha shout at her sister to get the animals fed in a hurry.

"We'll see you there, May."

I breathed a sigh of relief. "Oh, thank you, Bertha. You can leave church early if you want—I just have to talk with you. It's really important."

"Got it. Oh. By the way. Our little ferret disappeared after you visited yesterday. Do you have any idea where he went?"

I squeezed my eyes closed. "No," I said in a small voice. "No idea. Sorry."

Here I was, lying on a holy day. Maybe I wouldn't have to fake a bleeding ulcer or a stroke after all. God has ways of punishing bad deeds. I just hoped He would hold off until after the morning service.

"Who was that?"

I whirled around, startled.

Ted stood there with his towel twisted on top of his head. The tail end of it wasn't tucked in properly and it kept falling in front of his face. He jerked his head to get it in place, but it wasn't cooperating. I walked over and jerked it off, telling him he looked ridiculous. He had a full head of hair and it stood up like a bush. Then, I felt bad and pasted a smile on my face.

"I thought it would be nice to invite Bertha and Inez to church this morning."

"That was thoughtful." Ted took the towel from my hands and bent over. He tried again to get the turban in place. "The shower's free. I'll get breakfast ready. Müeslix for me, though."

"Still on your health kick?"

Ted stood upright, the towel in a wad on his head. He crouched and boxed the air. "I feel like a new man."

What an invitation. I sidled over, reached out my hands, and squeezed his bottom. "Nope, you feel the same to me."

Ordinarily Ted would have taken that as an amorous come-on, but I was moving too fast that morning. I was in the shower within seconds, formulating my list of questions for the sisters.

I gussied up in record time, tossed down some breakfast, and grabbed my Bible on the way out the door. No time for the life-alert necklace, and I hadn't retrieved my good earrings from last night, so the dangling silver ones sufficed. When I walked out the front door, I knew there was no chance of a relaxing drive to the church. Snow had continued to fall throughout the night and our garage door was barricaded by a good foot of powder.

"Looks like the Hum-V this morning, Maybe Baby."

Ted couldn't have looked more pleased at this sad turn of events. My Camaro was miserable in the snow, but the Hummer was a dream. I hated it. It sat in front of our house, a bright banana-yellow. I remember the day Ted had brought it home. One of his many arrested-development purchases; he'd even given it a name. He called it The Big Banana. I could just imagine him now, showing it off to his nurses.

"Come on out to the parking lot, gals, I want to show you my big banana!"

Sigh.

There was no point in arguing, and there was no time. I scooted through the snow and crawled into the beast. I fit the seatbelt into its latch.

"Now I can show you what this thing can do!" Ted settled himself into the driver's side and stuck the key into the hole. The engine turned over with a rumble.

"Wait a minute, Ted, I want to grab the Sunday paper."

I left the growling Hummer, shuffled back through the snow, and retrieved the paper from the front porch. Back once again, I had the paper open while Ted buckled me into my seat. My shoes were full of snow and I kicked them off, looking quickly through the pages for notice of Gerty's funeral, memorial service, or—better yet—an indication that her death was being investigated as something suspicious. No luck there, but what I did find jarred me nearly as hard as the jolt I took when Ted peeled away from our house.

"Ted, would you look at this?" I flipped the paper over to the business section. "They're auctioning off all of Gerty's paintings! Look here. Look here!" I smacked the paper for emphasis. The nerve.

"I guess her husband needed the money," Ted said lightly, as he revved the gas like a teenager.

"Exactly." I folded the paper onto my lap and narrowed my eyes. "Seems a little suspicious, doesn't it?"

Ted was ignoring me as usual. His face was lit up and he wore a grin a mile wide. Get the man behind the wheel of a behemoth like the Hummer and any conversation was lost to him.

"Hold on, May! We're running a little late. This could get hairy!"

Ted stomped on the gas and whipped the Hummer onto the road, skidded toward the center line, and dodged an oncoming snowplow. We were covered momentarily by a white sheet. The world went invisible.

"Ted, do you mind?" I grabbed for the dashboard. "I'd rather get to church late than dead."

"Don't you worry about that, my little chickadee—this is one primo machine. It'll get us there just fine."

"Then why are you driving with your head out the window?"

"I think the windshield wipers are frozen. Can't see a thing."

"Oh, for Pete's sake."

I got my window down and batted at the snow with my paper. That cleared a spot that was followed immediately by fog on the inside of the window. You would have thought this would cause Ted to slow down, but it didn't. We headed down the South Hill at breakneck speed.

"Ted, slow down! How can you see anything at all?"

An oncoming car passed us, honked loudly, and rode the sidewalk for a minute until Ted brought the yellow beast back into his lane.

"Maybe I should have let the Hummer run for a little while." Ted was still grinning. The vehicle bumped over a slight rise, and Ted leaned over the steering wheel, navigating a curve. "It's still a little hazy up here."

I hit the defog button and shouted, "Pump the brakes for heaven's sake! We'll never make the next corner! You'll kill us for sure!"

They didn't call it the South Hill for nothing. Our busy little road went straight down. After about three miles of narrow twists and turns, it ended in a busy intersection. By the way we were going, we'd shatter every traffic law getting there.

"Brake, Ted, brake!" I dropped the crumpled, soggy paper onto the floor and braced my feet against the underside of the dashboard. I reached my hands out and dug my fingernails into the icy dash. Up ahead, the most formidable curve rushed to meet us. It was a Y where the road split, where two one-way streets became the two-way road climbing up into the residential area. We were barreling toward town and Ted showed no sign of slowing. In fact, it felt as if we were accelerating.

"Brake, Ted, for the love of all that's holy!"

"No can do, May, see?"

I looked at Ted's feet as he demonstrated the problem. He pumped the brakes, but aside from causing the back end of the Hummer to whip side to side, it didn't slow our momentum at all.

"Ice?"

"One long, solid sheet." Ted glanced in his rearview mirror. "Maybe I should have put on those studded tires last week."

"Ted!" It was all I could say. Whatever I had left on my lips I swallowed, along with a mouthful of blood-curdling screams as we careened down the hill, toward the Y, completely out of control; but bless his heart, Ted was trying.

"Maybe if I do this." Ted lifted his left leg and aimed for the emergency brake.

"No!" I slapped at Ted's head. "Don't do that!"

"Grab something, May—I can't control 'er!"

Twenty-five yards now. The Y was seconds away. I wondered who would write my obituary. To make matters worse, a large, brick medical building was at the center of the Y. If we kept to the right, we could get down the hill maybe in one piece. Swept over to the left, though, and we would be going in the wrong direction, directly into traffic. Straight through the center, and we'd be making a new wing in the medical building with our Hummer. There were businesses on either side of the road, parking lots, parked cars, sidewalks, telephone poles, utility boxes—no cushy fields or runaway ramps here—and they were whizzing by at a tremendous speed.

"What are you going to do?" My voice wobbled, and my heart thudded. The Hummer, uncontrollable now, started a violent sideways slide and ricocheted over to the left lane. Approaching the Y, Ted strained to bring the car back to the right, but it was no use. We might as well have been sitting atop a toboggan. The medical building got closer with every second, and I braced myself for the collision.

Just seconds away from crushing our skulls against the wall of the brick fortress, the Hummer clipped a utility pole, sending us into a backward skid, down the hill, onto the one-way street, going the wrong way.

My husband remained cool, and with all of his wits about him, he gunned the engine. I peeked out of one eye just long enough to see what he had done. Instead of going backwards into traffic, we were now heading the right way—back up the hill.

Five minutes later and we were cruising past our house again.

"Welcome home, May!" Ted said joyfully.

"Oh my gosh. We're really late now," I huffed.

"Yeah, but the windshield's clear."

Any other day and I would have ordered Ted to let me out at

the house. I would have taken my purse, my Bible, and my last nerve, and I'd have held my own worship service in a bubble bath. But knowing Bertha and Inez were waiting at the church, I endured a slightly less hair-raising trip back down the hill to church. Ted snaked through the back roads, making the trip more manageable, but, as I feared, we were terribly late when we finally pulled into the church parking lot.

I jumped from the Hummer and walked toward the church like I had an orange between my knees. I didn't want to hazard a slip on the ice. Once inside the vestibule I noticed Bertha and Inez sitting on a bench just inside the front door.

"I'm so sorry I'm late." I was breathless.

Bertha stood and gave me a hug. "It's okay, we just got here ourselves. The pastor made us feel real welcome." She nodded toward a short man I did not recognize.

"Look, May, I went and got some pearls just like yours. Do they look good?"

Inez did have a string of beads around her neck, but I wouldn't be the one to tell her they were paste and probably worth several hundred dollars less than mine. Real pearls aren't what you get when you shop at the dollar store. Still, she was quite proud, and I complimented her good taste.

"May! So good to see you!" Mrs. Shoe, the wife of one of our deacons, floated out of the sanctuary to take my hands in hers. "I understand you brought some visitors this morning."

I'm pretty sure Mrs. Shoe lived at the church. It would not surprise me at all to find a dresser full of her clothes downstairs in the kitchen. She organized every welcome dinner, every Bunko game, every potluck, picnic, and tent revival, and, I learned, had for thirty years or more. Apparently, she never slept. She wore an attractive navy suit with matching pillbox hat. She wore white gloves on her hands.

"Hi, Mary. Yes. May I present Bertha and Inez Peach."

Inez stood to accept Mary's outstretched hand. Mary, usually very composed and cheerful, was suddenly speechless. I soon understood why.

Bertha and Inez, not ones to attend church frequently—or attend social gatherings of any kind, to my knowledge, aside from the occasional lunch—nonetheless had made every attempt to dress for the occasion. Unfortunately, what they wore fell short of the traditional Sunday fare.

Bertha was squeezed into a pair of black woolen leggings topped by a shimmering green Lycra bodysuit. While the collar with all of its ruffles and taffeta might have been pretty, the snapped crotch looked a bit out of place. She wore attractive heels, though, with straps over the insteps, but even I knew white patent leather was quite out of season.

Inez had come in a more conservative ensemble. In addition to the bargain pearls, she wore a short, thin flowered cotton dress, its hem falling just below her bloomers, full of static cling. The short skirt showed a lot of bony leg, absent of hose, and on her feet she wore leather sandals. Her hair looked nice, though, twisted up on her head, the white streak tucked behind one ear, secured with a bobby pin. If you squinted, it did look a little bit like a French roll.

"Mary"—I took the attention away from my friends—"where's the pastor?" I hadn't seen him at his usual position by the front door.

"Oh, May, it's so awful." Mary put her gloved knuckles to her mouth. "From what I heard, he's at home recovering from a terrible beating."

I gasped. "That's horrible! What happened?"

"He was at the grocery store. An angry mob accused him of stealing a grocery cart and nearly pummeled him to death!"

I felt weak. "Is that so? Pummeled? What is the world coming to?"

"He should make a full recovery, but in the meantime, we've called in a pastor from Cheney. He's not as good as Pastor Robinson, but he's all we could find at such short notice."

"That's nice."

Mary smiled at Bertha and Inez, invited them to Wednesday's potluck, and floated off to greet a family coming through the door. I looked around for Ted, but he was nowhere in sight. Just as well. He was probably showing off his big banana to some of the deacon's wives in the parking lot.

"Okay, what is it you had to talk to us about?" Bertha pulled me onto the bench.

Here I go, I thought, and took a deep, cleansing breath.

"I've been thinking a lot about Gerty." I looked from Bertha to Inez. "I know the paper said she died of a heart attack, but she sure didn't look sick to me when I had lunch with you all."

"Nope, fit as a fiddle." Bertha sniffed.

"Don't you think it's a bit odd that she would just die like that? Didn't you wonder why the reports said she died of natural causes?"

Inez and Bertha exchanged glances.

"What are you getting at, May?"

"Well, is there any reason that you can think of for someone to, well, want her dead?"

Inez and Bertha looked at each other again. Neither spoke.

"What?" I demanded.

"You always were a smart cookie, May. Didn't I tell you? I said, she knows something's up." Bertha talked to Inez.

"You thought it was strange, too, didn't you!" I leaned in toward the sisters, speaking quietly but forcefully. I was quite excited. My suspicions were correct. Gerty didn't have any coronary disease, so there had to be some other cause of death. The girls were really getting nervous and I thought I might have struck a chord. Could it be? A confession right here at the Hills

Baptist Church? I couldn't think of a more appropriate place. I could hear my pastor now: *confess your sins!*

"There was someone—" Inez started, but got a glare from Bertha.

"Be careful," Bertha warned.

Darn, I thought. No confession, but something was definitely making the gals gauge their words.

"I think she should know," Inez said.

"What should I know?" My hands grew moist in the palms.

"I thought we should have told you, but Bertha said no." Inez ignored her sister's glare.

"What?"

Inez opened her mouth to speak, but a loud bell suddenly interrupted us. Ted appeared by my shoulder.

"Time for Sunday school, girls."

I tried to hide my disappointment. "You don't have to stay if you don't want to." I stood and extended my hands to the sisters.

Bertha took my hand. "Are you kidding? I didn't get all dressed up to turn around and go home. Just lead the way, May Bell. We're right behind you."

CHAPTER TWELVE

I was beginning to think Bertha and Inez, while not particularly troubled by their sister's death, weren't responsible for it. Maybe they knew who might have had a motive to kill Gerty, and maybe they didn't want the death investigated, but why? My idea that this was a murder was moving from a diluted hunch to a fortified level of certainty. I couldn't be happier.

After greeting friends and introducing Bertha and Inez around to the members of my Sunday school class, I took my chair and opened my Bible. Ted sat to my left and Bertha and Inez found seats directly behind me. It was a cozy class, in a small room, with only about fifteen in attendance. The Senior Saints, we were called. The teacher stood behind a lectern at the front of the class. Today's lesson, part two of a theme, was "Food for the Soul." I settled in for some spiritual nourishment.

Before the teacher, Mr. Black, had a chance to get his first teaching point out, I heard a commotion behind me. All eyes swiveled around to Bertha, who was wildly waving her hand in the air. I stifled a groan and bent over my Bible.

"Sir, you said the lesson was on food for the soul? I have some teaching aids if you'd like."

I peeked over my shoulder. Bertha rummaged in her purse and came out with a large bag of potato chips. She held the bag between two meaty palms and pressed inward. The bag exploded with a loud "pop!" Her taffeta shuddered.

"Just pass them around," Bertha instructed. Inez scooped out a handful of chips, placed them in her lap, and handed the bag to the lady sitting next to her. Mrs. Dugan politely took a chip. Soon the bag had made the rounds while Mr. Black patiently waited.

Mr. Black cleared his throat. He was a soft-spoken, diminutive man, with a sharp nose and no lips at all, just two years retired after spending thirty-five years as a competent CPA. It wasn't in his nature to come across in a forceful way, but all of the smacking and chewing made it hard for him to project.

"If you'll turn in your Bible to—" Mr. Black started.

"Huh?" Bertha said loudly. "I can't hear ya, honey. You've got to speak up."

Mr. Black blushed, but remained composed.

I glanced around again. Inez was licking the salt from her fingers and winked at me when she caught my eye. She'd made a table out of her skirt. Her legs were spread apart in an unladylike fashion.

Caught off guard, Mr. Black was furiously trying to locate his passage of scripture. He gave up after a futile page scan and went with plan B.

"Why don't we have a discussion today," he said. "With our newcomers, it wouldn't be quite fair to jump into the middle of our lesson anyway. Last week we talked about heavenly healing. Have any of you found your prayer life changed by the direction I instructed in petitioning for medical intervention?"

"Oh, yes!" Mrs. Farnsworth, an ancient little lady known for her arthritis treatments and lavishly adorned hats, answered around a mouthful of chip. Today she wore something purple with lots of feathers on her head.

"An answer to prayer," she said. "My neighbor gave me some of these copper bracelets for my arthritis, you know, and I can say, my knitting has never looked so good!"

Bertha snorted. "That old trick? It's just a bunch of hooey."

I gasped.

Mrs. Farnsworth blanched.

"Everybody knows pine tar is what you need," Bertha said. "Slather it on good. You'll get those kinks worked out in no time. Hey you. Keep those chips coming." Mr. and Mrs. Pollard were hogging the chips. They moved them along after snatching a couple more.

"But I prayed," Mrs. Farnsworth defended.

"Of course you did, dear," Bertha said. "And you can pray just as hard over some pine tar." She then reached into her purse and came out with a can of diet coke. She popped the top with a loud psshht! She guzzled and then shared with Inez. "Pass it around, Inez."

Thankfully the can was empty when it got to me.

Mr. Black continued. "Anyone else have some miraculous healings since last week?"

"Oh my gosh!" Bertha said. "I have these hemorrhoids. Did May tell you? If someone here can give me some advice about what to do, I'd really appreciate it."

I slid further down in my chair.

"Maybe we can lay on hands?" Mrs. Farnsworth was trying to be helpful.

Ted guffawed. I shot an elbow his way and he nearly strangled on his own tongue.

"What? The pine tar didn't work?" He whispered in my ear.

"Sticky buns?" Inez found a crumpled package in her bag of goodies.

I quickly looked at Ted. He was about to lose it, so I gave him another jab.

Poor Mr. Black had lost his class. Bertha and Inez were busily exchanging prostate potion recipes and goiter treatments with the Senior Saints, who enthusiastically scrawled ingredients on their church bulletins and pumped the sisters for advice. It seemed there was nothing the gals didn't have a remedy for, and nothing the seniors didn't need help curing.

I tried to assist Mr. Black by gently suggesting to the class that it was getting close to choir time and some of us would have to be going.

"Oh yes, May, don't you have a solo this morning?"

Mrs. Hoblitt, a woman who wore large, plastic wraparound sunglasses, scanned her bulletin.

"Not this morning, Eloise."

"Oh yes. You're listed right here under 'special music.' "

I felt my pulse quicken. "Oh dear. I've simply forgotten!" A little bead of sweat popped out on my upper lip. This was very bad.

"You? A solo?" Bertha scooted her chair up close to mine. "I didn't know you sang. Inez is quite musical too. She could do a duet with you."

"Sure, May, I can help you out there," Inez said.

I vigorously shook my head. "No, that's okay—I'll just pick something out of the hymnal. I'll be fine."

But I didn't feel fine at all. What I'd planned to do was skip the sermon, get Bertha and Inez into a back room, and wear them down. They had something they weren't telling me, and I needed to know what it was. The paper had cinched my decision. That thing about the auction. All of Gerty's paintings! This was certainly peculiar, not to mention the fact that Gerty had died of a nonexistent heart problem.

"Really. Inez, why don't you give the class a taste of what you can do?"

"Yes, Inez! We'd love that!" Mrs. Farnsworth clapped her hands. The rest of the Saints joined in, thumping their Bibles, fanning their bulletins.

"Yes, Inez, please bless us with your talent!" Mr. Black said.

Inez smiled shyly. "Oh, if you insist."

"You just get up there, girl," Bertha insisted. "Mr. Teacher, let her have the podium. She's really got talent."

Inez made her way up to the front of the class. She looked at everyone with her buckteeth and bug eyes. I waited for what was to come.

Inez pulled her glasses off, gently closed her eyes, and stretched her upper lip down low, forcing it over those big teeth. She brought her lower lip up and formed a funnel.

And she started to whistle.

I stared at Inez, not daring to look at Ted. The song was "His Eye Is on the Sparrow."

She blew out a long note, her face in deep concentration. The notes warbled like a bird. "His eeeeyyye is on the sparrooow-www. And I knowwww he watchesssss meeee." I have to admit the music was beautiful. She didn't miss a beat; her mouth pursed and flexed, rounded and yawned, her eyes occasionally opening then closing again in meditation.

I glanced around and saw most of the seniors, too, sitting wistfully with their eyes closed, their chins raised to the heavens, a smile on their lips. A few were singing quietly along with the accompaniment.

We were coming to the crescendo. Inez drew a deep breath into her lungs. Her chest heaved. There was a moment when it seemed like all of the air had been sucked right out of the room. There wasn't a sound from the audience.

Then, with piercing clarity, she did it. She blew for all she was worth. *"Hie eyeee is onnnn the sparrowww, and I knowww he watchessss meeee!"*

The bell rang as Inez drew out the last note. The seniors erupted in grand applause. Mr. Black sat down hard in a chair.

No matter what hymn I chose from the hundreds of selections, I knew it would be just a sad second place to what we'd all witnessed that morning.

CHAPTER THIRTEEN

"You're off the hook." Ted caught up with me just as I was slipping into my choir robe.

"Huh?" I felt Ted's hand on my arm and let him pull me away from the rest of the singers, out into the hall where I was greeted by Bertha and Inez.

"I told the choir director you haven't been feeling well. A bad case of laryngitis flaring up, and you couldn't possibly strain your vocal chords this morning."

Bless his heart. Sometimes it's good to be married to a doctor.

Ted grabbed my robe and lifted it off over my head. "If you know what's good for you, you'll get out of here before they have you doing nursery duty."

"Take good notes." I kissed Ted and gave the sisters the high sign. "Come on, you two, we've got to talk."

The sisters and I slipped from the church and piled into their clunker. Inez drove.

"Let's go back to your place," I instructed. My, I was getting rather bossy, but this just wasn't the time to pussyfoot around the issue. There were questions to ask, and I had a captive audience. The long drive back to the Peach residence would give me some valuable interrogation time.

Bertha sat in back and leaned over the seats. I craned around as best I could to see her, while keeping my other eye on Inez.

"You said there was something strange about the way Gerty

died so unexpectedly." I left it at that, allowing Bertha time to explain. Inez was busily navigating the slick roads, so I let her concentrate.

Bertha hesitated and then said, "She was seeing someone."

"Seeing? As in a boyfriend or something?"

"Yes. She had a lover."

Oooh. This was a nice juicy tidbit. "Did you meet him?" Or her, I almost added, not knowing which way Gerty tacked her sails.

"No, never met him. But she did tell me he would come to her house. So's she could paint his portrait."

"Did she tell you his name?" I was happy it was a him.

"Nope. Only that he was pretty beefy, and very young."

I tried not to imagine that union. Old wrinkled Gerty making out with a young buck in her studio.

"Was that something she normally did? Paint subjects at her home?"

"No, and that's why this is all so strange. Mostly she did landscapes, still life, that kind of thing. Also, it was a bit weird when they said she keeled over from a heart attack. My sister was a vegan."

I gasped loudly and covered my mouth with a shaky hand. "Oh, my! She'd been married all that time, and still a virgin?"

"Not a virgin, May, a vegan!" Bertha said.

"A vegan!" Inez shouted. "She didn't eat no meat, no milk, no eggs, nothing good like that. She was the poster child for healthy living. No heart problems. Never."

"But didn't her husband say she had a history of heart problems?"

"What would he know? They lived under the same roof, but they pretty much went their own ways. I have no idea why he said she had heart problems. Doesn't make sense. And even though they were traveling in different circles, I'm bettin' when he found out about her boy toy, that got his attention."

"So the marriage wasn't good." I sighed.

Inez shouted again. "She was gonna ditch her husband."

"Is that true?" My heart started thumping. Motive. Motive.

"Oh, Inez, she's been threatening that for years." Bertha rummaged in her pocket for a lifesaver and popped one in her mouth. She talked and smacked at the same time. "Never was serious about ditching Bernard before, but the last time I talked to her, she was going on about closing us down. Said she was going to file some complaint same time as her divorce papers and her updated will."

"Busy day at the courthouse," I said under my breath. "Do you know if she got a chance to file the papers? Did she change her will after all?"

"I know what you're thinking, May—didn't I tell you she was sharp as a tank, Inez? I don't know. But that sure would make things interesting if she didn't get around to it, wouldn't it? Only problem is, she wasn't a rich woman. Even if she did change her will, her husband didn't stand to lose a whole heck of a lot. Maybe some of her paintings, a little savings, nothing big, or I'd know about it."

Inez slowed and stopped at a red light. I was quiet for a minute, pondering the latest bombshell. So Gerty had a dude. What would Bernard think of that? More importantly, what would he do about it? Was it enough to make a man kill his wife? Sure it was. Happens all the time. Just how to prove it. That was something altogether different.

The light turned and Inez slowly pushed the gas pedal. She was a good driver, which made it easy to concentrate.

Inez spoke up. "Wait a minute, Bertha—she wasn't doin' too bad with her artwork. One of her paintings sold for five hundred dollars last month. Remember?"

"Oh, yeah. I forgot about that. But that's sure not enough to kill her for."

I casually asked, "And you two were mentioned in her will?"

Bertha scoffed. "She thought she could use that little trick as a bargaining chip. 'I'll keep you in my will if you shut down the Hooch,' she'd say. 'I'll cut you out of my will if you don't shut down the Hooch,' she'd say. Pain in my arse."

"But that didn't really matter to you." I scrutinized the faces of Bertha and Inez in turn, looking for any sign that they were lying.

"Forget it. Just one more thing to hang over our heads. She threatened us all the time, and then she'd get real nice. Close down the Poochie Hooch, she said, and she'd put us up in style. Maybe even move us into one of them places up on the South Hill."

I shuddered. That would be interesting. Bertha and Inez and an upgraded Poochie Hooch right there on the South Hill. Mr. Fitz would be having fits if that happened.

"But no way were we going to give up our business. Means too much to us," Inez said.

"No way," Bertha concurred. "So then she got mad, said she was going to drop us from her will. We wouldn't get a thing, and after she divorced Bernard, he wouldn't get anything either."

"Sounds like she had a lot of rage," I said.

"Spoiled brat," Bertha said.

"And you said she didn't have any kids, so who would get her money?" I was breathless. Maybe those paintings were a lot more valuable than we thought. One thing I remembered from my TV court cases was to follow the money.

"I guess FETA," Bertha said.

"FETA?"

"It was her life. I don't know for sure, but that would be my bet. All her money would go to FETA."

We were nearing Hunker Hills. Inez slowed.

"What about this auction?"

"What auction?"

"The paper said there was going to be an auction. All of her paintings are up for sale."

"Well I'll be snookered. That's her no-good husband for ya. Couldn't wait to get his hands on whatever money he could milk out of her artwork. Slimy snake."

"Listen. I think we all know her death was no accident. We've got to find out how she really died and who killed her. Since you're her sisters, you'd have reason to ask for the autopsy report."

"No autopsy, hon."

"No autopsy," I said, disappointed. I had been afraid of that.

"No reason. You got an old lady, history of heart problems, who dies in her own home. Cops barely even looked the place over. According to Bernard, they just asked him a few questions and left the rest to the medical examiner."

"But you said she didn't have heart problems."

"I know that, and you know that, but the police don't know that. They just went by what her husband, the slimy bastard, said."

"Bertha, you really shouldn't use that word," Inez admonished.

"Okay, the sleazy bastard."

"That's better."

"Anyway," Bertha continued, "she's going to be cremated after her funeral tomorrow."

"No!" I said. "That's horrible! If you thought something wasn't right, why didn't you tell the police? Why didn't you insist they investigate?"

"Investigate what? She's out of our hair. We weren't going to get any of her money anyway, and what do we care if her paintings get sold off to the highest bidder? Good riddance, I say."

"Honestly, Bertha!" I frowned. "What about justice? What about due process? What about all that's right and honorable?"

Bertha sulked and looked out the window.

Inez leaned over to me. "That would spoil our plans, May Bell. Tell her our plan, Bertha." Inez pulled up in front of their home and killed the engine.

"I don't know." Bertha frowned.

"My lips are sealed," I said seriously and buttoned my lips with my fingers. What were they talking about?

"Guess it couldn't hurt," Bertha said, looking more cheerful. "We had a good idea that maybe it was her husband that knocked off Gerty. We thought we'd be able to ask him for a loan. You know, suggest we knew some things and—"

"Bertha!"

"Come on, May, why not? If he killed Gerty, I'm pretty sure he'd be more than eager to send a little hush money our way."

I put my hands to my mouth in horror. "Oh, my gosh, Bertha! He might do more than that. He might want to send someone to hush you up, but good! You don't know what these nefarious types can do!"

"Hadn't thought of that." Bertha frowned again. "Maybe it's not such a good idea." She opened her car door and pushed her way out. "Come on, girls, let's get something to eat. I'm starved."

CHAPTER FOURTEEN

While grazing at the Hooch house table, Bertha, Inez, and I did some brainstorming. Bertha suckled the business end of a cold drumstick while Inez ground her way down a cob of corn. With those teeth of hers, it was a spectacle worthy of Ripley's. The bug-eyed woman chewed three rows simultaneously, back and forth, a flip of the wrist and she was plowing her way along another three lines without a breath. Butter dripped from her chin and clung to her mole hairs. She paused and looked at me for a minute, asked if I wore dentures, and when I said I didn't, she complimented my dental work and asked for the name of my orthodontist. I said I'd find the number for her. She thanked me and went back to work on her corn.

I sipped a Coke through a straw. "Look," I said. "Sounds like Bernard had good reason to kill Gerty. We all agree it's rather strange that she just keeled over when there was no history of illness, and even more strange that her husband would tell the police she had heart problems, but we have no proof he did anything to her."

"Nope, none." Bertha tossed her naked chicken bone across the kitchen into the garbage can and lifted a bag of seasoned croutons from the table's center. She popped a handful in her mouth. The scent of garlic and onion wafted through the air.

"So how are we going to find out if he had a hand in this?" I asked.

Inez waved the corncob by her ear. "Not by sitting here, I'll tell ya." Her teeth were littered with yellow corn skin.

I sighed heavily. "So what should we do? Write him an anonymous note, get him worried, hope he'll say something? Or maybe we can hide a video camera in his house, catch him hiding evidence. Maybe we can tap his phone. I'm just thinking here, gals. Jump in any time."

Inez sucked on her teeth. "We could ask him."

Bertha snorted. A plume of garlic-onion dust blew out of her nose. "Oh, yeah, that's good, Inez, Hey, Bernard. Did you kill Gerty? Inquiring minds are just dying to know!"

I discretely wiped my seasoned blouse front, thankful I was wearing the tan one today. "Wait a minute, Bertha. Wait a gosh-darn minute! Why the heck not? Of course, we won't just come out and ask, but if we're clever—I mean, if we're really smart about this—we can get him to contradict himself. We'll just casually ask him about the night Gerty died. What happened, how he found her, who he called, if he dialed nine-one-one, that sort of thing. I'll watch his eyes, see if he shifts or if he fidgets or anything." I hit the palm of my left hand with my right fist. "It could work!"

Bertha dusted her hands together. "Inez, how much gas we got in the car?"

"Enough," Inez answered.

I blinked rapidly. "What? We're gonna do this now?"

"Why not? It was your idea, May." Bertha stood and went to the refrigerator where she pulled out four cans of Slim Fast. "For the road," she said.

Oh, dear. What had I got myself into this time?

After making a check-in call to Ted, the gals and I bundled up and got back into the clunker. The snowplows were busy piling up dirty snow in the Hunker Hills main district as we drove through. The redneck social club, AKA the Hunker Hardware

Store, was hopping. As we passed, I recognized a pickup truck I'd seen before. It was Stanley's beater. Guess he didn't work on Sundays. He was chatting with someone outside the store. Just as we passed, he looked up. I had a moment of fright, knowing it would blow my cover if he saw me in the car with the sisters. I quickly leaned over to avoid detection and smacked my head on the dashboard.

"Hey, May!" Bertha shouted from the back seat. "There's a dashboard in front of your head!" Both sisters screeched with laughter. I smiled weakly, blinked rapidly, and rubbed my bruise.

Catching sight of Stanley caused me to think of Jolene. The idea of her being jealous of her boyfriend's alliance with Gerty seemed more remote now considering the revelations of Gerty's recent activities. Still, it was curious that she didn't know about Gerty's death when Stanley did.

"Have you had any more trouble from Jolene?" I asked.

Inez shook her head vigorously. "As a matter of fact, she came by last night to apologize and give us convalescents."

Condolences? "What exactly did she say?"

"I don't rightly agree, Inez. She said she was sorry, May, that she didn't know Gerty had died until after she came bangin' on our door, but she still said she was going to try to get our place shut down. For Stanley. Sure. Mostly, she just needs to pick fights. If it's not one thing, it's another. No wonder she doesn't have a man."

I asked, "Who told her Gerty had passed away?"

"Guess it was Stanley. He'd have known because he worked with Gerty in that FETA group trying to get us shut down. He was over to her house last night." Bertha looked at her watch. "Expect we'll see Jolene in maternity shorts again by Christmas."

"Why don't she just move?" Inez growled. "If she hates us so bad she can leave. She don't have to live there."

"Yes. Why doesn't she find a nice little trailer somewhere

else?" I looked at Bertha.

"My guess is, she's afraid Stanley won't be able to find her new place if she does that. Too far to travel," Bertha said. "Besides. She don't hate us, she's just stickin' up for Stanley. I can't imagine the smell or noise bothers her, none. With all those kids she probably don't even notice. No, she's just whining for Stanley."

Mustering optimism, I suggested, "He could move, too. If the noise and smell are too much for him, he could take Jolene and their kids and go."

Bertha and Inez shared another loud cackle. "Are you kidding?" Inez crowed. "If he goes, I'm here to tell you it won't be with no kids. He's got the best of both worlds where he's at. You know what they say: why buy the cow if you can get the milk through the fence?"

I shuddered, and tried without success to keep the vision of Jolene's double-D tube top from popping into my mind.

As we neared the town of Harvest, the usual feelings of calm and serenity were replaced by the disconcerting idea of what we were about to do.

Confront a killer.

The Harvest Inn was just up the road, and I convinced the gals that we needed to make a pit stop. An injection of espresso was required for this sort of deed. Inez pulled in front of the covered porch and pushed the gearshift to park. We entered the lobby and sucked in the rich warm smell from the hills of Columbia.

Bertha thought the chai tea looked good; Inez settled on a mug of hot chocolate; and I ordered my usual. A two-shot latte. The girl behind the counter looked appreciative when I tipped her fifty cents.

Down a short hall, we found a small room empty of customers. At one time it had been a parlor or a bedroom, but it was now a reading room with musty-smelling books lining all four walls from floor to ceiling. Overstuffed, mismatched chairs were placed haphazardly. The sisters and I pulled the chairs close and settled in to discuss our plan of action.

I said, "We've got to get our questions together. What we'll say, what we'll ask—"

"So's not to sound too suspicious." Inez nodded and stirred her chocolate.

"Right. We don't want to tip our hand," I said.

"Tip our hands? You gonna slap him?" Bertha lifted her eyebrow.

"No. I mean, tip our hand. Like in cards, you know, when you're playing poker . . . Never mind. Let's just talk about what we'll say."

"I know what I'll say." Bertha placed her cup on an end table and pointed a finger. "I'll poke him in the nose and say, 'What did you do to our sister, you slimy bastard?' "

I groaned.

"Bertha! I told you not to use that word," Inez said.

"Okay, 'What did you do to our sister, you sneaky jackass!' "

I groaned again.

The sisters collapsed in a heap, two braying old ladies.

"Shhh! Quiet. The whole place will hear you!" I looked around frantically.

Inez unfolded and wiped her bug eyes with a sleeve. "Seriously, May, we'll behave. We promise."

"Promise." Bertha giggled, which caused another eruption of laughter from the girls.

My hands tightened around my latte cup. "Just let me do the talking. I was her friend, too, sort of, and I just want to pay my respects, I'll say. I'll go in—"

"And ask the bastard, 'What did you do to my friend, you

slimy jerkface!' "

That did it. The girls were gone—off rolling around in their big overstuffed chairs, laughing like they'd gone brainless.

Now normally I would have joined in the fun. I do have a pretty good sense of humor, but with the serious business ahead, there was just too much thinking to do. It was clear the sisters weren't going to be much help unless they pulled themselves together. I looked at Inez. She was now in a full spasm. One knee was pulled up; her other long, bony leg was out straight, pointing at Bertha, screaming in laughter; the tears were rolling and she clutched her stomach. Bertha had slid all the way to the floor. She wasn't even laughing aloud any more. Her face was bright red, and after a while both sisters simply bent forward and back, their shoulders jumping in breathless glee.

My purse was on the floor by my elbow. In my purse was a super-size bottle of Excedrin Migraine. I might just need the whole bottle before this day was over. Biding my time while the girls exhausted themselves, I felt around in my purse for the Excedrin bottle.

When I brought the bottle up, a tuft of hair came with it. Ferret fur clung to my damp fingers. This caused me a moment of panic. Had the girls seen? I'd already told them I had no idea where their Horace had gone. Quickly I shoved the bottle back into my purse and my fingers grazed my notebook. It was as if Gerty were giving me a nudge. What kind of detective was I, anyway? The pages were woefully empty. I pulled it out and busied myself writing all of the things we'd learned so far.

Bernard finds Gerty dead late Friday night, tells police his wife has history of heart problems—untrue.

Did Bernard call ambulance?

Did police investigate scene for evidence of a crime?

Gerty had threatened to close down Hooch, and had solicited help of Stanley.

Jolene wanted Poochie Hooch closed; didn't know about Gerty's death.

Gerty had art that may have been more valuable after her death.

Husband auctioning off paintings after Gerty's death.

Gerty prepared to have her will changed. FETA stands to inherit funds from Gerty's will.

Sisters happy to have Gerty out of their lives.

The last entry gave me pause. Bertha and Inez were very happy to have their sister dead and gone. They had conveniently dropped hints about Bernard as a prime suspect. They'd also offered information about Gerty's love interest, but couldn't be more specific than what she'd allegedly told them. He was young and beefy. I think that's what they'd said. Elusive—and all hearsay. How could a dead woman challenge their words? For that matter, they admitted interest in Bernard's inheritance. Could they have stalled the will update with some promises of their own? Yes, Gerty, we'll close down the Poochie Hooch, just keep your will the way it is and we'll close up shop by next week.

Well, Gerty was dead, and the Hooch was still operational. The whole thing was awfully suspect if you asked me.

When I looked up from my notebook, Gerty and Inez had regained their composure. Hurriedly, I shoved my pen and pad into my purse, not wanting to give them a chance to ask what I'd been writing.

"Let's get going," I said.

"Think we should call and tell him we're on our way?" Inez pulled Bertha to her feet.

"No, we don't want to tip him off." I took a big gulp of my latte and motioned with my head. "Come on. We'll just show up on his doorstep. Watch his reaction."

"What if he isn't home?" Inez talked while we walked. We passed the front counter, left our cups on the ledge, nodded to the girl, and headed for the parking lot.

"We'll cross that brick if it comes," Bertha said. "Besides, I have keys to the house. We can break in if we have to."

I stood by the car. "No. No breaking in. If he's not home, we'll wait."

Inez opened her door and buttoned her coat. "That could take forever. He spends all of his time at the VFW hall."

We slid into the car. "Is it open on Sundays?"

Bertha adjusted her seat belt. "If not, he's got his other selections of favorite watering holes. Drinks like a fish."

"Do fish drink?" Inez revved the engine and backed away from the inn.

"They do if they're married to Gerty," Bertha said.

Inez shrieked.

"You two are horrible." I snapped my seat belt into place.

Chapter Fifteen

Gerty had shared a beautiful home with her husband, Bernard, before her passing. A two-story 1960s farmhouse, ivory in color with green trim, hidden in a thick cluster of snow-shrouded ponderosa pines at the end of a long, pitted dirt road. There were shutters on the windows, a brick walk to the front door, and Gerty's love of the countryside was evident everywhere. Hummingbird feeders hung, empty and frosted, outside the kitchen window; squirrel perches were littered with dried corn; and deer salt licks were placed among hay bales under a cluster of blue spruce.

I'd been here before, that time when we'd fetched Gerty for our lunch date. I remembered the kitchen; warm and smelling of biscuits and vegetable stew. But now as I trudged up the wide porch steps, there was a haunted feel to the place, and out here in the wilds of Harvest, where the next-door neighbor was a mile's walk down the road, it was unnaturally quiet.

No one would have been able to hear her scream.

I stood before the front door and had a look around as I gathered the courage to give the broad wooden entry a knock. The porch had been swept clean of snow. Small powdery mounds ran the length of the porch on the ground just under the railing. There were brush strokes along the wooden slats, and an industrial-sized push broom leaned against the house by the front door. Gerty and Inez huddled behind me clutching each other's arms. "Do you think he's in there?" Inez whispered.

"The windows are awful dark," Bertha said quietly.

"Shhh," I said.

Inez gave me a nudge. "Push the bell, May."

"We're right behind ya," Bertha whispered.

"Can I help you?" The voice was strong and deep, and it was coming from behind us.

There was a lot of commotion on top of that porch; I'm here to tell you. Bertha and Inez were tripping over each other trying to take cover behind my skirts, and I was so startled I did the one thing that came naturally. I grabbed up the broom and went into a fighting stance. I faced the man standing below us, and jabbed toward him with the bristles. I'd learned a thing or two about broom fighting with Ted, and this time I kept my eyes open. The broom was so heavy, though, I only got it about three inches off of the ground. A vein in my neck popped and my knees buckled, but I didn't go down.

The man seemed unfazed. He studied me curiously and adjusted a large bag of rock salt under his arms. He wore a plaid wool jacket, and an Elmer Fudd hat covered his head, flaps up. His cheeks were ruddy and unshaved; his ears were fat and rubbery-looking—perfect for holding up his horn-rimmed glasses. When I looked at the large lumberjack boots on his feet, I put the broom down. No way could I hold my own against this mammoth. Maybe begging for mercy would be more effective. Before I could go into a genuflect, though, Bertha stepped forward.

"Hi Bernard," she said coolly.

"Bertha . . . Inez." Bernard addressed the sisters, and then seemed to search his memory when he looked at me.

I dropped the broom and held out my hand. "May. May List, Bernard. So good to see you."

Bernard didn't take my hand, probably because his arms were full. I should have seen that. Instead, he hefted the bag of salt and trudged up the steps. He dropped the bag by the door and picked up the broom. The sisters and I scuttled away, out of reach. He gently propped the broom against the wall, pulled open the front door, and walked into his house without a backward glance.

My face grew hot with embarrassment. This poor man had just lost his wife, and I hadn't even offered my sympathy. Naturally he would have been aloof and short with me.

"Think we should leave?" Inez put her hand on my sleeve. She breathed heavily through her nose, making a funny whistling sound. That talent might come in handy during our next Sunday school class. I felt kind of bad for the woman; her hand was trembling on my arm, and her eyes were popping more than usual. Her glasses were barely hanging off the tip of her nose. Bertha was acting strangely, too. Her brow was creased and she had a haggard look about her. The gals were spooked.

"What's wrong with you two?" I hissed. "We're just going to pay our respects. Ask him a few innocent questions. Maybe make him a sandwich. There's no harm in that."

"He ain't actin' right," Inez said. "He's never been this way before."

"Yeah. Giving me the creeps, is what he's doin'," Bertha said.

The girls' fear was catching. My knees turned to liquid and there was an uncomfortable thudding under my blouse. Since I'd never met Bernard before, I had to believe Bertha and Inez when they said there was something peculiar about his behavior. Something peculiar about Bernard and—judging by Bertha's pale, drawn face—something sinister. It looked like we were right in assuming that he'd had something to do with Gerty's murder.

"How does he usually act?" I insisted.

Inez stuck out her thumb and tipped an imaginary bottle toward her mouth. "He's usually sloshed!" One white eyebrow went up and she leaned her head toward me. "Looks like he's in the wagon."

Bertha nodded vigorously. "Afraid he'll say something to give himself away."

I sighed heavily. "Is that it? You're worried because he's sober?"

Bertha put her hands on her hips. "Well, wouldn't you be?"

A response eluded me. I pulled my purse straps over my shoulder and squared up. "We can't just stand here all day. Get a grip, you two, we're going in."

I cracked the door open and poked my head through. "Yoo-hoo! Bernard?" The girls pushed against my back and I shrugged them off roughly. "Bernard?" No answer. I took a step into the house, and then, gathering courage, I walked forward far enough to give the girls clearance. I motioned them in. "Shut the door," I told Bertha.

"Do you think that's such a good idea?" Inez asked. "What if we have to make a run for it?"

"Shut the door, Bertha," I repeated.

She complied reluctantly, but reminded me that our only avenue of escape had just been blocked.

I scowled and called again. "Bernie! Where are you? Bern?"

Inez said, "He ain't answering, May. He probably went upstairs to take a nap. We might want to get out of here." She looked at her sister for support. Bertha looked at me.

I held up my hand, listening. The old farmhouse was as cold, and as quiet, as a morgue. My own analogy gave me a shudder, but a good detective must remain unemotional in times like these, so after pursing my lips and patting my up-do, I gave a loud shout.

"Bernard! We want to talk to you. Where are you?"

No answer still. It was giving me the willies. I turned on the light switch by the door. The rest of the house was dark. I crossed quickly to the kitchen, turned on a light there, found no Bernard, came back to the front vestibule.

"Where is he?"

"Did you get a knife from the kitchen? A good sturdy one?" Bertha asked. She and Inez hadn't moved from near the front door.

"Don't be ridiculous," I said, and then could have kicked myself for not thinking of it myself. I was unarmed, defenseless, but I did have my life-alert necklace under my blouse. I reached to rub it for luck, but it wasn't there. Shucks. Forgot I'd left it at home.

"Bernie, please talk to us," I said loudly, but heard a warble in the "please."

Imagine my surprise when a tired voice came from the direction of a room immediately off to our right. It was at the end of a long hall. "Come on," the voice said. "I've been expecting you."

"Let's go," I whispered, and took Bertha's hand.

Three pairs of feet shuffled across the hardwood floor, tracking the voice of Bernard. Three gals keeping close, hanging on to one another for support and confidence, moved toward the voice, wondering what we would find when we looked into the room. For a little while it appeared that we were making no progress at all. Perhaps the trepidation of going into the unknown was paralyzing us. I've heard that for a person in the midst of a traumatic event, time slows, even seems to stop, and the senses become acute. That was probably it, I mused. However, when I looked down at my feet I saw the source of our trouble. A medium-sized throw rug had gotten bunched up and we were scooting along an inch at a time dragging it with us.

"Pick up your feet, girls," I commanded forcefully. "Lift your knees, now."

It had been cold on that porch, and the lubrication in my hip joints was sluggish at best, so when we all started marching toward the door it sounded like hinges swinging on a rusty gate. See? My auditory senses were definitely keen. Some might argue, but it's what I heard.

"Well, come on in," Bernard said when we got to the room. He was sitting on a chair in the middle of the room with his hands squeezed between his knees. The room was dark, with the exception of a muted lamp casting an amber glow, which made everything shadowed and distorted. It was Gerty's studio. A round room, custom built to her specifications, with plenty of windows, cluttered shelves, and cabinets spilling out canvasses and rags, assorted supplies for the creative genius.

The first time I'd seen it I'd found it charming. It had been bright out that day, not dim and snow-shrouded like today; the room was alive and full of yellow sunlight, its white walls clean and decorated with her colorful paintings. The paintings were gone now, the room a sterile place smelling of oils and solutions I didn't know enough about to name.

Bernard sat in a chair reserved for models or baskets of fruit, whatever Gerty was working on. Bernard studied the floor. Never before had I seen a man so broken—so void of affect. It was as if his spirit had gone and the body had stayed behind.

"Bernard, I'm so sorry—" I began.

"This was her favorite room," Bernard said. He slowly put his hand to his head and slid his hat off. He placed it on his lap. "Did you know that?" He looked over at me, then back at the floor, but not before I caught the empty look in his eyes.

Bertha and Inez stood with their mouths gaping. Not what they expected, I could tell.

Struggling for words, I said, "Yes, I can see she must have spent a lot of time in here." This was an easy reply, because it didn't take a Sherlock to see Gerty had, indeed, whiled away the hours in this place. She'd taken great care in her studio design; it was fitted with indirect lighting, an artist's table, and a shelf overflowing with paints, thinners, brushes, rags, and other colorful paraphernalia important to the artist's life. There was a chair in front of the table, slightly off kilter, and a large smudge on the floor, probably a spill, or—I gasped. This was the murder scene! That smudge was undoubtedly some of Gerty's bodily fluids left behind after the paramedics had tried to work a miracle. Whoever had tried to clean up hadn't done a very good job.

Casually I made my way over to the table, with the pretense of admiring her latest portrait, a half-finished canvas propped against an easel. But what I was really doing was examining the smudge and anything that might give me a clue.

Oh, he's a clever one, that Bernard. Play like the grieving husband, knowing it would throw me off balance. It was her favorite room, did you know that? I'm so sad, I'm grieving so hard, I'm so distraught! Ahhhh! Well it's not gonna work on me, big boy. Not this detective.

I pivoted quickly. "Where are her other paintings, Bernard?" I squinted at him, daring him to lie. I pointed to the half-finished portrait and said, "Why is this the only one in here? I know she had an exhibit just two weeks ago. I saw her paintings, and there were dozens of them. Where are they now?"

Bernard looked stunned and blinked rapidly.

Inez wagged a warning finger by her waistline, out of Bernard's line of vision. She was telling me to shut up.

I ignored Inez. "I'm awfully sorry about your loss, Bernard," I challenged, "but I happen to read the papers. And this morning, what do I find? Much to my surprise, I see you're planning an auction. An auction to get rid of Gerty's paintings. Now I'm thinking to myself, I'm thinking, May, now isn't that awfully quick? I mean, the old gal's not even in the ground—oh, and by the way I know you're planning to have Gerty cremated, so that's pretty handy, too—and I say to myself, May, it's awfully funny that Bernard is having all of Gerty's stuff sold even before she's in the kiln . . ." I had to pause to catch my breath. I looked at the girls, who were having spasms. I ignored them again.

I was on a roll and nothing was going to stop me. Finding testosterone I didn't know I had, I walked over to the astonished Bernard and poked him in the chest. "So I'm asking myself, May, why in the world would a grieving husband want to get rid of his wife's treasured paintings, and in a mighty big hurry, I might add. Did I already say that? Well, in a big, bloomin' hurry, unless he needed some quick cash. And maybe, just maybe, he figured out a way to get his wife removed, so to speak, so he could get at her cash, and he needed to sell her paintings before anyone got a chance to take a look at that will of hers, that I know, by the way, was changed to leave you with nothing! What do you say to that?" I pushed at his chest a second time.

Bernard swatted at my hand and rubbed his breastbone with his fist. He kept his fist balled and I jumped back and took a pugilistic stance, once more, daring him to gouge away.

"What in the heck are you talking about, lady?"

"Ohhh," I shuddered the word, "don't you act coy with me, buster. You know what I'm talking about." I looked at the girls and held up a thumb. Piece of cake.

Bernard stood and glared. "First of all, Gerty didn't have anything to leave in her will. Second of all, I cleaned out my savings to give her a proper memorial service and bought her a nice urn for her ashes. I even had to take out a second mortgage on the house. I have to auction off her paintings just to pay my bills! Death doesn't come cheap, you know."

I sucked in my cheeks. Hmm. This certainly was unexpected. Bertha jumped in.

"Now Bernard, that might be so. But there's something I've

been wonderin' 'bout since I heard Gerty was dead. And that's the thing you told the cops. You said she'd had heart trouble. And we know that ain't so, don't we?"

Bernard paled.

I winked at Bertha. Good one.

"So what is this? You think I killed her?" Bernard asked. He was getting the picture.

Inez waved her hands like she was washing windows. "No, no, Bernard, we ain't saying that at all, are we, girls?" She stepped in close behind Bertha and put her hands on Bertha's wide shoulders. She peeked out over Bertha's head.

"Well, did you?" Bertha snapped her elbows back to put her hands on her hips and caught Inez in the solar plexus. The taller sister said something like "whoosh!" and doubled over.

At that point, Bernard did something I would never have dreamed he would do. Never in my wildest nightmares. And it was really creepy.

CHAPTER SIXTEEN

After accusing him of murder, I expected something dramatic, like an angry rebuttal, or refusal, or protestation, from Bernard, so you can imagine how shocked I was when he placed his head in his hands and began to weep.

Though muffled, I could make out Bernard's words. "I had to come up with something, some reason why Gerty died like she did. What else could I tell the police? That it was my fault? I had to think of some reason why she died, and a heart condition was all I could come up with off the top of my head. I even changed the labels on my pills, and good thing, because they looked. I just got her name off one of her prescription bottles when she had pneumonia last year and pasted it over my name on my bottle of heart medication. If I didn't tell them something fast, they would have investigated."

Gently I placed my hand on Bernard's back. Quietly I asked, "That was pretty fast thinking, I'll give you that, Bern, but tell me. Why would they have investigated?"

Bertha's face turned crimson. "Because he killed her! You were right on the money, May Bell. You are a sharp cookie. Didn't I tell ya, Inez? She had it figured right all along."

Bernard looked up at me with tears pooled in his eyes. "You really thought I killed her?"

Inez was still bent over after Bertha's elbow to the gut, hands on her knees, but she managed to unfold and said breathily, "No, no, Bernard, May didn't think any such thing. Did she,

Bertha?" She shot a beseeching bug-eyed plea at Bertha, but when the husky sister looked away and crossed her arms, Inez said, "We've all been . . . well, just a little bit stressed out since we heard Gerty died, haven't we, Berth? May here wanted to come and pay her respects. Tell ya how sorry she is. We all did. It's okay, really. She didn't mean nothing." Inez smiled, but it was forced. "It's hard to lose a loved one, Bern, you know that. We've been pretty broken up about the whole thing."

Bernard wiped his nose with the back of his hand. "Come off it, Inez. I know you and Gerty hated each other, and I don't blame you for that. But that makes me think you and Bertha didn't come up here because you were heartbroken that she's dead." He pulled off his glasses. They'd fogged up pretty good and he wiped them with the tail of his shirt. "In fact, you're probably happy she's out of your hair."

Bertha cocked her head to one side and tapped a toe on the wood floor. She stared at Bernard. "That may be true, Baby Cakes, but I'd bet my last dollar you ain't torn up about having her out of your life either. Admit it. She was a pain in the rear. Our own mother would say that about Gerty, and she's loony tunes."

Inez glowered. "No, mother's loons all right, but she wouldn't say that. She'd say Gerty is a horn in her side, but not a pain in her ear."

We were getting away from the important subject. It looked like Bernard was composing himself but that meant we were in danger of losing ground in this investigation. Opportunely, we'd caught Bernard at a vulnerable time. He'd more or less admitted to lying to the police, and he was visibly nervous and worried about the events surrounding his wife's death. I wanted to know why.

There was a trick I'd seen on *Court TV.* It was a tactic police used to force a confession. Sympathize with the perp and tell him you could understand why he might have done what he did. Be concerned, caring, pretend you're on his side. Throw out a safety net, make a believer out of him, and he'd squeal for sure.

This might take a while and I needed to be comfortable. I shrugged out of my coat, placed it on the arm of a chair, and signaled for the girls to do the same. They acted confused, but complied. Bernard had returned to his position, bent over, head in hands, glasses back on his nose. He was rocking ever so slightly. Gone away into a world of his own. I was pleased to see we were back on track. Quietly I ordered the girls to go put on a pot of coffee. They sulked a little, but did as I'd asked. After they reluctantly left the studio, I pulled a chair up to sit beside Bernard.

My fingers found their way to the back of his neck. I tugged at his collar and he allowed me to pull off his coat. I folded it and set it on the floor. Not something I would normally do, but I couldn't risk leaving to hang it in the hall closet. The confession was just inches from my grasp.

Then I grew worried. Bernard seemed to have drifted off again, not even aware of my presence. In order to keep him focused, I trailed my fingers back to his neck and squeezed tenderly, feeling the knotty muscles. Man, this guy was meaty. He had the normal corrugated, weather-beaten skin and flush of a heavy drinker, but there was a lot of tone under his wrinkled skin. He was obviously younger than Gerty had been. Maybe even by ten or fifteen years. She definitely had a penchant for younger men.

At first, when I massaged his neck, Bernard tensed. A good sign. At least he was coming out of his stupor. Then, as I continued to probe and manipulate, working my way up to the hairline and back down again, he relaxed. Surreptitiously I watched his face. His eyes closed and his jaw relaxed. The position was cumbersome and clumsy, so to get a better position and for maximum effect, I stood and moved around behind him where I could knead those big shoulders with both hands. I leaned over slightly and said in his ear, "No one will blame you for what you did, you know."

"It was horrible," he said.

"Yes. Horrible. What was horrible?"

"What I did. It was unforgivable."

"But surely she gave you good reason." I pinched and squeezed.

"I couldn't take it any more."

"No, of course you couldn't. She pushed you to it."

"She wouldn't stop nagging. Nagging and nagging. Nothing I did was good enough. I could never be good enough for her."

"No man should have to live with that." I rubbed the back of his head, twirling my fingers through his hair.

"If I forgot to do something she screamed at me. If I remembered to do what she wanted, it wasn't right and she yelled more."

"She was a demon."

"If I touched her wrong she slapped me. If I forgot to touch her she whined."

"What a big baby. She was just begging to get it."

"It was because of her I started to drink." Bernard wrung his hat into a ball. "Just to drown out her incessant nagging."

"It's understandable. I would have done the same." I faked a sniff of sympathy. Let him think I was moved by his plight.

"She just provoked me."

"Yes. Provoked."

"She wouldn't shut up. Nothing I said or did could make her shut up!"

"No. Nothing could shut her up."

"And then she told me she was in love with someone else.

She was having sex with someone else, that she was leaving me for another man!"

"Anybody would have done what you did. She pushed you to it."

"I was furious. She ripped my heart out and smashed it to pieces!"

"Little bits and pieces! Smash! Smash!"

Bernard crumpled. He bent over his lap and the tears began to flow again.

I moved around beside him, reached under his dribbling chin, and gently removed his glasses, still the good cop. "Here. Let me get these for you," I said. This interrogation was falling apart and I frantically searched my *Court TV* memory files for where to go next. What did the police do at this point? Get in his face?

The sisters didn't allow me this opportunity. They returned with steaming cups of coffee. From the quick turnaround it must have been instant. They weren't the types to be left out of a juicy interrogation.

Before they could interrupt the mood with chatter, I held up my hand, not wanting them to break the spell. "Here, Bernard. Take this." I handed him a cup of coffee and took one for myself. Thankfully, the girls were silent. I think they were mystified by the scene unfolding in front of them. They scooted chairs up to sit across from us, and it felt like we were telling campfire tales. If I wasn't careful, we might be tempted to hold hands and have a séance. To add to the tenor of the moment, the sun had dipped down, early as it did this time of year, and it grew darker in the studio. The light from the adjoining hall and the small lamp allowed us to see each other, but only in shadow. I was inches from a confession, and my stomach was wrapping itself up in knots.

No one could hear her scream.

What if Bernard suddenly came to his senses and realized what he was saying? We would all be dead for sure! And me without a good steak knife. Too late to worry about that now. I pressed ahead.

"Talk to me, Bernard. Unburden your soul. Cleanse your conscience."

Bernard sighed heavily and raised his head. I caught his tortured expression in the lamplight, and then he turned away, hiding his face in the shadows.

Bertha said, "Bernie, you look like you've been rode hard and put up wet. Just what in the hell happened here?"

I didn't chastise Bertha; after all, it was a fair question, and I was out of ideas.

Bernard stood slowly, painfully, with great effort. His hat slid to the floor. He held his coffee cup in one hand, his finger wrapped through the handle, took a sip, and then stepped on his hat as he walked between the sisters and over to Gerty's drawing table. He stopped there and ran a finger over its edge. We all watched.

When he turned back to us, I knew he was about to say something important. He took another drink of coffee, placed the cup on the drawing table, and sighed heavily. And then he told us a story—a tale horrific enough to curdle your blood and curl your toenails, unless of course you were a hard-core homicide investigator.

And I was not hard core.

CHAPTER SEVENTEEN

What Bernard told us was shocking. Inez, Bertha, and I sat spellbound as he recounted the evening he'd found his wife dead. While he talked, he paced in front of Gerty's drawing table, lifting and replacing her brushes or her paint tubes, looking over her things, rubbing the table top with a thumb, sipping nervously at his coffee. At first, his voice was soft, trembling, and emotional.

"That night . . ." he said, and paused.

"Yes. That night," I encouraged.

"That night we had a terrible fight. I was getting ready for bed; she had her dentures out and was brushing them by the sink in the master bath.

This was a serious time and no room for jokes, but the image took a little of the fear factor away momentarily. I cleared my throat.

"Was this, uh, a normal activity? I mean, did she always take her dentures out before bed?" I had no idea why I was asking the question. But as it turns out it was a good one.

Bernard nodded. "She took great care in her personal appearance." He turned to look at me and there was fire in his eyes. "But. *But.* She was taking a little too much time. It was her habit to brush her dentures, leave them in the glass by the sink, and then go downstairs to paint."

"She, er, popped them back in that night?"

"Not only that, but she put some of that perfume she had

behind her ears. And then she put on a little negligee that I'd bought her last year. She'd never done that before. And it sure wasn't for me, I can tell ya now. When I look back on that night, I'm sure she was provoking me. How could a woman get all sexied up like that just to walk off and leave her husband wanting?"

I quickly interjected before his commentary turned R-rated. "Okay, Bernard, she brushed her teeth, put on some perfume, and wore her sexy little negligee. That probably made you wonder what she was up to. Right?" I was working on that sympathetic angle for all I was worth.

"Yeah, that was all weird, I'll admit. But what really got strange was when she went downstairs and made me a drink. It was a doozy. A Long Island iced tea."

The temporary quiet from Bertha was shattered. "Oooh! That'll knock you on your can!" she said.

I held up my hand. "She didn't normally do that, I take it."

"Oh, please," Bernie said. "She was always complaining about me drinking, and here she was smiling, fluffing my pillows, even turned on the tube and brought me a drink. She put one of those little umbrellas in there. The drink was loaded, and pretty soon—so was I.

"Where was Gerty while you were drinking your tea?" I spoke softly.

"She went down to paint. Now you've got to wonder. What was an old woman doing painting landscapes in a negligee? I started to think about that. Up in my room, propped up on the bed, drinking my tea, watching David Letterman, I started thinking. I was going over everything in my head, and I was getting mad. She was up to something. With a little liquid courage, I was going to make her talk."

"Bernard, I know this is difficult. But I need to ask. Did you know Gerty was filing for a divorce?"

A strangled sound came from Bernard's throat. "Yeah. I knew it. She'd been telling me for a long time she was going to do it, but it had always been a way to get me to do whatever she wanted. She was forever threatening." He lowered his head. "I was weak. Denying it, running off to the bar to drown my sorrows, pretending she really didn't mean what she was saying."

"Sounds like she was pretty good at her little games." I made my voice sound angry.

"Like I said, I was weak. I just let her go on."

Bertha piped up again. "Well, Bernie, why the heck didn't you leave the wench?"

"You did have good reason," Inez added.

"Yes, why didn't you leave her?" I asked.

"That's the funny thing." Bernard looked around the room. "I couldn't. For all the trash she threw my way, I still loved her. I know women go through menopause and lose their marbles for a while—maybe it was that. She did have her good qualities, and when she had her teeth in she was very attractive. You know how it is with creative types. Moody and unpredictable. It's what drew me to her in the first place, not to mention she was quite a contortionist. Her strange behavior had to let up eventually. Did I mention she was quite a contortionist? I figured I'd just stick it out."

Bertha shifted loudly in her chair. "I hate to tell you this, Bern, but you could stick it out all over the place and it wouldn't have interested Gerty. She liked fresh meat, or didn't you know that? You were Mr. Beefcakes when she met you, but she prefers 'em young, and you were having birthdays quicker'n snot."

Poor Bernard. He had to know Gerty was well past menopause-laden mean streaks. The man had forgiven, overlooked, and made excuses for her cruelty—and she'd walked all over him. Had he finally snapped?

"Please go on. We're listening." I put my elbows on my knees.

It was all I could do to keep myself from reaching for my purse. The notebook needed data, but I refrained. That would come later.

"I think she figured I'd get souped up and fall asleep. It was her plan. Because what she was doing down here was a little bit more than painting."

I held my breath. Here it was.

"So I finished off my drink, put on some socks, and crept down here. I had to see what she was doing."

My hands went to my mouth.

"I stood outside the studio door and listened," Bernard said. "She was laughing and talking to somebody."

I chewed on my knuckles.

"There was no light coming from under the door. Pretty hard to paint in the dark, if you know what I mean, and I hear some man's voice, and I hear Gerty again laughing, giggling. I was so mad I was shaking. I went to barge in on the two of them. I was gonna flip on the light. Catch 'em by surprise, you know, maybe kill the SOB who was diddling my wife, but I was too drunk. I accidentally fell against that little table before I had the chance to surprise them. I fell over it, it crashed over onto the floor, and the noise gave me away."

I turned and looked at a tiny table in the hall, pristine, upright, with doily and vase. Somebody'd cleaned up.

"Even though I was drunk, it wasn't hard to make out what was happening in here," Bernard said. "First, Gerty stopped talking for a second, then she said something like, 'Oh my gosh! I think I heard Bernard! He'll see you! Get up, get up! Get off me! He has a gun in the house, don't you understand? Get out! Hurry up!' I was getting to my feet when the studio door flew open and somebody ran right past me in the dark. Whoever it was hit me hard. I went down again and he took off out the front door."

"Did you run after him?" I squirmed and felt my pulse race excitedly, imagining a hot foot pursuit.

"No time for that. Besides, I was on the floor. I heard a motor start out front, I heard gravel spinning, and he was gone. Then Gerty was standing over me. She was pulling up the strap on her negligee, kicking at me with her naked toe, and yelling at me." Bernard adopted a voice eerily similar to Gerty's "Bernnnnn! You're drunk. You're worthless. Look at you lying on the floor like a big blob. You're just a stupid idiot. Why aren't you passed out in bed like you should be?" Bernard rubbed his nose with a fist. "And that's when I got really mad. I was sick of it all. She'd gone too far this time. I knew she'd been playing hanky panky with some other guy and it was going to stop." Bernard was trembling with anger.

Softly I encouraged, "What did you do?"

"I got up off the floor. Then I pushed Gerty back into the studio. She was yelling the whole time, waving her arms around, screaming at me, clawing at me like some wild animal. I dodged her. She didn't get her hooks in me, but she looked wild and wicked and dangerous, and I decided to call it a day. I spun her around, gave her a big shove, and closed the door. And then I locked her in."

"How did you do that, Bernard?" Nervously I counted the steps to the door. Just in case.

"This is an old house. The doors lock with keys. There was always one over every door. I just got the key and put it in the lock and trapped her in here." Bernard lowered his gaze. "I shouldn't have done that."

I stood up and went over to Bernard. I placed my hand on his arm. "Bernard, surely she could have gotten out if she wanted to. There are"—I counted—"six windows in here."

"Yeah, she could have crawled out a window, but I yelled at her, told her I was locking the front door. Even if she'd gotten through a window she couldn't have come back into the house, and she didn't have the car keys. Our closest neighbors are miles away and she was just wearing that little nightie. No, she wasn't going anywhere. She had plenty of things to keep her busy, and a couch to sleep on. I was just ticked off."

"Then what? What happened then?" I asked.

"Yeah, Bern, what happened then?" The sisters were wide-eyed.

"The booze was hitting me pretty good. I thought I'd wait an hour or two, sober up, get my head together, and let her out. Then we'd have a long talk. But when I got to my room I fell asleep on the bed. The next morning I woke up pretty hung over. I couldn't even remember what had happened the night before. Until I looked over and noticed Gerty's side of the bed hadn't been slept in. Then it all came back. I didn't hurry to get downstairs; actually I was pretty worried about what Gerty would do to me when I let her out of the studio."

Bernard sighed, and went on.

"It took me a minute to find the key. I thought I'd brought it upstairs with me, but after I looked and looked, I found it back over the studio door where I must have put it. Force of habit, I suppose. I'd just put it back in its usual place. When I found it, I opened the door." Bernard pointed to the studio entrance. He swallowed hard. "And I found her." He stood up and pointed to the drawing table. "Here. I found her here, slumped over. There was a terrible stench in the room. She'd fallen over, probably fell asleep while she was working on that painting"—he pointed to the half-finished portrait—"and got her paintbrush stuffed up her nose, caught the edge of the cleaning fluid jar, and tipped it over. Her face was covered in it. She must have been overcome by the fumes. The rags were soaked, the floor was a mess." Bernard stopped and took his glasses off. He rubbed them with his bare fingers.

I whispered, "Was she dead?"

"Yes." Bernard was barely audible. "She was dead."

Bertha and Inez gasped.

"What did you do?" I asked.

"The room was full of the stench. I ran around getting the windows open but I could feel myself getting dizzy. I had to leave and go outside because of the smell. I started vomiting and went to my knees. It wouldn't have taken long for her to die."

"No, I don't think she suffered." I stood up, walked over, and comforted Bernard, touched his back, rubbed his neck. "But, didn't Gerty know how dangerous it was to paint in a room without ventilation? She's been painting for many years. Don't you think she'd have taken precautions?"

This comment seemed to surprise Bernard. He looked at me. His brow furrowed. "She had a ventilation system installed. It was an air purifier. Come to think of it, I don't hear it. It usually makes a terrible racket." Bernard stood quickly and walked out to the hall. I heard him say, "That's strange. It's been turned off."

Bertha, Inez, and I followed him out to the hall. We looked at the little control box on the wall. The switch had, indeed, been pushed to "off."

"She never turns that thing off," Bertha said, her brow furrowed.

"No. Never," Inez said.

"Why don't we finish our conversation in the kitchen," I said. "I'll put on another pot of coffee." I went into the kitchen. The studio was feeling too creepy at the moment, and it had become completely dark now. I flipped on all of the kitchen lights and went in search of coffee, filters, and the coffeepot. I saw the instant coffee jar by the microwave. That just wouldn't do when a man was confessing to murder. We needed fully leaded stuff.

I ran the water in the sink, filled the carafe, and had the coffee gurgling in no time. Inez perched on the counter, Bertha leaned against the wall with her arms crossed. Bernard found a chair and sat with his head in his hands.

Once the coffee was finished, I went back to the studio for our cups. Entering, I turned on a light. My coat was still there, draped over the arm of a chair, and the sisters' coats were thrown here and there. I made a note to remember them before we left. Then my eyes fell on the unfinished portrait. Could this be a painting of the man Gerty had been with the night before her death?

"Bernard," I said when I returned to the kitchen, "who was Gerty painting? Who was sitting for that portrait in there?"

"Probably the man she was sleeping with. I don't know. I don't think anyone will be calling for it, if the guy knows what's good for him."

Bertha poured the coffee. "So what did you do when you found our sister dead? My guess is you didn't call the police right away."

"No. Not immediately. I was in a panic. So ashamed at what I'd done, and so scared. When I looked at her I saw some small bruises on her shoulders where I'd shoved her back into the room. And I was sure someone would have been able to tell I'd locked her in the room. Also, there were a couple of scratches on my arms. I guess she got in some licks after all. It looked really bad for me, and I just went crazy. I had to clean everything up and make it look like she'd died of natural causes. So that's when I thought up the story about her heart condition and changed the prescription bottles, and hoped the police wouldn't go so far as to check her medical records or anything.

"When I went back into her studio the smell was so strong, making me sick and really woozy, that I went out back to the shed and got the mask I use when I spray the attic for bugs.

Then I got some rubber gloves and a mop. And I cleaned up. I got rid of the cleaning fluids; I put everything in plastic bags and refilled her cleaning jar with new fluid. I even washed her face and hair. It took me a long time, but after I was finished, it just looked like she'd fallen over and died of a heart attack. Nothing else. The paintbrush was lodged pretty good and I couldn't get it out, so I left it. I guess I did a pretty good job because the paramedics didn't even suspect anything. They just came in, checked her pulse, noticed she was stone cold and let the police take over. They hardly checked anything at all. Asked me a few questions and told me to call someone from my funeral home of choice to haul her away. It was easy."

"What did you do with all of the stuff?" I asked.

Bernard looked puzzled.

"The stuff you cleaned up. The mop, gloves, rags, all of that."

"I threw them away. Bagged everything up and tossed them in the trashcan outside. There was a thermos I didn't recognize in here, too. I just figured it was the guy's who was with my wife. It's all out back. I was gonna haul it to the landfill tomorrow. Why?"

It was an important detail. If Bernard was telling the truth, there was a way to confirm his story. I needed to get a look at the evidence. But what if he wasn't telling the truth? Or, what if he was? At the very least, I could get at that thermos. There was bound to be some spittle DNA on the lid. But what would that prove? We all knew there had been someone in the studio, but he'd gone long before Gerty had died. Proving who she'd been sleeping with probably wouldn't mean a thing.

Darn. If things had happened the way he said, poor Gerty had simply died by sucking in cleaning fluid. She would have known how dangerous it was to breathe that stuff, but someone had turned off her ventilation system. Bernard was cleverly surprised to find this had been turned off somehow. That was awfully convenient.

My suspicions were well founded. There were dozens of ways Gerty could have saved herself. She could have opened the windows before she started painting; she could have put the lid back on her fluid jar. She certainly wasn't the kind of woman to be this careless. No, this was still an open case in my opinion. Maybe Bernard hadn't intended to kill his wife, but she was dead. Then again, there was the matter of the other man in her studio. Who was he? I was struck with an idea.

"Bernard, can I have that picture in Gerty's studio, the one she didn't finish?"

Bernard waved his hand. "Take it. I can't sell it. It's not done. I was just going to burn it anyway."

I looked at my watch and gasped. It was nearly five o'clock. Ted would be wandering around the house wondering why his wife didn't have dinner on the table.

"It's time to go. I'm terribly late and Ted will be worried." Then I turned to Bernard. "I'm so sorry about all of this. You said there is a memorial service. Is that tomorrow? I'd like to come."

"No, it's on Tuesday. Afterwards, Gerty's body will be cremated. This whole thing has been a nightmare. But at least one good thing has come out of it." Bernard attempted a weak smile.

"What's that, Bern?" Bertha dumped her coffee in the sink.

"I'm not drinking any more."

"The VFW will go bankrumpt," Inez said under her breath. She slid off the counter and kissed Bernard lightly on the cheek. "Sell her paintings, take the money, and go to Hawaii. You deserve it."

Bernard walked the girls to the front door while I went for our coats. I lifted the painting and tucked it under my arm. When I tried to lift my coat from the chair's arm it got hung up on a screw. I reached under to pry it loose and felt a tuft of something soft and furry. I got to my knees and looked under the chair. There, tangled around the screw along with the fabric of my coat was a tuft of brown hair. I plucked it out and held it close to my face. It looked familiar. Strange, I didn't know Gerty had a cat. That's probably what it was, I guessed. A cat had crawled under the chair, scraping some of his hair on the screw. I rolled it around in my fingers. Never mind. It was getting late. The hair fell to the floor and I stood, quickly piled the coats in my arms, took my painting, and headed for the door.

We said goodbye to Bernard and headed out. I passed the coats around and we crawled into the car.

The car lights poked holes through the dark cloak of evening as we traveled back to Hunker Hills. "What do you make of all that?" Bertha asked.

"He's telling the truth." Inez blew her nose on a tissue while she navigated the country road. "I can tell. He's telling the truth."

"What about this mystery late-night visitor? What do you make of that?" I reached over and held the steering wheel to allow Inez the use of both hands. She honked a second time into her tissue.

"Does it matter?" Bertha stretched out in the back seat, placing her feet up. She crossed her ankles.

"Maybe." I gave the wheel back to Inez. She handed me her tissue. I took it without thinking, and then released it onto the floor of the car. Oooeee.

"I'm just thinking—"

"I know what I'm thinking, I'm starved! Do you want to make a drive through McDonald's before heading home?"

Inez perked up. "Yeah. Let's get burgers."

That sounded pretty good to me. Maybe if I picked up some extra burgers Ted would forgive me for standing him up. I quickly made a phone call and told my husband I was bringing home dinner. He sounded breathless.

"Honey, I was getting ready to call out the posse. Where have you been?"

"Just visiting Gerty's husband. He needed some support."

"You've been there all that time?" Ted's voice was fading in and out. At first I thought it was the cell phone giving me trouble, but it wasn't.

"I'm doing my push-ups." Ted groaned. "Just two more to go."

"How many have you done?" I acted interested.

"Five. Just two more." Ted groaned again. "Just one more. Urrrrghh."

"Done?"

"Think I blew out an intestine. Don't know. Hurry, I've worked up a pretty good appetite."

"You're incredible, Ted." I kissed the phone and hung up.

"There they are, the golden arches. Get your orders ready, gals, we're going in." Inez pressed the gas and steered.

"Just one more question before we call it a night," I said. "Did Gerty have a cat?"

"Gerty?" Inez pulled up to the order box. "Are you kidding? Gerty was allergic to cats. She never had animals in her house. Never even came into our home or our Poochie Hooch, for all the noise she made about it. Thought it was a crime to keep pets anyway. Let them all be *freeee*." Inez waved her hand. "What'll it be girls?"

As we placed our order I puzzled over what I'd found under the chair. Gerty didn't have cats? Then what was that fur I'd seen under the chair? Something for my notebook. It was a small detail. A little thing. I had no idea whether or not it was significant, but I wrote it down just the same. As chance would have it, it was one of the little things that would eventually turn the investigation upside down.

CHAPTER EIGHTEEN

Security lights (installed by Ted during a previous house-improvement frenzy) were blazing across our yard when I pulled into my driveway. The snow had melted somewhat, leaving our sidewalk and front porch a slippery mess. Ted swung the door wide when he heard my car. He'd taken the time to shower. His hair was wet and tousled about his head. He was dressed in a robe, fluffy slippers, and, I would soon discover, nothing else. He greeted me with a big hug. Mr. Fitz was across the street spying on us. He was in silhouette with a shovel in his hand, pretending to be scooping slush. When Ted stepped aside to let me into the house the front of his robe fell open, causing Mr. Fitz to drop his tool. It made a metallic clang.

Ted chuckled. "That'll make him feel inadequate."

"That will get you arrested," I said as I walked into the house. "Where are your shorts?"

"No need for those anymore. I'm letting my skin breathe. Good for the pores. Now. Whatcha got for daddy?"

I shoved the McDonald's bag at his chest. "You might want to nuke it."

Ted opened the bag and peered in. "Feast of cholesterol."

"You'll get over it," I said. I hung my coat in the closet and dropped my purse, phone, and keys on the kitchen table as I passed. "I take it you weren't called in to deliver the twins this evening."

"Not tonight." Ted followed on my heels. He plucked out a

fry and chewed on it. "So how's the detective work going?"

I turned, prepared to defend myself, but I decided, judging from his encouraging expression, that the man was genuinely interested. His face didn't have the usual wash of sarcasm or even a hint of condescension. Now this was a thrilling change, and I couldn't wait to share. My last investigation had been complicated, but Ted had immersed himself completely in the mission, and he could be pretty resourceful. Perhaps he could be of some help this time, too. There were still questions surrounding the reasons Gerty had died. I needed Ted's medical expertise, but first, I'd need to soften him up.

Figuratively speaking, of course.

"I'll tell you what," I said. "You eat your dinner and I'll take a quick shower." I gave Ted a smile and tugged on his robe. "Let's meet up in the bedroom and I'll tell you what happened today."

Ted's eyes opened wide and he choked on his French fry. He coughed in spasms and lunged for the microwave, tossed his burger in, and pressed buttons like nobody's business. Turning to me he said, "This'll just take a minute. Maybe less." Punch, punch. The microwave hummed.

"Take your time," I sang out. On the way up the stairs I began to drop clothes. "We can always talk tomorrow if you'd like. I'm pretty tired and I might just fall asleep in the shower." Oh, how shrewd I was.

Ted called after me; his voice sounded panicked. "No, no, I'll be quick—almost done here!"

I laughed heartily once the bathroom door was closed behind me. Ted—so easy.

The shower was heavenly. I soaped and loofahed and sponged all the folds and creases. What had happened to the tight muscles and milky skin? Instead of sporting a tan in the outline of a bikini I now had liver spots and suspicious-looking moles. Gone were the perky mounds of desire, replaced by sagging, uninspiring folds of flattened flab. I'd lost an inch or two in my spine, my inner thighs overlapped and chafed, my chin skin drooped, my feet had spread along with everything else, but— Ted still wanted me.

Feeling fine, I tilted my head back under the shower spigot and filled my mouth with water. I spewed upward. What a nice little arc that made. I tried it again. Spew, spew, spew, nice little fountain. Next I filled my cheeks with water and punched my fists against my face. Oh, my, that was a good one. Nearly hit the ceiling. What if I add a little shampoo? Get some bubbles going? I opened the bottle and took a swig. Nasty, but if I didn't swallow it was okay. I swished it around in my mouth a little and blew. Following a stream of suds, the most marvelous bubble came from my lips. I opened my mouth wide; the bubble stretched.

"May, what in the name of all that's holy are you doing?"

Ted gave me quite a fright. My reaction was immediate. I gasped, sucked the bubble up my nose, and sneezed violently. I nearly popped a lung.

"Ted! Why are you poking your head into my shower?" I twisted the knobs and quelled the flow. Darn. I'd had a good thing going.

"I thought you might need a towel. Then we can talk about what you did after church." Ted threw a towel at me and hurried out of the bathroom, undoubtedly to warm up the bed. I knew talking was the last thing on his mind, but I played along.

Wrapped in the large towel, I ran a brush through my hair, wiped off my eye makeup, brushed the suds out of my teeth, and went to my husband.

"How nice, Ted. Candles." Dante's inferno blazed merrily in our bedroom. Ted had found my Christmas stash and red wax dripped everywhere. The smell of cinnamon and pine circled the room.

"I thought you might like that." Ted grinned sheepishly and patted the bed. He was stretched out on top of the quilt, still in his robe, black socks on his feet. His legs were crossed at the ankles.

I dropped the towel on the floor and stood for a minute, giving my husband time to behold the vision. Turning slightly, I stood just right, angled a little, allowing the candlelight to accentuate my finer points. Transforming my lips to pouty, I added sloe eyes and a sultry voice, and you could hardly blame the man for succumbing to my womanly ways.

"Come over here." Ted's voice was high pitched and squeaky. He cleared his throat. "Come over here," he said again, this time in baritone.

Of course I lingered. Slowly I spread my arms and then reached behind my head to cup the base of my skull. I lifted my hair and twisted my neck around seductively. I thrust a hip out and swiveled like my joints were made of butter.

Ted pushed a corner of the quilt into his mouth and started chewing.

I crooked a finger at him and gave him the "come hither" sign. This was undeniably a change in our standard modus operandi, fueled by a surge of schoolgirl pluck. *What is she thinking?* Ted's expression seemed to ask, but judging from the contour of his robe, he was delighted at the unexpected turn of events.

Ted crab walked across the bed toward me. His robe fell away, revealing his intentions.

"Sit here," I said huskily and pointed to the edge of the bed.

Ted scrambled and hung his legs over the tall bed frame. Oh, this wouldn't do at all. The man looked preposterous in this position, but I knew to laugh at this point would spoil the moment. I had to think fast.

"Now, reach over and pull yourself up," I said.

Ted grabbed the frame, hands on the outside of his legs, and did a stomach crunchie. A vein popped out along his neck and he was straining in the candlelight. Amazingly he maintained a look of expectancy. Now, what would I do?

I improvised. "Now, er, lift one leg," I commanded, running my fingers over the tops of my elongated breasts. He complied. Another vein popped out on his forehead and he had started to sweat.

"Now the other one," I whispered.

At this point Ted's legs were practically over his head and I was out of ideas. Wait. He was pretty spry. Time to put that fitness program to the test.

"Now do a backwards somersault."

That did it. Ted tried. He didn't want to spoil our fun, but this was just out of his league. He threw his legs over one shoulder and promptly shot off the side of the bed. Luckily Trixie was there to break his fall. She spat and yowled and darted away and saved herself with just a glancing mash to her tail.

I didn't bat a lash. "Perfect," I said, "just where I want you."

The floor proved to be more exciting than I'd ever imagined.

By the time Ted and I clawed our way back up onto the bed it was eight o'clock. The candles were nubs and Trixie was running sprints up and down the stairs.

Ted pulled me close. "Now. Tell me about your day."

His eyes were at half-mast, so I hurried through the story Bernard had told the sisters and me in the studio. My husband was an attentive audience, but I could tell he was struggling to stay awake, so I punctuated my findings with gestures, accentuated with excitement in my voice, and poked at him now and then. When I was finished, though, he was less than enthusiastic.

"Let's recap, May," he said around a yawn. "Why do you still think Gerty was murdered? Bernard himself said he'd locked her in the studio and that she'd been there still, alone, when he found her the next morning. Was there any evidence that there'd been a struggle or a break-in? Any real reason anyone would have wanted her dead?"

I shook my head, feeling miserable and disappointed. What Ted was saying was true and I could see the writing on the wall. There wasn't anything fishy here; nothing to really make me believe someone had killed off Gerty, no matter how many enemies she'd made. No, no evidence at all.

I said, "He found her facedown in the cleaning fluid, and there was no sign of a struggle or anything having gone afoul. He did say there were a couple of bruises on her shoulders where he'd pushed her into the room, and a paint brush up her nose, but that was probably because she fell and just happened to land on it when she passed out from the cleaning fluids. Still, nothing big enough to make the paramedics nervous as far as I know."

"Well, I'm sure if the signs were worth noting the police would have been called, don't you think?"

I chewed on a fingernail. "Yeah, I suppose. But, Ted, why was she painting that night? I saw the place; there are all sorts of chemicals, paints, solvents, stuff that was dangerous. Don't you think she would have known better to work in there without having a door or a window open?"

"Maybe she knew better than to paint in an unventilated room, but she did."

"And another thing. She had a ventilation system, but it wasn't working." I realized then what I'd said. Gerty probably thought it was working; that's why she didn't think it was dangerous to paint that night. But wait. "Bernard said it makes an awful clatter when it's on. Don't you think Gerty would have noticed it wasn't working?"

"Maybe, maybe not. We just don't know. The fact is, she made a terrible mistake. She was probably upset after Bernard found her with whomever and confronted her, and she took some time to work on her painting. Work off a little nervous energy. Get in just one more dab with her brush, just one more minute at her easel, and it had cost her her life. It was a horrible tragedy, babe, but I think you're making more of this than any real investigator ever would. You're looking for suspects when there are none.

"Real investigator, Ted? Real investigator? That's a low blow."

Ted stroked my leg. "Honey, I didn't mean it." He yawned again. "It's probably a good idea if you just let this one go. Why don't you take some time off and go to Belize. Patty would love to see you."

"I do miss her."

"Just promise you won't put any pressure on about grand-kids."

"It is about time, don't you think?"

"Her husband's busy. They have all of that immunization work to do before they come home."

"Jack's a good man. We got lucky there." I sighed. Maybe Ted was right. Get a plane ticket, visit my daughter and her husband in Belize, and put all of this behind me.

Ted closed his eyes. "Go to Belize, pick up some knick-knacks."

"Knickknacks?"

"See Patty and Jack."

"Patty and Jack."

"Yeah. Knickknack, Patty, Jack."

I certainly wasn't about to follow that up with anything about dogs or bones. My previous surge of energy was waning. Ted's mouth drooped and he began to breathe heavily.

I rolled over and stared at the wall. Ted was right, of course. Nothing I'd written in my detective notebook meant anything at all. So what if Gerty was fooling around with someone? My bet was on the curator—the guy Bertha wouldn't kick out of bed for eating crackers. He was probably the man in Gerty's studio, the man Bernard had collided with in the hall. Gerty was his bread and butter. His meal ticket. His girl toy. He wanted to keep her happy . . . and painting. No reason for him to want her dead.

I could check the rags and things in Bernard's trashcan, knowing I'd find just what he'd described. No, he hadn't killed her. The FETA sanction? Oh, yeah. Conspiracy theories were popular these days—and I didn't buy it. That left . . . the sisters? Jolene? Ridiculous. I squeezed my eyes shut. Forget it, May. Go to the grocery store tomorrow, order flowers for Gerty's memorial service, do some laundry, mail some letters. Go to Bunko and Bingo or Belize, and finally, finally start that first chapter of your novel. Get on with life.

As I lay in my bed, thinking over everything I knew, everything I'd learned about Gerty and her husband, everything I knew about this investigation, those old feelings of disappointment greeted me in the still, dark, quiet of the night. I was just a bored old lady with nothing to do.

But I wasn't tired.

I turned on the lamp by my bed and nudged Ted.

"Are you hungry?"

Mr. Macho snorted and opened his eyes, blinking against the light. He was propped up on a mound of pillows. He looked like he was on drugs.

"I could eat," he slurred.

"You wait right there. I'll be back in a flash. I'll make nachos." I jumped up, grabbed Ted's robe, and shrugged into it.

To tell you the truth, dismissing myself from the case was liberating. No more worries about clues and details. No more poking around in dastardly deeds. Nachos—everything would be fine after nachos.

"Oh, May. I almost forgot to tell you. That police friend of yours called while you were gone. He said he wants you to come down to the station tomorrow evening. He has some kind of award for you."

"What? Really?"

Ted's voice was fading. "He said it was some civilian appreciation thing. He wants you to be there in time for roll call. Three o'clock, he said."

"Well. That's certainly a surprise, isn't it, Ted?"

Ted mumbled something and closed his eyes.

I stopped with my hand on the doorframe. "You know what? Maybe we'll just turn in early." I hesitated, waiting for him to come alive and ask me all about my civilian award. Instead, he dropped open his mouth and started to snore.

Ho hum.

I covered my husband with a spare blanket, kissed him on the forehead, switched off the lamp, blew out the candles, and went about closing down the house. I thought about what Ted had told me. An award! Imagine that. I could hardly wait to get back to the police station, and back into action. Maybe there were some other cold cases I could help them on. Forget Gerty. Officer Murphy would probably be more than happy to give me a chance as a prostitute decoy. Belize could wait.

Downstairs I put a few dishes in the dishwasher, turned off a lamp in the living room, and then checked the back door. Locked. Now to the front. While turning the dead bolt on my front door I was struck with a feeling that I had forgotten something—something critically important. What was it? What had I missed? Oh well, it would come to me tomorrow. Tonight,

I needed my beauty rest.
 If it were only that easy.

CHAPTER NINETEEN

I woke up in the middle of the night. Actually, it was two a.m. by the numbers on my clock but who's to quibble over details? Two, three, straight-up midnight, it didn't much matter; the fact was I was awake when I should have been in the middle of my REM, and I didn't know why.

Not until I heard the noise.

Something was happening in my driveway, and it had alerted my ever-keen instincts. I stared from my pillow, straining to make sense of what I'd heard.

There! A sound like metal on metal clanking down below.

My breath was hot and fast on my upper lip. I puffed rapidly through my nose, my senses alive and spiked to full attention. The light from the window washed over the bodice of my nightie, showing the erratic hammering in my chest. Should I wake up Ted? Maybe it was just Mr. Fitz up for a late-night shoveling spree.

Clank!

I covered my mouth with my hand. Someone was down there! I thumped Ted's shoulder. "Ted! Ted! Somebody is in our driveway. I think they're doing something to one of the cars!"

Ted moaned and snorted, rolled over, and settled in.

"Ted!"

"Two more to go!" He cried out, and then relaxed again.

"Oh, for Pete's sake." I threw my blanket aside and crept over to the window. I peered out through the curtains. What I saw nearly crippled me.

I whispered as loudly as I dared. "Ted! There's a man down there by my car! He's got something in his hand! Ted, wake up!"

"Just one more push!" Dr. Ted uttered, evidently in the midst of a birthing dream.

Calm, May, calm. You're on your own for this one, girlfriend. I turned again to the window, moved the curtains over with a shaky finger, and tried to get a bead on the man accosting my Camaro. The security lights were still on, but from that angle I could only make out a bulky form. He was at the back of my car, fiddling with the trunk.

I gave up on Ted.

Clinging to the banister, I padded down the stairs on wobbly legs, one step at a time, except that third step. It always creaked, and I stepped over it. Running on my toes in slippered feet I got to the front hall and slowly opened the closet door. My cell phone was still in my coat pocket, and I rummaged as quickly as I could to retrieve it. The intruder might have cut the phone lines. I wanted to be prepared.

Clang!

The noise was louder on the ground floor.

I nearly dropped my cell phone. It juggled around in my hands, then I got it steady and started to punch the nine-one-one buttons. But wait. If I called the police, it would take them minutes to get there and the intruder might just be in our house by that time. Maybe he was trying to steal my car, or maybe he was . . . he was . . . wanting to rape an old woman in her sleep!

Clank! Scrape!

I swallowed hard. No, if he'd wanted to do that, he wouldn't be trying to jimmy the lock of my Camaro trunk right then. He'd be crawling up the trellis under my bedroom window, that's for sure.

Creak! Bang! Clang!

Where was Mr. Fitz, the busybody, when you needed him? I'd pull weeds, he'd be there; if I ran for my mail, he was there. If I forgot to close my blinds while undressing, he was leering (and that was the reason Ted and I had moved our bedroom upstairs). But now, the nosy neighbor was probably cowering in his bed.

Thanks a lot.

Ted was comatose, the police were miles away, and my neighbors were of no help.

Look out, Mr. Robber-Man. Here I come.

With my hand on the front doorknob and my cell phone in my robe pocket, I gathered my courage. Instantly, I considered the attack-and-restraint maneuvers I'd learned from watching *Cops, Tomb Raider,* and *The Matrix.* I eliminated high-flying roundhouse kicks, head butts, or sleeper holds. I passed on the blitz attack with a fireplace poker. Too aggressive. He'd be expecting that. A good detective would be stealthy and rely on the element of surprise. I backed away from the door and felt my way through the house to the rear entrance. Even as I pushed through the back door I could hear the clanging and banging coming from the location of my car. What was he doing, anyway?

Now I'd like to say I was pumped up, high on adrenaline, filled with righteous indignation at what was happening to my personal property, full of rage and fury, but truth be told, my knees were collapsing with every step through the mushy snow, and there was no saliva left in my mouth. No really good plan had come to mind.

Oh, why had I planted those bushy hedges along the side of my house last spring? There was no chance of me slithering along with my shoulder to the siding like I should have, hunkered down, low and hidden in the shadows. It was dreadfully cold, my breath was puffing out, but my trembling wasn't because of the weather, and there was no time to worry about wind chill. Pulling Ted's robe around me, I crept along the house and after a few yards I was close to exposing myself under the front security lights so I fell to my knees, struck an errant rock and grunted, went to all fours, and crawled forward quickly. Unfortunately, Ted's robe was long and uncooperative. When I crawled, my knees would run up the front of the robe and pull my face down abruptly to the ground. I kept adjusting, yanking the robe out from under me, crawling forward a couple more steps, jerking my face down, pulling the robe out, and doing it all over again. Inch by inch, I was nearly there.

Then. The clanking stopped. There was a dead quiet in the air. Had he heard me? Seen me? Was he standing by my car, a weapon in his hands or pocket, searching for his prey? I fell to my belly like I was trying to make a snow angel. I didn't move.

I was there in that position for quite a long time. Long enough to feel the wet seepage of melting snow turn my husband's robe to ruin and my torso to marbled frost. The clanking didn't return, but I heard footsteps. Fast-walking footsteps coming toward me. The steps crunched, slogged, and mushed over our expensive sod.

He'd seen me! He knew I was stretched out prone and defenseless by our decorative shrubs and he was coming to kill me.

Not if I had anything to say about it.

I waited until the footsteps were inches from my face and then I attacked. I rose up on my knees, screamed, waved my arms, and snarled and hollered. Spittle flew from my lips. Fire flew from my eyes. I was a wild woman.

That was when I saw him for the first time. The big man, a big black shadow blob, really, was so shocked by my demonic outburst that he screamed horribly (it really is horrible to hear a man scream), pinwheeled his arms, slid to a stop, and whirled around.

The last I saw of him were the soles of his shoes beating a hasty retreat down the sidewalk. I was disappointed. I wouldn't be able to identify him in any police lineup (unless we were lucky and I could finger him by a long scream) because I hadn't seen his face.

But I'd shown him. When I planted a foot to get up I stepped on the robe and yanked my face down again. Well, it wasn't pretty, but I'd gotten the job done.

I pulled the dry parts of Ted's robe around me and went to examine my Camaro. There wasn't anything at all amiss. Despite a few scratch marks near the trunk's lock I could see no other damage. Maybe the thug had been looking for something. Was it a random theft? A coincidence that someone would be poking around in the wake of my investigation?

Oh! I put my hand to my mouth as I remembered.

I'd left Gerty's painting in the back seat of my car! I cupped my hands and peered through the car's window. A corner of the frame was visible. I could see it on the floor of the Camaro where I'd left it. Could that be what the man was after? Would he return for a second attempt? If so, I was in serious danger. He'd been surprised the first time, but now I was sure he'd be ready to catch me on a return attack. I wasn't safe here. Not safe at all.

I peered once again through the car window with one hand against the canvas top of my car. The guy wasn't very bright; a sharp knife and he could have ripped through the convertible top like it was made of cheese. That got me scared; maybe he was going back for that knife. A really long, sharp, pointy knife. He'd slice my throat first, and then . . .

I raced around the house to the back door, my hair and robe tails flying. I cleared the back steps in a single bound. I grabbed the knob and threw my shoulder into the door, and nearly knocked myself unconscious.

The door was locked.

Three minutes of ringing the doorbell and hammering on the door brought nothing but sore knuckles and one step closer to hypothermia. Ted would pay for this later. I needed to find a way back into my house, and I needed to do it fast, before that guy came back with his machete. If I'd been a woman in labor, my husband would have jumped up, ready to go. As it was, nothing short of an atomic blast was going to get him out of bed this night.

Ted was a pretty handy guy, I'll give him that. He'd done really well installing that security light around the front, but the illumination fell short everywhere else around the house. This is why I had such a hard time figuring out a logical port of reentry. Breaking into your own house sounds like an easy enough thing to do. After all, you know where all of the weak points are, which windows are flimsy, what swivel locks don't always hold, and, conversely, which windows are painted closed and not worth the effort.

After trying three windows without success, I found myself standing in front of the trellis under my bedroom window, a window I knew to be unlocked, since it was on the second floor and you'd have to be pretty desperate, or downright foolish, to shimmy up the brittle, icy, wooden structure. Until this evening I'd never considered locking it. Before, I never thought there might be rapists outside looking for access—some uncomplicated way to snatch an old lady from her bed.

Maybe I was waiting for Rapunzel to let down her hair. Maybe I was crazy enough to think my husband would come looking for me. Maybe I just thought if I stared up at the second story of my house long enough I would wake up from this bad dream and Ted would be standing beside the bed with a nice, hot cup of coffee, dressed, and on his way to work.

But wait! I had the cell phone. How could I be so dense? I flipped it open, ready to call my husband, but I got . . . nothing. The darn thing had run out of battery juice. I'd had it all day and hadn't thought to charge it up. How stupid. I stared at the trellis again. Maybe I could throw snowballs at the window.

A car passed in front of my house in a slow roll and gave me the inspiration I needed. It could be the perp, casing my house, on his way back to finish the job. The car passed, its headlights disappeared in the distance, but I wasn't going to wait around to see him circle back. More than likely he was slamming a magazine into his Sig Sauer at this very moment.

Everything within me screamed to get moving! So, common sense be damned, I reached out and took hold of the trellis with both hands and winced at the instant frostbite. I shook the long sleeves of my robe over my hands and tried again. Better. I crawled up a couple of rungs. The wind kicked up and blew the tails of my robe out from under me, causing a great shudder to ripple up my spine, and I wished with my whole being that Ted hadn't asked me to put on that ridiculous teddy after our romp on the floor.

Step by step, hand over hand, I was halfway up the trellis when the car came back again and made another slow pass in front of the house. I froze. Figuratively, of course.

The car continued on its way.

"Hey, May! Whatcha doin' up there?"

The voice of Mr. Fitz beckoned from the earth below, and startled me violently. On reflex, my fingers gripped the trellis so hard my hands slipped right off. I grabbed frantically and caught hold thankfully, but at that same moment my feet lost purchase. I swung away from the house like a trapeze artist. The trellis strained and held, but bowed out dangerously close to its breaking point.

"Why are you up there swinging from the side of your house at this time of night?" Mr. Fitz asked.

As if some other time was okay to be hanging with from your trellis with your bloomers showing.

That sneaky old man was standing down there, and from that point he was certain to know the brand of my panties (with matching baby-doll top)—Victoria's Secret if you must know.

My fingers were sliding away again, and I scrambled to get my toes back onto something solid, but just as I was getting things under control, my slippers shot off my feet and I was swinging again, this time in a wide arc. If there had been a rope handy, I might have given the circus trick my full attention. Maybe I would have slipped a bare ankle into a rope loop, hung upside down, spun around gracefully with my robe billowing out like an accoutrement. As it was, I just wanted to keep from breaking a hip.

"Ya need help up there, Mrs. List? You look like you might be needing a hand or something." I glanced down quickly to see Mr. Fitz in flannel pajamas, black snow boots on his feet, with the pant legs shoved inside the tops. He had a floppy hat on his head and he wore mittens. "I could get you a ladder if you want."

I started to shake my head, and knew immediately this added movement was a mistake. The trellis gave a long moan, and snapped away from the house. It's one of those moments when you just don't know what to do. There was no planning, no preparation; I just hung on and rode the blessed thing all the way to the ground.

Mr. Fitz, for all of his annoying habits, did his best on this occasion to be the gentleman. During my free fall, I screamed a death knell and watched his gyrations as I hurtled toward the lawn. He dodged left, then right, held his mittened hands out as if he was preparing to catch a touchdown pass, and stuck his tongue out like Michael Jordan.

Bless his heart.

I plowed into him at a bone-crunching speed. I literally felt the breath as it whooshed from his diaphragm and blew past my face. When I opened my eyes, grateful nothing was shattered in the hip department, I felt him squirming under me, trying really hard to breathe. His mouth yawned and his jaw pumped. I would say he was gasping, but no air was coming or going.

"Oh, I'm so sorry!" I said, and rolled off to his left. He immediately sucked in air as if he were coming up from a long forced dive.

"May? What in the world are you doing down there? And who . . . ? Is that Mr. Fitz?"

From above me, Ted leaned out of our bedroom window. Sheesh. Now he comes to my aid. I wanted to say, "Why, yes, Ted, this is Mr. Fitz down here. He's met me for a midnight tryst. I was so inspired after our little hee-haw earlier that I thought I'd give the rest of the guys on the block a try."

But I didn't. It might encourage Mr. Nosy.

"Do you know what time it is?" Ted called out.

I got to my feet and fiercely brushed the dirt from my robe. "What time it is? What time it is, Ted? Is that all you're worried about? Your wife is on the ground, on your front lawn, having been, I might add, just nearly accosted by a midnight stalker, saved, I might add, by our good neighbor here—" At that point I reached out a helping hand to Mr. Fitz, who accepted it graciously. "And you're worried about the time?"

"Your midnight stockings cost you what?" Ted had one hand on the windowsill, the other cupped around his ear.

"I'm glad you're okay, Mrs. List. I thought I heard some commotion over here," Mr. Fitz said, now on his feet. He massaged his lower back.

Ted shouted, "What? You went to buy some lotion?"

Ignoring Ted, I turned to Fitz. "Yes. Someone was trying to break into my car." I tied my robe belt in a quick knot and found my slippers. Since my feet were completely iced numb by this time, I put them on just for show.

"That's not good," Fitz said. "Somebody breaking into your car and all, not good. No. I guess you were coming down from your bedroom there?"

"Not exactly, Mr. Fitz. It's a long story and I'm freezing here. I'll explain it all in the morning." I turned to the window. "Ted, will you please come down here and let me in? The door's locked."

"I'm on my way!" Ted called out and pulled his head out of the window.

"Maybe it's time I say goodnight. I mean, uh, if you don't need me, I should just go," Mr. Fitz said.

"Yes. And thank you once again." I shook his hand and watched him jog back across the street. By the time he was inside of his house Ted was unlocking the front door and I was standing on the porch ready to enter. I didn't speak to him right away; I had to get that painting out of my Camaro, and fast. No telling when the nasty perp would return. I hustled over to the table, grabbed up my car keys, and ran out the door, past Ted's perplexed face, and got the painting in record time.

Back up the porch, I put the painting under one arm, grabbed the front door handle, and—broke a nail. Ted had locked the door behind me.

The door flew open and Ted stood there grinning. "Just kidding," he said joyfully.

"You need help," I said and shoved him aside.

"Should I call over Mr. Fitz? He seems eager to please."

"Very funny, Ted." I love my husband with all my being, but he does have a way of making me crazy. I placed the painting on the table and went to the laundry room for a change of clothes. My back ached, my knees hurt, my hands stung, and my feet were beginning to thaw. I had to grit my teeth against that pain, which was probably a good thing, since this meant I wasn't able to bark at Ted with my jaws clenched like they were.

Well, you don't make it through medical school if you're an idiot, so Ted caught on to my temporary discomfort quickly. He waited until I got back to the kitchen before gently putting his hands on my shoulders.

"Why don't you tell me what happened tonight? Have a seat and I'll make the coffee. I'm dying to know why you were mud wrestling with Mr. Fitz."

Ted poured water from the sink. I sat at the table and stared at the painting. Sleep was out of the question. Even Ted had to admit something strange was afoot at the List house.

This was going to be a long night.

CHAPTER TWENTY

"Someone was after this painting, Ted—someone was out there trying to break into my Camaro to get it." I looked at the painting on my kitchen table. My feet were almost completely thawed, and the cup of coffee in my hand was a warm comfort.

"This thing? It's not even finished." Ted lifted Gerty's portrait and tipped it left and right. "It's not even that good."

"Really? You don't think so?" I took the portrait from Ted. My fingers smudged a bottom corner where the colors blended in a pale blue and light violet color. It was painted in oils and still tacky. The background had been finished, but the beginnings of a man's torso were taking shape in rudimentary brush strokes. The only things with any real detail were two masculine hands with sharp knuckles, short coarse nails, and ropy veins cutting across his wide wrists. These looked like the hands of a working man. I was taken by surprise.

"You know, Ted, I just assumed Gerty was painting her lover, but I thought she was fooling around with her curator. He wouldn't have hands like this."

"Why not? Have you seen him?"

"No, I've never met him. Wait. Let me think. There was that art show I went to a couple of weeks ago."

"He would have been there."

"Yeah, but I can't remember if Gerty introduced me to him. There were so many people . . ."

Ted leaned over my shoulder and peered at the painting.

"Those certainly aren't the hands of a pansy."

"Ted. I never said the curator was a pansy."

"Look. She even captured the grease under his fingernails."

"I thought you said it wasn't that good."

"Well, even I can paint black grease marks like that." Ted touched the paint and smeared it a bit.

"Ted. You've messed it up."

"No, I didn't."

"Yes, you did. Let me see your finger."

Ted held up a finger but the paint hadn't transferred at all. Maybe it wasn't as wet as I'd thought.

"See? That's not a smear—it's something she was painting on his hand."

I gasped. "Ted, get the magnifying glass, quick!"

Balancing the painting on my lap I waited while Ted rummaged in our junk drawer. After a lot of shoving and spilling, he hurried back to me with the glass. He seemed as eager as I was to get a better look at the blurry thing in the painting.

"Here," he said, triumphantly.

"Whoa," I said. Excitement danced a jig in my stomach. "It's a ring. Not very clear, but it's a ring, all right."

"Yup, that's definitely a ring."

"It could be a clue!"

"What else would it be?"

"You're making fun of me again."

"No, I'm not."

"Just . . . do we have a more powerful magnifying glass?"

"I could get the binoculars."

"And I could ask Mr. Fitz to hold it up across the street. Get our reading glasses."

Ted hurried off again. I heard him turning over furniture, opening and closing drawers. Eventually he jogged back into the kitchen with two pairs of glasses on his face. "Give me the magnifying glass," he ordered. I handed it over.

"Well, I'll be. It looks like a college ring of some sort. What do you think?"

I donned the two pairs of glasses, and stared through the glass as Ted had done. "No, I don't think it's a college ring, but there's an image of some sort on it. Too bad it's not finished. The details aren't very clear, but it's a symbol or something. Can you make it out?"

"What difference would it make? If you're right, and this isn't the curator she was painting, what do you deduce?"

"Deduce? I deduce, as you put it, that this isn't the curator."

"Brilliant deducing."

"What else do you want me to say? Aha! I've solved the crime; this is actually a portrait of Mr. Fitz, the man she was rolling around with in her studio late at night after knocking her husband unconscious with lethal tea bags!"

"He does turn up in unusual places."

"The curator?"

"Mr. Fitz."

My blood pressure was building. How did I know what the ring meant? Oh, the weight of responsibility!

"May, you're exhausted. You've had a long day. Don't forget I have to go to work some time this morning, and you have to be fresh and perky for your award ceremony at the police station."

I withered in my chair, feeling bone tired. "Thank you for remembering, Ted, but I don't know where I'll find the strength. I'm exhausted."

"You'll be okay. Chew on some coffee grounds or something."

"Okay," I said weakly, thinking it might not be a bad idea.

Ted took the portrait and placed it on the table. "If, as you said, someone really wanted this portrait, then I'd imagine that someone might be the one wearing the ring."

"Oh my gosh, Ted, you're probably right. And listen to this. I surprised whoever was trying to get into my car. That's why I was on the front lawn. I got locked out and tried to make it up the trellis. That's why Mr. Fitz was down there. He was trying to break my fall."

"Isn't that just a little too convenient, that he'd be up watching out for you at this time of the morning?"

"He's just a nosy-body. I saw the robber guy when he went past me, and it sure wasn't Mr. Fitz."

"Did you get a look at this guy's face, or maybe his hands?"

"No. And now I'm mad that I didn't chase after him." I didn't tell Ted about my crawl along the house or how terrified I'd been. I probably wouldn't be able to describe the man if I'd seen him face to face. My mind was blocking out the trauma.

Ted stretched and yawned. "The painting is safe, and I doubt seriously that we'll have any more late-night visitors, especially now that we have the neighborhood Fitz-watch out holding sentry. I wouldn't doubt it if he's loading his sawed-off shotgun as we speak."

"Don't even joke about that."

"Who's joking? I've seen it."

"His gun?"

"It's a monster."

"When did you see his gun?"

"Just a few minutes ago. Look."

I stood up and went to the kitchen window. The morning sun was rising, and I followed Ted's pointing finger. Mr. Fitz was pacing back and forth across his lawn, a large black weapon at port arms. He was still in flannel pajamas, boots, and mittens, but he'd thrown on a camouflage jacket, obviously in a hurry, because it wasn't zippered in front. He had a motorcycle helmet on his head.

"I think we should seriously consider relocating," I said.

"What? And give up all this?"

Ted and I caught a few more minutes of sleep before he shuffled off to work. I vaguely remember kissing him goodbye, and think I plucked a square of toilet paper off of a razor cut on his chin, but it's all a little hazy. After the Hummer disappeared from view, I fought the urge to curl under my quilt again before the spot grew cold. There was much to do, and I wanted to be alert for my police award later in the afternoon, so I showered and dressed for the day. If I had known what kind of day I was dressing for, maybe I would have borrowed some of Mr. Fitz's army fatigues.

As it was, nothing could have prepared me for the upcoming events, and so I was dabbing my lashes with mascara when the phone rang, causing me to flinch and rake the black gunk across to my temple. I whispered a forbidden word or two and dropped the mascara into the sink before answering the phone.

"Hello?" I rubbed my stained face with the back of my hand.

"May. You won't believe what happened."

"Hi, Bertha."

"May. We was robbed! Can you believe that? Someone broke into our trailer and went through our stuff."

I gasped. "What did they take? When did this happen? Are you okay? Who did it?"

"Can you come over? Inez is in shock. She's eating everything in the refrigerator."

"Did you call the cops?"

"Not yet. I don't think they got anything, I asked Inez to do an inventory but she won't get away from the crisper."

I heard Bertha shout at her sister, something about spitting out a cucumber, I think. There was some commotion, and then Bertha was back on the line. "Just come over, May. Inez is in an awful state. We'll talk about it when you get here."

Bertha hung up and I stood there for a minute knowing, possessing the keen senses of a good detective, that my brush with death last night and their robbery were somehow connected. I flew through the rest of my Mary Kay regime, skipping the obligatory blend-and-smooth steps, and hopped into my Camaro.

The roads were as clear as they could be after a good snow, since most of it had disappeared from some warmer temperatures. This gave me confidence behind the wheel, and I was blazing over the asphalt.

I navigated the highway, jerked over the lane markers left, and then right, passed motorists like nobody's business. My elbows were out; my chin thrust forward; my back not even touching the leather chair covering or lower back support pillow. The sisters needed my assistance and I wouldn't fail them.

Hold on girls, I'm a-comin'! I'm a-comin'!

I went a little crazy, thumped over some of those sleep bumps on the shoulder, and rattled my teeth. I also rattled the spare tire in my trunk. I heard it come loose and every time I veered or changed lanes I heard it slamming side to side. Ted would have to fix that when I got home. It was quite annoying.

Bertha met me outside of the Poochie Hooch when I skidded to a stop. She waved her arms and told me to park there. The spot in front of her trailer was too muddy, she said when she helped me from the car, and I'd have a high old time getting my car out if I got sucked down in it.

"Step on those rocks, May, come on. Inez went through everything in the deep freeze and she's moved on to the pantry. We'd better hurry."

I trotted along behind Bertha, stepping carefully on the stepping-stones. This was urgent business. My purse swung furiously on the crook of my arm.

"Inez!" Bertha hollered when we stepped into the trailer.

"Put those down!'

Inez looked up, eyes wide, her face pale and drawn, her eyebrows arched. She stood inside the pantry, and had a mouthful of pretzels. They stuck out in a chaotic array and she chewed frantically, trying to down them before Bertha stepped over and swatted the half-empty pretzel package out of her hands.

"Get hold of yourself, girl." Bertha wadded the cellophane. "May's here now. You can relax."

"Yes, Inez, why don't you come over here?" I gently guided the chewing sister over to the table. "Now, sit down and tell me what happened." Inez allowed me to push her toward the little kitchen space without an argument. She sat down and fingered a bowl of plastic fruit. Bertha slapped her sister's hands.

"When we get up this morning, the front door's standin' wide open," Bertha said.

"Yes, it feels a little chilly in here." I pulled my jacket around me. It wasn't my good coat—that one was on its way to the cleaners—but the spare was warm enough. Unfortunately, the fresh air had also carried in the stench of Hooch doo-doo and it was worse than I'd ever remembered. I could feel the smell burrowing into my second-best coat. The cleaners would make a mint off me this month.

"Whoever came in here did a pretty good job of trashing our stuff," Bertha said. She pinched her mouth into a wrinkled ball. I'd never seen her so furious. I looked around at the clutter, not seeing anything out of the ordinary. How would they know?

"I'm pretty sure it wasn't the first time someone was in here. They just got careless and forgot to close the door this time. Maybe we surprised them. I think they're the ones who took Horace the other day."

Inez made a strangling sound in her throat. Her eyes pooled with big fat tears. Her glasses immediately fogged.

"They took Horace? Your ferret?" I wondered if my face gave

away my guilt. I thought of telling them where Horace might be found, imagined a loaded rat trap under Sherman's desk, and thought better of it.

"Yeah. I think they took Horace," Bertha said. "And they took other stuff."

"What other stuff?"

"I don't know yet, but we have some pretty valuable stuff in here. We've been collecting for years."

"You don't know what they took?"

Bertha shook her head. "Inez was supposed to look. I called you right away, but she was supposed to be going through our drawers to see what's missing."

Inez blinked and a tear fell. "But I just started eating," she said.

"Yeah," Bertha took my hand. "With you here it will be better. Why don't you sit with Inez and I'll take a look-see."

I squeezed Bertha's hand but didn't let her go. I looked around feeling nervous. "Could someone still be in your house?"

Inez squeaked.

Bertha whispered, "I'll take a look. Don't move. I'll get my gun."

Her gun? What is this? Does everyone in Spokane own a gun? I needed to pay a visit to the Hunker hardware store. I was definitely in need of some hardware.

Bertha moved off to her bedroom and then I heard a scream. The scream was echoed by the answer of a zillion barking dogs, and Inez fainted dead away.

CHAPTER TWENTY-ONE

After the scream, I was on my feet in a flash. I leapt over the unconscious body of Inez and raced toward the bedroom. The Poochie Hooch was in a deafening frenzy next door.

"What is it? What's wrong?" I called out, certain the robber was still in the house and Bertha had unwittingly found him under her bed or in the closet. I needed a weapon and I needed one fast. The only thing I could think of, and the only thing handy, was the philodendron. I grabbed its woody trunk as I passed and wrenched the thing out of its pot. A spray of dirt and roots littered the floor. I kicked at the bedroom door, holding the tropical plant like a javelin. Dirt showered down the back of my blouse.

"My gun! They stole my gun!" Bertha sat on the edge of her bed beside an empty drawer. Its contents were dumped on top of the rumpled bedspread—a hairbrush, a mirror, some bobby pins, and a clump of pencils held together by a rubber band. "It's always in here. They stole it!"

"Are you sure?" I sputtered. The philodendron dirt trickled down my neck.

"Of course. Sure as I'm sittin' here. Inez! They stole my gun!" Bertha yelled. The barks started anew.

Inez didn't respond, and then I remembered she was lying on the floor. I rushed back to her side, tossing the philodendron back into its pot on the way. I reminded myself to put some Miracle Grow in there later when things calmed down. It was far too dry.

Inez moaned and writhed around on the stained green carpet of their kitchen space. Her eyes showed a lot of white around the pale blue center and her glasses were hanging from one ear. I yelled at Bertha to get her something cold to drink.

Bertha thundered down the hall behind me, snatched open the refrigerator, and then appeared by my side. "Here," she said, and shoved a can of Slim Fast in my hands. I popped the top. I tipped it up, cradled Inez' head, and ordered her to sip. It did the trick. Inez glanced over at my shoes. "Are those alligator?" she asked, and slumped again. A few more drops of the cold drink and Inez was back sitting at the table in no time. She sipped the Slim Fast and fingered the plastic fruit. Bertha slapped her hand.

"Okay. They, or he, or she, whoever, stole your gun. You're not hurt, and it doesn't look as if they took anything else. No harm, no foul, I say." The attempt at soothing Bertha's nerves didn't work.

"They stoled my gun, because they want to shoot us with it!"

"Bertha, if they wanted to shoot you with it, why would they wait to come back and do it later?"

"Don't you remember? They left the front door open. I think they got spooked. Maybe the dogs started barking. As a matter of fact, they were making quite a commotion last night, and I got out of bed to tell 'em to shut up."

Inez went pale again. "You probably just missed the robbers! We're lucky to be alive!"

"Bertha, if you got up to tell the dogs to shut up, wouldn't you have noticed the front door was open?" I asked.

"Right, May, I would have noticed. That means one thing." Bertha paused and looked at her sister. I could read her mind. The robber was still in the house when Bertha got out of bed. He probably fled after she went back to her room, leaving the door open. We looked at each other, knowing it was best not to say anything. Inez looked as if she would take another face plant into the green carpet, so we just talked with our eyebrows.

Inez stood up unsteadily. When she spoke, her voice was weak. "I've got to feed the dogs. They're probably starving, and we're expecting our first appointment in a few minutes."

"You haven't been out to the Hooch yet?" I stood, too, and took charge. "You'd better let me go in first. Whoever came in here last night might have gone out there too."

"Probably not, May. Those dogs would have made such a racket it would have woken up the whole neighborhood."

"Well, you did say they were making a lot of noise."

"Yeah," Bertha said. "You'd better take a look."

I paused and looked at both sisters. "Before I do, there's something you should know. I don't think what happened here last night was an isolated incident."

"Huh?" Inez plucked at her white streak.

"I had a visitor myself."

"Last night?"

"Yes. Someone tried to break into my car. I scared him away, but it's quite a coincidence that we both had someone trying to steal our stuff."

"Why would they want to steal your car?"

"Not my car, Inez—I think they wanted what was in my car. Remember Bernard gave me that portrait Gerty was painting? I left it in my car. I think that's what they were after."

"I don't know, May," Bertha said. "How would they know the painting was in your car?"

"And how would they know where your gun was?" Inez asked.

"Only one way," I said firmly. "He or she's been watching us."

"Ohhh!" Inez said, and slithered onto the floor again.

"You stay here, Inez," I told the unconscious woman. "Bertha and I will be right back." I jerked my head toward the Hooch. "Let's take a look."

We took a collective breath to steady our nerves and, trembling, I put my hand on the doorknob. Who knew what we would find inside the sisters' place of business?

Bang! Bang! Bang!

It was like an explosion. Three deafening shots rang out. Bertha grabbed me by around the neck and together we hit the floor.

Bang! Bang! Bang! "Bertha? Inez? I know you're in there. I need to talk to you!"

Bertha rolled her eyes. "Jolene."

Inez lifted her head. "She's out there again," she said.

"You just rest, Inez. I'll get it." I dusted myself off, feeling just a little foolish, and helped Bertha to her feet.

I opened the door just as Jolene was ready to bang it down. "Where's Bertha and Inez? I need to have a word with them."

"Nice skirt, Jolene," I said. It was made of denim with a ruffle around the hem. She didn't seem to care that it was two sizes too small, or that her thighs could feed the whole Donner party.

"Jolene." Bertha stood beside me. "I thought we worked all of this out. I'm trying to keep the dogs quiet, but there's really nothing I can do about it."

"It's not that," Jolene said. One of the straps on her halter top dropped down and she let it stay. "Have you seen Stanley? He ain't been over in two days and I can't find him. It's not like him. He never goes two days."

"Maybe he's at work." Bertha looked bored.

"No, I called. They said he took the week off." Jolene put a cigarette to her lips and sucked on it hard.

"Where are your kids?" I looked over her shoulder.

"They's with my mama. I thought Stan and me was gonna

go away." Jolene blew out a long stream of smoke. "That's what I thought. Now I can't find him. You don't think he run off on me, do ya?"

Jolene sucked on her cigarette again.

"No, Jolene, why would he do that?" I tried to comfort the woman; she was trying hard to act calm about all of this, but I could see the worry in her eyes. Bertha opened her mouth but I stopped her, fully expecting her to say something about the cow and free milk. "Maybe he's buying you flowers or something. Have you seen his truck?" I could see Bubba's trailer but no truck.

"I ain't seen him or his stupid truck in two days. I thought I heard it last night, but he didn't come over. He don't miss two days in a row."

"I'm sure he's just out doing something, like . . . oh, you know how men are. Well, my husband disappears for hours. Sometimes he's getting the oil changed, or he has to work late, or, well, you just never know."

Jolene shook her head. "It's not like him. Bertha, you tell me if you see him?"

"Sure thing, Jolene," Bertha said.

"Okay." Jolene trudged back toward her trailer. Her bleached orange hair waved in the cool breeze. I shivered.

"She's really upset," I said.

"Yeah. He probably took off."

"I guess she'll know soon enough. Now let's go take a look in the Hooch. I'll help you feed the dogs and clean out the kennels."

The Hooch looked just as I remembered it. Stinky, loud, and in need of a fire hose. We hurried about cleaning and feeding. Bertha stopped by the cage I'd seen earlier. "Oh looky! May, they've got their eyes open!" Bertha reached in and pulled out one of the little bald dogs. "This one is yours. I'm good at matching dogs with people and this one has May written all over him."

I cringed again, thinking this was just about the most horrid-looking creature I'd ever seen. It had "May" written all over it? I'd better take a little more time with my makeup.

"I don't know, Bertha," I started, but when she shoved the little bundle in my arms it was as if I had been handed a baby. Even the skin felt human. It was a strange feeling, and not just the skin. All of my mothering or grandmothering instincts took hold, and I'll admit it was hard letting that little mutant go back into its cage when I was done cuddling.

"So, we know everything is okay in here. No broken windows, jimmied locks, no sign that anything is missing, right?"

"Yeah, but we know somebody broke into our house and tried to break into your car. If what you said is true, who would be the one most likely wanting to steal that painting?"

"Who is the one most interested in Gerty's art?"

"The curator!" We both whispered simultaneously.

"Yes. We haven't even talked to him since Gerty died," Bertha said. "Are you still thinking she died surreptitiously?"

"Suspiciously? I don't know. What Bernard told us makes sense. She probably just died of breathing cleaning fluids, but I'm wondering about this curator friend of hers, and who is nosing around in our stuff. Maybe someone was out to make some money off her paintings after all. Think about this, Bertha—if the curator thought there was a piece missing, he might have been trying to get it. Maybe it would complete a set or something. I don't know."

"That makes sense, May, but why would he steal my gun?"

"I've been wondering about that. It could have been he was trying to see if you and Inez had some of her art in your house. You know, maybe she gave you something, and he found the gun by accident, and, well . . ." I was plumb out of ideas.

"Oh, yeah. He accidentally found the gun while looking for one of Gerty's paintings in my drawer?"

Like I said, I was plumb out of ideas. But I could do something.

"I'm going to go talk to him."

"What? He might blow a hole in your head, May! What are you saying?"

"Not if I catch him at work. He wouldn't dare. Now, let's get back to your house. You just write down his name and his work address, and I'll be on my way."

"And then what will you do after you talk to him?"

"I'll just worry about that when the time comes," I said.

We left the "closed" sign on the Hooch door and trotted back to the house. We found Inez eating cereal out of the box. Grape Nuts. They made a horrible noise, grinding between those splayed teeth of hers.

"Looks like you're feeling better, Inez," Bertha said. She scribbled something on a piece of paper and handed it to me.

"Good luck, May, and call me when you're done."

I patted the cell phone from outside of my purse. "Will do. You two stay safe, now."

And with that, I was gone. Hunker Hills flew past, the hardware store was humming, but no sign of Stanley. Poor Jolene. She'd had such high hopes. The spare tire in the trunk of my car had come completely unhinged. It thudded and bounced, so I pushed in a tape to drown out the noise. I lost track of my driving for a minute and heard someone mash their horn. I mashed mine. So rude. Nobody gives a little courtesy to their elders any more.

I checked my watch. No time for dilly-dallying; I needed to catch the curator before he left for lunch. I made it to downtown

Spokane in minutes. A quick interrogation, and then I'd be on my way to the Harvest Police Department. I sure hoped I had some information to share with Officer Murphy. Who knew? I might have this whole case wrapped up by dinner.

The Spokane Art Department was in a beautiful old building made of red stone and lots of glass. I had to pay five dollars for parking, and roughly handed the attendant my money while thinking it was a crime. He didn't care, and took my cash. I parked and moved quickly along the sidewalk. I entered the building and stood to get my bearings.

A lovely woman dressed in a green silk suit greeted me and asked if I needed help. Was that a loaded question? I asked her to take me to the curator, that I had business with him, and she floated along in a cloud of perfume, leading me toward the back. Her heels clicked along the marble floor. "He's right in here." She whispered for no apparent reason. "I'll let him know you need to speak with him."

"Thank you," I whispered back, a little sarcastically maybe, but it was with the practiced air of a doctor's wife, and she didn't notice I was mocking her. I patted the back of my hair and came away with a clump of dirt and a philodendron stem. I smiled. She smiled.

"Mr. Bottox? A Mrs. List is here to see you, sir." The woman floated away on her cloud of perfume and I was left facing a desk. Behind the desk was a man seated in a leather chair. The chair squeaked when he rose to accept my outstretched hand. Fast as lightning I looked at his hands. He wore several rings. That didn't help. It was just like him to make things complicated.

"What can I do for you, Mrs. List?"

"Hello, Mr. Buttocks, nice to meet you."

"Bottox."

"Excuse me."

"Happens all the time."

I felt a flush surge up like a neap tide. "I can see it might get confusing."

"Yes. Now, I'm rather busy," he said. "Can I help you with something?"

"Actually, I'm here at the behest of Bertha and Inez Peach. You do know them, don't you?" I looked for a waver in the Bottox man.

Mr. B stuck his lower lip out and stroked his chin. "Can't say as I do."

"Gerty's sisters?" I probed.

"Gerty Knickers?"

"No, Gerty's sisters."

"Pardon, that's what I said. Gerty Knickers' sisters?"

"Yes. Mrs. Knickers, the deceased. God rest her soul."

"That is a shame. She didn't seem ill at all. But she was getting up in years."

"And how old are you, Mr. Bottox?"

The man looked surprised. "I passed sixty-three last year. And how old are you?"

What brass! "Let's just say I have a few good years left. Nothing wrong with this ticker!" I poked at my breastbone.

"That's nice."

"Enough with the pleasantries, Mr. Buttocks—"

"Bottox."

"Yes. Well, I need to know what happened to Gerty's paintings. I know you were representing her, and I know her artwork was worth a great deal of money. Now, my clients, Bertha and Inez Peach, feel they are due some of the moneys garnered by these pieces, but they haven't seen a red cent, and we're looking at litigation."

"How are you representing them? As their attorney?"

"Yes. I'm their attorney." I started to sweat and envisioned the tap dance I was pulling off, but not very well.

"I'm not very fond of attorneys, Mrs. List; frankly I find them a pain in my—"

"Bottox?"

"Yes?"

"I don't really care what your feelings are about attorneys; I simply need you to answer my questions. Where are the paintings?"

Mr. B drew a heavy book across his desk and started flipping pages. "They've all been claimed by her husband."

"Bernard?"

Mr. B turned the book around so I could see it. "Yes. He signed for them. Right here. Mr. Bernard Knickers. They're all gone."

"Looks like Mr. Knickers will be a rich man if he sells the paintings, doesn't it?"

"I seriously doubt it; they were poor in quality at best. I just handled her work as a favor. You know, local artist—it was a charity case."

"A charity case? Her paintings weren't worth anything?"

"Hardly the canvas they were painted on. From what I understand, her husband plans to auction them off. He might do better to hawk them at a garage sale. The frames might bring a few dollars. He might even make some money if her family picks them up, but they aren't professional quality."

"I guess you weren't too upset about letting them go, then."

"Actually, it was a relief. I couldn't get them out of here fast enough. We needed the space."

"Well, then, Mr. Buttocks."

"Bottox."

"Yes. Well, then, that's all I have for you today. I'll be in touch."

"Do you have a card, Mrs. List?"

"A card?"

"Yes. A business card. In case I need to get in touch with you."

"No. And I wouldn't think you'd want one after your insults. Good day, Mr. Buttocks."

"Bottox."

"Yes. Good day, sir."

Mr. B rose, took my hand, and bade me a fond farewell. He hadn't blinked, flinched, bit his lip, broken out into a sweat, or turned any funny facial colors. The man was telling the truth. Gerty's paintings were worthless. Nobody wanted them for the financial gain, and that made the whole case that much more intriguing. I hurried out to my car and opened my purse. I was gathering data faster than I ever had before, and I needed to get it on paper before it got confused and jumbled. On my notebook I scribbled for all I was worth, organizing facts and jotting details.

As I wrote, I also added questions about the break-in at the Hooch house, the missing gun, my midnight thief, the unfinished painting, the mystery man in the painting and in Gerty's studio, and Bernard's confession that he'd had a hand in Gerty's death. Then I slapped my forehead. I hadn't even interrogated the curator about his personal involvement with Gerty, and I hadn't gotten a really good look at his rings! Yikes. I would have to go back in.

However, when I found the perfume lady, she told me Mr. Bottox had left for lunch. Was that an unusual thing for him to do? I asked.

"Very unusual," she replied. "The man always eats at his desk."

Quite intriguing.

CHAPTER TWENTY-TWO

I couldn't wait around for Mr. Bottox to come back from his atypical lunch break; I had a date with the Harvest Police Department. Although it wasn't rush hour, the traffic was heavy and there was a lot of starting and stopping before I got clear of the city jam. Ted really needed to get that spare tire pinned down. It kept bumping and sliding, making me cranky and edgy. On top of everything else, I hadn't had my morning coffee, and I'd missed at least three nights of *Forensic Files*. Laundry was piling up at home, Ted was reduced to fast-food meals, and Trixie had let me know she wasn't happy about being neglected. Just last week I'd been complaining about being bored, and now I was letting my wifely duties slide because there was simply no time to do everything.

A young girl in a slick new sports car darted in front of me, paying no attention to my front bumper, and sped away. I wanted to warn her not to be in such a hurry. Life is too short, and before you know it, old age creeps in, making you want to rein in the years and get back all those miles you put on your car, or your bod, but . . . she'd learn one day.

I was thinking all of these things as I approached the Harvest Inn. I had a few minutes to kill, and I sure could use a latte.

I walked into the coffee bar and searched out the face of the girl behind the counter. The place was a warm haven away from the biting autumn cold, like a friend's hug or a homemade quilt.

The smell of books made me reel with familiarity. It was as if old chums like Agatha Christie or Ann Rule were smiling, beckoning me over: "Sit a spell, May. Let's have a chat. Share a moment of your life."

At the counter I ordered my drink, imagining how I would act during the upcoming award ceremony at the police station. Should I bow prettily? Should I throw kisses to the uniformed crowd? Would the mayor be there? Perhaps they would want me to salute. I'd made a pretty good drug bust, but I really wished it had been a thwarted robbery or even a curtailed kidnapping. That might have gotten me an honorary position on the force. If I could be successful in solving the Gerty mystery, it could happen. Deep in thought, I made a right-handed, quick movement toward my forehead, just to practice the salute, and saw the girl behind the counter raise one eyebrow, followed by a nervous glance around, probably looking for backup if this crazy old woman at her post did anything dangerous.

My hand came down in a flash, and then to cover my gaff I shot it up to my forehead again and scratched. It looked pretty natural.

"That'll be two-fifty," the girl said hastily. "You can pick up your drink at the other end of the counter."

She obviously wanted me away from her. I couldn't say I blamed the poor girl. When I reached into my purse for my money, I noticed, much to my embarrassment, that there were Horace hairs stuck all over my eelskin wallet. They flew and scattered and landed next to the tip jar. It was nearly impossible to visit the Peach sisters without coming away with the stuff on and in everything. I shook off my wallet, much to the disapproval of the counter mistress (Connie, it said on her name tag). She swiped the counter with a wet towel while giving me a nonverbal admonishment.

"Hair of the dog, Connie," I quipped, feeling quite clever.

Connie looked brain-dead and smiled with an expression she probably reserved for the mentally challenged.

After counting out exact change and dropping a quarter in the tip jar, to show my goodwill, I moved down to the end of the counter and picked up my boiling cup of energy. After some quick, hard, cautious sucks on the straws, the coffee drink gave me renewed energy, not to mention a steep rise in my blood pressure and a little scald across the roof of my mouth. I took the steamy cup to the car and made it to the police station within minutes.

Sherman, the desk sergeant, was at his post. He watched me approach the tall desk. He had a pencil in his hand and ran the eraser back and forth across his mustache. He looked bored, annoyed; he had the face of a man whose better years were behind him. Used up, burnt out, turned in.

He didn't even ask if he could help me. Just kept erasing his mustache.

"Good stuff." I tipped my drink at him.

Sherman blinked twice in slow motion.

"I'm here to get an award. I suppose Officer Murphy told you I was coming."

Sherman quit erasing to look through his paperwork. He'd turned his mustache an interesting pink color. I thought about telling him, then decided against it. He didn't look the type to tell me my slip was showing, so why should I tell him he had an art-gum lip?

"While you check your documents I'd like to freshen up a little, if you don't mind. Can you please direct me to the ladies' room?" The level of coffee in my cup was at the dregs, and I needed sudden, urgent relief. It had snuck up on me quickly. Without looking up, Sherman pointed his pencil at a corner by the front door. I thanked him and ducked away, happy to be afforded a minute to dispose of some water weight and check my face in the mirror.

Once in the bathroom, I chucked my coffee cup into the trash bin and scooted into a stall. I sat relaxed on the cold porcelain, rested my purse on my lap, and took out my compact. I directed the mirror at my mouth and dabbed on fresh lipstick. Then I spritzed a cloud of perfume around, hoping to cover any doggie smell that might be clinging to my clothes and hair.

At first, I didn't think much of the tickling on my legs. My trouser socks were sliding down my calves, I surmised, as they sometimes do when the elastic loses its stretch, but when they started sliding up my legs I glanced down in wonderment at this anomaly and was horrified to see the beady little eyes of Horace. In a second, he turned and darted back down into my pant leg. The tickling was unbearable.

I didn't panic this time. No. Instead, I clamped my hands in a tourniquet around the upper portion of my ferret knee and squeezed, sort of like you would squeeze a tube of toothpaste. Hand over hand; I squeezed down, moving little Horace back the way he'd come. His scrabbling little claws tickled and scratched my skin, twenty little needle pricks, giving me the heebie-jeebies, making me bounce and rock around on the toilet seat.

When a patch of fur emerged, I bent double and grabbed for the scruff of his neck.

"Aha! I got you!" Quick as a bunny, the ferret fiend was back in my purse, locked down tighter than an inmate at Alcatraz. He bumped and protested some, but settled down in no time, probably chewing his way through my lip gloss.

"Mrs. List? Everything okay in there?" A rapid knock at the door and a friendly voice hurried my bathroom process. The voice was that of Officer Murphy. If I didn't show myself soon, he'd probably bust down the door. Cops like to do that sort of thing.

"I'm coming!" I cried out.

I whipped out a strand of toilet paper, which kept coming, a long train of it rolling out and out and out. Most of it ended up on the floor. Never mind that, I was comporting myself as best I could, grabbing at my waistband, hitching at my purse strap, blushing uncontrollably. Things kept falling and slipping, and in my hurry I banged a few times against the metal stall door. Eventually I got everything together.

"Any problems?" Murphy sounded genuinely concerned.

"Nooo, no problems!" I gathered up the quilt of toilet paper, shoved it into the toilet bowl, and unlatched the stall door. And then I whipped back around to face the toilet. I'd almost forgotten to flush.

Loath to put my hands on anything unsanitary in a public restroom; especially in one visited by druggies and prostitutes, I tapped the toilet handle with my toe, hurrying to get to the sink. Murphy was knocking urgently.

"Do you need help?"

"No, no. You just wait out there, I'll be out in a jiffy."

The toilet didn't flush. I tapped again. Nothing. Then, with more force, I jabbed a heel at the toilet handle. I guess I must have smacked it too forcefully, because the handle went down and stayed. The toilet flushed, then the water came back, rising, rising, rising, then over the top of the bowl. Disintegrated particles of toilet paper swam around like feathery, white guppies.

Horrified, I lunged from the stall with just enough time to give my hands a quick rinse before the floodwater cascaded and splattered onto the bathroom tiles. I darted out of the bathroom and leaned my back against the door. My shirt was quite moist under the arms, my hair was drooping, I was breathing hard, but I don't think I was in enough disarray to give myself away.

Murphy was waiting a few feet away, polite and calm as I

remembered, smiling brightly.

"Roll call in a few minutes. Are you ready?"

I smoothed the front of my shirt, cleared my throat, and took his elbow. "Lead the way, Officer."

As we walked away I cautiously took a backward glance in time to see a trickle of water fingering its way under the bathroom door, making its way toward the police station waiting area. A little something to brighten Sherman's day.

CHAPTER TWENTY-THREE

Roll call at the Harvest police station was as much a social event as a professional obligation. A dozen or so cops were gathered in a moderate-sized classroom, sitting atop tables, leaning against walls, chatting together, coffee cups or Big Gulp drinks in hand. It was a place where blue was the fashion-favorite color.

At the front of the classroom was a lectern and behind the lectern was a green chalkboard. On the board someone had scribbled *Sherman's a dork*. Although I agreed, it still wasn't very nice.

Mike introduced me around. I tried to remember names, but it wasn't necessary since they all wore nametags. A guy named Parker said hello, then shot a rubber band across the room and nailed Baxter in the thigh. Baxter returned the favor by firing back a thick spit wad through his Coke straw. Parker dodged and the spit wad stuck to the wall, hung there for a second, and then slid onto the floor.

A female cop pulled an aerosol can from somewhere near her holster. I thought she was getting ready to mace anyone who dared get her into a tangle, but instead, she tipped the can up and proceeded to lacquer her hair. A cloud of Final Net settled over her poof of blond. The woman looked savvy, and I imagined she had a good reason for this maneuver. Hair was something perps would occasionally grab to get the upper hand in a fight, and this gal was thinking ahead. Let anyone clutch her coiffure and they were goin' down, sticky fingers and all. She shoved the can back into her belt.

A man entered the room and the temperature dropped a couple of degrees, conversation ended abruptly, and everyone scurried to find seats. It reminded me of a kindergarten class when the principal came through the door. The man took his place behind the lectern and busied himself with some notes. Mike took my coat, then pulled out a chair near the front of the room and offered me the seat. I sat, and rested my purse near my ankle. I felt a little motion from down there. Horace was getting antsy, but I don't think anyone noticed. Still, I pushed him farther under the table with my heel.

"That's Captain Kovach," Murphy whispered in my ear, explaining the man at the lectern. "He'll make the announcements. I'll present the award. Then you're free to go if you'd like, or you can stay for the rest of the roll call."

"Of course I'll stay," I said. "I don't want to be rude." Also, I thought, there might be some juicy bits of data to gather at this meeting. No harm in educating myself to the ways of the underworld.

Captain Kovach looked out over the crowd and everyone sat in rapt attention. He opened his mouth to begin the meeting, but before he got through his "good afternoon," a holler arose from the outer waiting area. It was Sherman, yelling for all he was worth. He was cussing a blue streak.

I'm sure I went pale; of course I knew what had made him come unglued. The flood had obviously coursed its way over to his desk. Naturally, I said nothing. Sherman was really having a tantrum out there and a couple of cops rose to their feet, but Captain Kovach waved them back down.

"Hold on. I'll handle it," he said.

When the captain was out of the room, things changed. Parker drew out a wad of cash and tossed it on his table. "My money is on the rat," he said. "Nothing gets Sherm worked up more."

Baxter threw down a twenty. "Nope, it's the ex-wife."

The female detective snorted. "No, no. Sherman just got a call from his doctor. I'll bet he had a procedure when he was born and just learned he's really a woman. Match that twenty and I'll raise you ten."

"His mom forgot to put mustard on his sandwich," a fourth cop said, and the betting grew heavy.

To think I could have cleaned up that day, and I'm not talking about the septic problem. All I had to do was identify the real reason Sherman was throwing a hissy, toss down a ten spot, and Trixie could have dined on prime rib. I said nothing, but found myself tugging nervously on my collar—a gut reaction to guilt.

Mike chuckled. "I'm pretty sure he had a run-in with that rat again. It keeps trying to get into his drawers."

I sniffed. "Well, maybe he shouldn't wear boxers."

"No, his files. It's already chewed through half of his paperwork. We tried to put down traps, but that got her going." Mike jerked his head at the blond lacquer queen. "She sicced FETA on us, and we were ordered to capture the thing in a humane manner, whatever that means. To tell you the truth, we've all gotten a little satisfaction knowing Sherman is the only one it messes with. For now, we've made it the unofficial Harvest PD mascot."

"Hmmm. FETA, huh?"

The mention of the organization jolted me. I didn't know they were so popular or powerful in this part of the country. I was still fairly new to the Spokane area, was quickly learning about the environmentalists, and had developed a newfound sense of respect at the levels they would go to, to save plants and animals. Still, chaining yourself to a tree was going a little too far. That brought me back to thoughts of Gerty and her involvement with FETA, and I wanted to strike myself. I hadn't even investigated this part of her life! What was I thinking? That could be a crucial clue!

Kovach was still out, Sherman was still cursing, and I took the moment to ask Murphy a thing or two. "This FETA thing. Do they have enough influence to shut down businesses?"

"What kinds of businesses?"

"Let's say there's an animal business, and someone complains that they are treating the animals inhumanely. Would this be something FETA would take on?"

"Maybe, but I think that might be something the humane society would deal with together with the animal-control people. Still, FETA would probably get involved. They love a good fight."

"Hey. Do you know where I can get a list of the active local members? Do you keep that sort of thing on file around here?"

"Not unless they've broken a law. Their involvement might be written into the report."

"Great! Can you get that for me?"

Mike looked worried about me. For a minute I thought he might try to take my pulse.

"I mean, it is public record, right?"

"I suppose . . ."

"Mikey, this is great. I just have to check out something. It might be nothing, but then again, it might be just what I need to prove something."

"You still thinking about your friend?" Murphy looked at me with gentle eyes, probably thinking about his dear grandmother, who was more than likely spending time in an assisted-living facility, talking about the Great Depression and how it was coming to an end "any day now!"

"Just give me the goods, and I'll take it from there," I said with as much authority as I could muster.

"Come to think of it, there was a protest not too long ago. It got out of hand and we had to break up a fight or two. I think we still have some photos."

"Fantastic!" I crooned. "Perfect! We'll check it out after this."

No sooner had I swiveled back in my chair than the captain returned. He was sloshing, his shoes were a wet mess, and on his heel he trailed a soggy strand of toilet paper. That wasn't the most incredible thing, though; behind him, also sloshing, was my husband, Ted, grinning at me like a fool.

"Ladies and gentlemen, we have two special guests today." Captain Kovach began without any further ado. We were behind schedule.

"This is Dr. Theodore List. He's here at our request."

I beamed. My Ted. Here to watch his wife get her first cop award.

Ted shook the captain's hand, nodded to the crowd, and crossed over to me. He took my hand, kissed it, and helped me to my feet. And then he whipped his left hand from behind his back and presented me with a beautiful bouquet of red roses. I blushed crimson, took the flowers, and gave them a sniff.

"Let's not take any more time," the captain said. "We're here to honor a local civilian who helped capture a couple of drug runners."

The room erupted into applause as I stepped up to the lectern clutching my roses. Murphy followed and reached under the lectern. He came up with a wooden plaque. A small uniformed man with a camera scurried from the back of the room and took a pose.

The captain read from a paper, a formal missive about my feat, filled with a lot of professional-sounding jargon. And then he directed everyone's attention to a large-screen TV. Much to my surprise, the captain pushed a button and replayed the entire event of my drug bust. The cops erupted in screaming laughter when I shouted out my dismay over the PA. They hooted and roared when I shot out the perp's front tire, and guffawed when I pressed my foot down on the bigger criminal's neck, but it was kind laughter, and so I wasn't too embarrassed. Mostly I felt like I'd won a gold medal. I took the plaque from Mike and then it was my turn to address the group of officers.

I said my thank yous, ignored the cursing still coming from Sherman behind the closed doors, and said simply, "Never underestimate the support you get from the civilian population. We're here to assist our police officers in any way we can. We really care."

Feeling the moxie, I kissed my husband, shook hands all around, and after taking my seat again I waited out the rest of the Captain Kovach's announcements in a warm glow.

It didn't take long to get through the rest of the meeting. Nothing much in the way of high crime, so I didn't pull out my notebook. Not that I would have anyway; Horace was down there thumping and thudding. I needed to get out of there, get the ferret home, and hope Mike would have that photo before Gerty was cremated. I only had the rest of the day and maybe part of the next morning. I would have to act fast.

As Mike and Ted walked me out to my car, we passed the cursing Sherman on the way. He was rubbing a mop around the floor and I took a sick satisfaction in that.

Standing outside the police station, Ted kissed me again and said, "Well, May, honey, congratulations."

My return kiss left a smudge of lipstick on his cheek. As I wiped at it with my thumb I said, "I was surprised to see you. How did you get away from the hospital?"

"Oh, I only have the one delivery, Mrs. Davenport, and she was dilated to six when I left. Plenty of time."

"Ted, doesn't she already have five children?"

"Oh, yes. You're right. Come to think of it, baby four shot out before the first push. Better get back to work." Ted turned to leave, and then asked, "Did you tell the officer here about our late-night visitor?"

Murphy lifted his eyebrows.

"I didn't think to mention it." I turned to the officer. "It was nothing, really, Mikey. Someone tried to break into my car. But I stopped him before he did anything."

"She thought she'd tackle him in our driveway," Ted said.

Murphy walked to my car. "You're sure they didn't do any damage?"

"Nothing a little touch-up paint won't fix. Whoever it was tried to jimmy the trunk. See?"

I walked over to Mike and pointed to the scratches by the rear lock. "But they didn't get in."

Officer Murphy held out a hand for my keys. "Why don't we take a look inside? Just to be sure they didn't take anything."

"Okay." I started, wondering how I was going to get the keys out of my purse without releasing Horace. Ted saved the day.

"Use my keys," he said. "I have a spare."

Mike took Ted's key and inserted it into the lock.

"By the way, Ted, the spare tire's come loose. It was bouncing all over the place. We'll need to get that fixed."

Mike lifted the trunk lid.

"No problem, May." Ted looked into the trunk.

"I don't think it was the spare, May," Mike said, and he sounded sad. Very sad indeed. "I think your problems are a lot bigger than that."

"What?" I peered down into the trunk and shrieked.

"Who is it?" Ted said, cocking his head to the side.

"I'm not sure, but whoever it is, he didn't feel a thing," Murphy said.

I shrieked again. There was a body in the trunk of my car, a body with a little black hole in the center of his chest. The body was none other than that of Bernard Knickers.

"It's Bernard!" I screamed, "and he's been shot!"

"Yup," Mike said, "and unless I'm wrong, here's the gun that shot him." With two fingers he pointed at a smart-looking revolver lying beside the body.

"What's he doing in my trunk?" I cried.

"That's what I'm wondering." Mike looked stricken.

"How should I know?" I started to panic. "This isn't even my gun!" Reaching toward the trunk, I was about to grab up the pistol when Mike swung an arm around and got me in a gentle but firm bear hug. Under other circumstances it would have felt good.

Officer Murphy quickly toggled a switch on his shoulder radio with one hand while holding me firmly. He spoke into it. "We got a DRT. Need assistance."

"DRT?" I asked, feeling the fear rise.

"Dead Right There. Police term."

"Oh. Oh, Mikey, you know I didn't have anything to do with this! I'm innocent!" I wanted Mike to release me, but Ted patted the air with his hands, telling me to calm down. I felt the tears well up in my eyes, and the corners of my mouth were twitching. I didn't want to cry, but it was hard not to feel terrified.

"I'm sorry, Mrs. List, but I have to do this." Murphy pulled out some handcuffs and started reading my Mirandas.

"Ted? Ted? What's happening?"

Ted frowned. Gently he took the citizen plaque from my hands and gave it back to Murphy. "May, you're being busted."

My roses fell and scattered onto the sidewalk.

"It's procedure, ma'am," Murphy said, all professional while he turned me around in order to shackle my wrists. "We'll get it sorted out in due time."

"Wait. I really had nothing to do with this," I protested. "Don't you think it's funny that I saw someone fiddling around with my car, and then here's this?" I flailed my wrists around and dodged the handcuffs while Mike kept reaching.

"Just be calm, now, Mrs. List."

"Be calm? No. I won't be calm. This is ludicrous!"

"I'm sure they'll work it out, honey." Ted touched my shoulder. "Let the officer do what he has to do, and then after I deliver Mrs. Davenport, I'll bail you out."

"Hmph! Where's my knight in shining armor, Ted? Where is my tough protector? Are you really going to let him haul me off to the pokey?"

"It's all a mistake, I'm sure, hon. But . . ." Ted checked his wristwatch. "I've really got to be running."

"Ted?" I glared at my husband.

"Hmmm?"

"I'm getting a bigger broom."

Officer Murphy clicked open the cuffs.

"Hold on, Mikey. Let me have a minute or two with my husband before you strip-search me, okay?"

"I don't do that, ma'am. That's the female officer's department."

"Whatever."

Murphy scratched his chin and looked the other way, a silent signal for me to talk with Ted before the cuffing.

I grabbed Ted by the sleeve and hauled him off to the side.

"Ted. Listen carefully. Listen like you've never listened before. Take my purse." I quickly reached in around Horace, grabbed my wallet and cell phone, fastened my bag again, and then thrust it into his hands. "Get this over to the Peach sisters' house. Give it to the girls." I gave him an address, hoping he'd remember. "Then call me on my cell as soon as you give them the purse. Don't leave it in the car, whatever you do. Tell them to look in my purse. But, Ted, don't open it until you get to their house. After that, call me on the cell to let me know it's finished." I gave myself ten points for remembering to charge it up.

"Honey, I doubt if you'll get to keep your cell phone in jail."

I almost started to cry again, but held it together. I cleared my throat. "Just call me. If the phone is nearby I'll hear it ring and I'll know it's you. Or leave a message or something. Just take my purse and don't forget to leave it at the Peach house. Please, Ted!" Again, I felt tears burning my throat. I'd been so proud of my plaque, and now Mikey had it under his arm. He was signaling for me.

"This sounds interesting, May, but I don't know." Ted looked at my purse. "Maybe the cops will need it for evidence or something. We don't want you in more trouble than you're in right now. Why do you—"

I cut him off. "Don't ask any questions! Just *do* it! And then go to the hospital, do what you have to do, and for Pete's sake come back and bail me out!"

"If I have to get all the way over to Hunker Hills and back to the hospital, the deed might already be done by the time I get there."

"So be it, Ted. I need you now. Don't fail me."

Mike crooked his finger at me. It was time to go.

"Don't worry, May!" Ted called after me as I was hauled away. "I'll deliver Mrs. Davenport, then I'll be back to bail you out." He winked. I breathed a sigh of relief. Horace would finally make it home.

"I'm innocent, Ted. I didn't do it, I promise!"

On my way into the police station for the second time, I kept wailing out my innocence. We passed Beer Breath, the dressing-room peeper, as he was being shoved into Sherman's waiting room behind me. "That's what they all say, lady," he slurred.

"Oh, shut up, Frank," I answered.

Sherman looked way too happy to do the paperwork on me. I'm sure he figured out who was responsible for turning his floor into a swamp. It was the first time I'd seem him smile, and I wanted to rip that pink mustache right off his face.

Lucky for me, a body in the trunk of a vintage Camaro didn't happen every day in the town of Harvest, and while the police station emptied out to look over my cargo, I had a free minute with Mikey.

In a rush, I said to him, "You know I didn't kill Bernard, and I can prove it. Get up to Bernard's house in a big hurry. There are some garbage cans behind the house, and in the garbage cans are some suspicious materials. Bernard put them there. They're double bagged," I explained, "and whatever you do, don't touch whatever is in the bags. In fact, wear gloves if you know what's good for you. Get the stuff to a chemist for analysis. Then you'll know I'm telling the truth. If my hunch is right, it will shed some light on why there was a dead body in the trunk of my car. And," I told him breathlessly, "we need to get a look at those FETA photos."

I had a feeling. Everything was starting to make sense. Everything that had happened was suddenly starting to come together. I prayed Mikey believed me. It was up to him, since there was little I could do while serving time in the pen. "And one more thing, Mikey. You've got to see if you can find that paintbrush that was lodged in Gerty's sinus. Dust it for prints. This is important! Can you remember all of this?"

"What's in the bags, Mrs. List?" Mike sounded interested, thank goodness.

"Please, just go get the stuff and have it analyzed. If it isn't a bunch of rags and brushes with plain old paint thinner on it, then lock me up and throw away the key. If you find my fingerprints on any of it, incarcerate me. You've got those on file, remember, but, Mikey, listen and listen good. If there's something in those bags that shouldn't be there, then you'll have to believe I'm innocent, right?"

Mikey whispered in my ear, "I believe you. I'll take a look. Let's just keep this between us, okay? Until I find out what's what."

If my hands hadn't been locked behind my back I'd have given Mikey a big hug and a smooch to boot.

I just hoped Ted could hurry and get back before it got dark. The last place I wanted to spend the night was at the Harvest Police Station. There's a limit to how far I'll go to gather data.

CHAPTER TWENTY-FOUR

I was booked, photographed, fingerprinted again, and locked in a cell with two prostitutes. Out of spite, I triggered the camera on my way to lockup, and smiled when it launched upwards. This time, the screw didn't hold and it fired off across the room. Sherman shook his finger at me.

My jail time wouldn't be a totally wasted experience. I got a lot of good stuff from the hookers. Leather and Spanky. Probably not their real names, but I wasn't going to pry. After I started my story, we became chummy and I learned that they were really nice. Leather let me French braid her hair, and then returned the favor by giving me some awesome dreadlocks.

Spanky discussed my wardrobe—I needed tighter skirts, she said. After the grooming, Leather took a seat on a cot and patted the place beside her, a signal for me to come and sit. "You said you were arrested for murder. Who, and why? You never did finish."

Mikey had taken my shoes, so I pulled my feet under me and nestled on the hard cot, my back resting against the wall. "I was arrested for killing a man." I sighed.

Spanky, interested in this, took the empty space to my other side and frowned. "Did he get rough with ya, baby?"

I patted Spanky's knee, looked at the moldy ceiling, and sighed again. "No, he was pretty nice, really."

"He liked it rough?" Leather poked at her braids.

"Not that I know of," I said, weary of the whole thing. "But

223

he did get physical with his wife toward the end." I thought of what Bernard had said about the way he'd shoved Gerty into her studio. It hadn't been a love tap, that's for sure.

Spanky put her arms behind her head and leaned against the wall beside me. "Oh, I see. Now we're getting down to it. He went and brought the wife in. Why do they always want to bring the wife in?"

"Happens all the time," Leather said. "And that's when the trouble starts. They bring in the wife, she says, 'Oh, yeah, I'll try it this once. Whatever you want, sugar lips.' Then they see the guy with another lady and they get jealous. They go berserk. I've seen it a lot."

"You have?" I looked from Leather to Spanky.

"And I'll bet his wife's the one who clobbered him over the head or stuck him with a shiv, or maybe shot him with the pistol by the bed, right?" Leather said.

"No. That's not possible. She was already dead," I told her, trying to think of who would want to kill Gerty, and who would want to kill Bernard, and how long I would be stuck in this cell.

Spanky snorted. "Well, that's just sick."

Before I could backpedal and clarify, Leather sat up and said, "You just can't never figure what some johns will want. I remember this guy, a real oily dude with a huge rubbery gut, but he was rent, you know? A smelly, feely guy—he didn't look like his skin ever was in the sun. Well, his wife had been dead a good two weeks, he said. He was really lonely, but he didn't want to admit his wife was gone. He just left her right in the bed where she died. He gave me a call and—"

"Please!" I put my hands over my ears. The description made me think of Sherman, and I wondered if he occasionally took liberties with his clients.

Spanky took one of my hands away to ask, "So you killed the stiff yourself, huh?" Leather plucked at a run in her pantyhose.

"No, but try telling that to the cop who found him in the trunk of my car."

"Oooh, yeah. You've got trouble, lady." Leather let her nylons go with a snap.

I withered. "I know. But how do I explain it? He just showed up in my car. I didn't put him there. He was alive and well, last time I saw him."

"Did you overcharge?" Leather asked somberly. "It's okay if you tell us. Maybe he got mad with ya, got your hands behind ya like this." Leather scrambled over my lap and grabbed Spanky's hands. Spanky got into the scenario and complied with the faux assault, even twisted her face into a terrified grimace. "And you had to defend yourself, right? It's okay, we understand."

"No. I didn't overcharge. In fact, I didn't charge a thing."

The girls' jaws dropped. Leather released Spanky. For a minute they were both speechless. I scooted over to give the girls a little more room on the small cot. We were practically sitting on top of each other. Then Spanky said. "Well for Pete's sake, lady, he probably dropped dead of shock! No crime in that, I say. Maybe I should try that trick a couple of times on my old cronies." Then she shook her head. "No, I'd never make my car payment then . . ."

I squeezed my eyes closed. "No, no, no. Nothing like that. I don't do . . . well, I don't do that sort of thing. Well, maybe I sometimes playact with my husband, but he doesn't have to pay or anything, unless you count room and board and the occasional night out or fur coat."

Leather rubbed her chin. "So, this guy in your car. You have a beef with him?"

"Not exactly. I accused him of killing his wife once, but he didn't seem too upset by it."

"So then, if you didn't pop the dude, who did?" Leather went back to examining her hose.

Spanky perked up. "Did he have ties to anything illegal or something? I mean, you accused him of killing his wife. Looks like they were both into something pretty bad."

I said, "Well, he was worried about some chemicals—"

Leather slapped her hands together, giving me quite a shock. She said, "Could have been a drug deal gone bad!"

"I doubt it. Bernard didn't do drugs. His drug of choice was Budweiser, I think, and Gerty, his wife, definitely didn't do drugs. She didn't even eat meat."

"How do you know that? Everyone I know does drugs," Leather said.

I looked at her, nearly blinded by the reflection of her heavy blue eye shadow glaring my way, and didn't doubt her for a minute. What a shame.

For a while we sat, the girls and I, alone with our own thoughts. The minutes dragged by, and just as Ted had thought, Officer Murphy had confiscated my phone and my wallet. There wasn't much I could do but hard time. I wondered where Ted was, if he'd made it to the Peach house, and what the cops had done with Bernard. There was no doubt now, though, that Gerty had been murdered. Someone was out there knocking people off, but who? And why?

Bernard was dead, Gerty was dead, the curator was a possible suspect, but there was nothing I could think of to give him reason to kill either Gerty or Bernard. He had nothing to gain. I kept thinking of that painting. I should have taken more time in Mr. Bottox's office. I should have found a way to look at those rings of his. At least I could rule him out if he didn't wear a ring like the one in the painting. But wait. I had looked at his hands, and he'd worn lots of rings. Rings that looked like they'd been wedged into his flesh for quite a long time. You can tell these things. How the skin sort of swells up around the ring. Wouldn't Gerty have painted all those rings and not just one?

I closed my eyes and leaned my head back against the cell wall. Bad idea. There was a wad of chewed gum on the wall and I came away with it in my hair.

Agitated, I started yanking at the back of my head, tearing out my dreadlocks.

"You trippin' honey?" Leather asked. "You need somethin'?"

"Oh, no thanks, just maybe a lude or a doobie, just something to take the edge off." I jerked at my hair. The irony went past the girls.

"Oh, honey. That ain't somethin' you want to get into. I should know. How do you think we ended up in here?"

"I thought it was for johns."

"Yeah, it was johns that got us all up in that mess."

"What mess?" I got most of the gum out, not interested in what got the girls thrown in the slammer, but they wouldn't stop talking.

"No, Spanky," Leather said, "it wasn't johns. It was Bruno. Don't blame this on the johns."

"Who's Bruno?"

"That's Spanky's pimp," Leather said. She got off the cot and went to a corner where she stood with her arms crossed over her chest. She narrowed her eyes at Spanky and pointed a long nail. "He's why we're in here. Tell her, Spank. He's lettin' us take the rap for his drug business, out there recruiting fresh hooch right this minute, while we're rottin' in this here rat hole."

"Why would he want to drop the dime on you two?" I asked, working the lingo. "Aren't pimps supposed to protect you from stuff like that?"

"Listen, girl, you gonna have to learn a thing or two if you're gonna be in here a while. Don't hand over your career to no pimp. He'll do you wrong." Leather stared at Spanky.

"Take that back, Leather. Bruno's not like that. He's trying to get us out right now. He just needs to get some cash together. And then, when he bails us out, he's going to pay my way to college. He told me so last night."

"Yeah? Zat so. Was that just before we got busted in his meth lab or after?"

The girls were getting steamed. I chimed in to keep the peace.

"I've heard about those things. Those meth labs. What are they?"

"You never tried meth?" Spanky seemed surprised, as if I'd said I'd never tried green beans or something.

"Sorry. It was on my list of things to do. Just never got around to it," I said.

"Well, if you ever need some spending cash, it's a good way to go." Leather brightened. She came back to sit beside Spanky on the cot.

"I tried it, once," Spanky said, running her fingers along her newly plaited hair.

"Methamphetamines?" I asked.

Spanky picked at the polish on her nails. "No. I only do coke. Keeps me awake while I'm doin' the deed."

"Oh, I know how that is," I said, "but you can get it in decaf now."

The girls looked at each other. Leather rolled her eyes.

"I'm not talkin' about sodas, hon," Spanky said. "I'm talking about something with a little more kick. But working the biz wasn't my thing. I tried to have a meth lab once. In my bathroom."

"Real good money," Leather said.

"Yeah, but it stinks like crap," Spanky said.

"No, Spanky, it stinks like rotten eggs or something. You're right. All those chemicals and stuff. It's enough to make you ralph." Leather got bored watching Spanky pick at her nails and dug at the paint chips on the cell wall.

"That's why I couldn't do it. It was putrid. I do have standards," Spanky said. "And then Bruno started his own lab and wanted us to work it for him. We were in his bathroom, all that stink and stuff everywhere, and I was telling him no way was I gonna do that, and that's when the cops come bustin' in. Bruno bailed out the window and me and Leather got tagged."

I was astonished. "You can make the stuff in your personal bathroom?"

"Sure, honey, get everything you need down at the hardware store, pick up a few things at the drugstore, the grocery store. You don't want to buy it all in one place. It's all out there, though," Leather said. She had worked a good-sized scar on the cement-block wall. There were lime-green paint chips all over the cot. She'd probably get an extra ten to twenty for that.

"But how do you know what to get? How to mix it? Aren't you afraid of blowing yourself up or something? How do you get that kind of information?"

Leather laughed. "Same place you get information about building homemade bombs, explosives, poisons, whatever you need."

"Yeah," Spanky said, excited and bouncing. "It's where I found my assault rifle."

"How? Where? From some underground information network or something?" I asked.

The girls chorused, "Off the Internet, baby!"

"Off the Internet!" I whispered, incredulous. "It's that easy? What is this world coming to?"

"Sho' thing, honey. Sho' thing." Spanky slapped away the paint chips and stretched out on our cot. Leather and I had to adjust to give her room. She closed her eyes and said, "It's a boomin' business, lady, 'specially around here. This meth-lab stuff is a way to make a living. If you can get away with it, and if you can stand the reek."

"Where are these labs? Everywhere?" I was breathing fast. Maybe there was something to this thing after all. Maybe Bernard and Gerty had been involved with drugs!

"Just about everywhere. People even make meth labs in cars. Drive them around so the coppers can't track them down. Now I wouldn't do that, myself. The stench! It'll ruin a good Volvo."

"The stench." I said, more to myself than to the girls. Why was that important? Why was this important in the Gerty investigation? With the force of a rogue coffee table ramming into my shins, I had an answer. I jumped to my feet and started shouting through the bars.

"Yoo-hoo! I need to talk to Officer Murphy. Yoo-hoo, anyone!" The police had taken all of my personal effects, so I didn't have a metal cup to run over the bars or anything; I just kept yelling until I got someone's attention. Luckily, it was Mikey who answered my pleas for help. He didn't look happy.

"May. What's all the noise about? You've only been in there two hours."

"Mikey, did you go to the Knickers' house? Did you find the stuff I told you about?"

"Yeah. I bagged it up and sent it to the lab. We'll know about it soon enough. For now we're pretty sure the ballistics will come back matching the gun we found in the trunk of your car. Good news—we've also run a trace on the gun and it was registered to one Bertha Peach." Mike was talking quietly. I don't think it was standard procedure for him to be sharing this information with a perp, but we had a special relationship.

"What? It was Bertha's gun?"

"Yeah. I think it was the stiff's sister-in-law."

"Oh, Mikey, I hate it when you talk that way." I looked hopeful, trying to hide my astonishment at the news about the gun. And another question immediately came to mind. Should I tell Mike the gun had been stolen? Why hadn't she reported the break-in? Well, I hadn't reported a dead body in my trunk, so maybe Bertha and Inez had their reasons. Too bad, though. Now they were in as much trouble as I was. "Still, I guess I'm cleared then, right?" I asked Murphy.

"Soon. We still need to hold you until everything gets worked out. I think your husband's been trying to call you on your cell phone. It's been ringing constantly. Sherman finally turned it off."

"Thank Sherman for me, will ya?" I grumbled, wishing now I'd flooded all the bathrooms. At least this latest about the phone calls was good news. That meant Ted had delivered Horace. Now where was he with the bail money?

Mike looked over at the hookers, who were trying to get his attention by exposing parts of their bodies. He looked uninterested and quietly motioned me closer to the bars. "May. I've got something else. I found the photo. You need to look at this."

Mike held up a black-and-white glossy. I gasped. It was a shot of some kind of civil protest by the looks of it. There were several people clustered around Gerty, who was sitting in front of a bulldozer. Among those present were Bernard (looking embarrassed and holding a beer); the curator, Mr. Bottox; several angry-looking hippie types; and right there in the middle of everything I saw him.

Stanley.

His fist was raised, his mouth open in a snarl, his scrubby face turned toward the camera.

It wasn't the fact that he was there with Gerty. The Peach sisters told me he'd been involved in trying to get them shut down and had called on FETA to help. It was something else I noticed in the photo that caused me to cry out and jump up and down. Mike took a step back.

"I've figured it out! I know who killed Gerty! I know who killed Bernard, and I know why!"

The hookers applauded. "Way to go, girl," Leather said. "Now where's Jimmy Hoffa?"

"Mikey! You've got to get me out of here! I think the Peach sisters are in trouble!"

"What's this about, May? What do you want me to do?" Mike was catching the fever.

"First of all, get my cell phone. Get it now. Hurry!"

"Okay!" Mike rushed away from the cell and through a door. He came back in a flash. "Here, Mrs. List."

I punched numbers and got Ted on the first ring.

"Ted! Why are you still at home? I'm rotting away in this jail cell, and you're at home?"

"I was just on my way, Maybe Baby, just needed a refreshment."

"Fine. Good. Anyway, I needed you to be home."

"You needed me to be home, and you're bustin' my chops because I am?"

"Not now, Ted. Go get that painting I got from Gerty's husband."

"The bad one?"

"Yes. Go. Do you have it yet?"

I heard Ted's footsteps crossing our kitchen tiles. "Got it. How ya holding up, honey?"

"Never mind. Look at the painting. Look at the ring on that guy's finger. Get your glasses or the magnifying glass if you need to. Hurry, Ted."

"Okay, looking."

I got Mike's attention and motioned for him to give me the glossy. He passed it through the bars.

"Now, Ted. What does the ring look like? What can you make out?"

"Not much. Wait. There's something here, it's hard to see, I don't know. It's a . . ."

"My gosh, Ted, what is it?" I stared at the glossy.

"I think it's a cross. Yeah. Looks like a cross. That's all I can make out."

"Eureka!" I screamed, and got another round of applause from the hookers.

"Ted. Get over here and bail me out. I think I've just solved Gerty's murder."

CHAPTER TWENTY-FIVE

"Mikey, get me out of here!" I commanded. "There are some lives at stake and we can't putz around at a time like this."

"Sorry, May. Not until your husband gets here with the bail money. Just sit tight."

"I will not sit tight. And what does that mean, anyway, sit tight? Can a person sit loose?"

"Come on, Mikey," the hookers crooned. "Let her out. She's just a little old lady. She wouldn't hurt a fly."

Mikey looked uncomfortable. He wanted to help. He really did.

"Why am I in here, anyway? The gun wasn't mine, I had no motive to kill Bernard, and there's absolutely no reason why you should be holding me."

Mike rubbed the place between his eyes and said, "Uh, aside from the fact that you had his dead body in the trunk of your car?"

"Hello," Leather said.

I waved Murphy away like he was a fly. "Sheesh, Mike, there are probably lots of dead bodies in people's cars and they don't even know it."

"I wouldn't think so if they're dead."

Exasperated now, I said, "You know what I mean. Now come on. I'm worried about my friends. They're in serious danger."

"I don't know, Mrs. List." Mike looked over his shoulder. "They're working on an arrest warrant right now for Bertha

Peach. I can't exactly let you go spoil that right now."

I pressed my face up to the bars and sweetened the deal. "Listen very carefully. How would you like to be singularly responsible for one of the biggest drug busts in the county? Would that interest you?"

"And how would you know about a thing like that?" Mike narrowed his eyes.

Uh-oh, now I'd probably said too much.

I stepped back and crossed my arms over my chest. "I have my sources." My tone was staunch; no-nonsense. I hoped my shredded dreadlocks didn't take away from my obvious resolve.

Mike didn't budge. Darn. I'd hooked up with a cop with principles.

"Wait," I said. "This is what you do. Go get those lab results. If there's anything on those rags besides the artist's cleaning fluid, you'll let me out, right? That'll prove I know something that you should be taking seriously."

"Deal." Mike looked pleased to take the barter. I know he really did want to give me the benefit of the doubt, but his professional ethics kept him honest. Good boy.

Mikey was gone a long time. I was certain, and worried, that he'd been called away suddenly on a robbery or domestic disturbance. I didn't know it took a while to analyze chemicals. On TV it just took fifteen minutes. When he returned, he looked excited. He had Ted in tow.

"You were right, May!" Mike was ecstatic. He explained it wasn't regular cleaning fluids on the stuff behind Knickers' house. It was something called trichloroethylene.

"Industrial degreaser," Ted explained. He looked as smug and proud as I'd ever seen him. "Good work, May. How did you know?" He paused. "Hey, I like your hair, May!"

I rolled my eyes. "This stuff. This trichlor-whatever is lethal, right?" I squirmed, feeling my suspicions were finally validated.

Mike shoved a key into the lock on my gate, letting me free. He had to shove the prostitutes back in when they threatened to rush him. They protested.

"The lab tech says in large doses it's horribly toxic," he explained. "If you get it on your skin, or breathe it, it can kill ya like that." Mike snapped his fingers. "In small doses it can cause liver damage, headache, nausea, heart problems."

I shuddered.

"I did a quick search on the Internet and found out they use it to clean metal parts or strip paint off airplanes," Ted said.

"Yeah. The kind you might find over at the Air Force base?" I said. We walked and talked.

"Maybe at one time," Ted said, "but I don't think they use it anymore. The information I got was that it was used at places like Boeing. It's strictly controlled, so it would be hard to come by if you don't work with it."

"But," I added, "maybe there's still a stash of it somewhere. And if someone knew about it, they could have access, right?"

"That makes sense." Mike hurried after me. "And another thing. I found a thermos in the garbage can. It looked new, no reason for someone to toss it, so I got it analyzed, too. There were traces of the trike in the thermos. It looks like that's how it was transported to the Knickers' house."

"I was right!" I cried out. "Nobody checks a thermos. If the stuff was controlled, it would be easy to smuggle out of a place like Boeing or the Air Force base. Just fill up the jug and walk through the fence. Past the guards. Somebody brought that stuff to Gerty and killed her with it!"

"We don't exactly know that for sure, yet, Mrs. List, not until the toxicology reports, which I've ordered by the way. I was just getting ready to head over to the lab . . ." Mike was talking, but I was on the move. It felt good to get away from the holding pen. I was practically running. Behind me, the hookers were blowing Officer Murphy wet kisses. I shouted back a goodbye. Pretty nice gals.

We passed Sherman's desk without slowing and I gave him a salute. He looked disappointed that I hadn't been convicted of murder—yet. He tossed an envelope with my personal affects at me and I caught it on the fly.

Still in the lead, I burst through the Harvest PD doors and out into the dark autumn air. It was cold, and Ted threw my coat at me as I skidded to a halt beside Mike's cruiser. It was idling, the exhaust blowing warm plumes into the biting night air.

"Mikey, I need your car."

"Oh, no you don't." Mike shook his head.

"Please. It's really important. I know how to use all the knobs, now, and time is of the essence!"

"Sorry, May. I've got to get to the lab and then up to the Knickers' house and secure the area. Then I have to make some calls to the Hunker Hills police station. You just go home with your husband. Let us take care of the rest."

I was beyond frantic at this point. I couldn't tell Mikey about my feelings that something terrible was going to happen to my friends if I didn't get over there in a hurry; there was no proof. I was going on a hunch, but I was sure they were in danger.

"Fine. I'll just take my own car." I rummaged through my personal property envelope but found no keys. "Where are my keys?"

"We impounded the car. You'll get it back in a couple of days. It did have a body in it, you know . . . it's being processed." Mike looked like he was sorry, but there was nothing more he could do and keep his badge.

"Oh for Pete's sake! Ted. Let's go." I'd have to involve my husband one more time in my investigation. Luckily the Hummer was robust. We'd need that if there was gunplay. Just then his pager went off. Ted checked it.

"Whoops, looks like the twins are ready to make an appearance," he said.

I knew what that meant. I'd have to go with Ted to the hospital. Valuable time would be wasted. I couldn't let that happen.

"Well, Mikey, thanks for everything. I'll let you handle things from now on." I smiled sweetly and took his hands in mine. "You've been a real sport. Now, will you do me a favor? I think I left my life-alert necklace on Sherman's desk. Will you be a doll and get it for me?"

Officer Murphy gazed down into my eyes and patted my shoulder. "Sure, Mrs. List. I'll be right back."

When Mikey went into the police station I pushed Ted toward his Hummer. "Go, Ted, get outta here! You don't want to be around when Mikey comes back."

With that, I spun around, jumped into the driver's seat of Mikey's car and threw it into reverse. The last thing I saw before speeding off down the road was my husband's astonished expression, and a big cloud of exhaust.

I put the hammer down. The Poochie Hooch was better than thirty minutes away doing the speed limit, but remember: I was in a souped-up, super-charged, high-performance police car. I hit switches, toggled doohickeys, and got the lights and sirens going. It was quite gratifying to see cars in front of me scatter to the sides of the road. I drove like a maniac.

I spun tires and careened along the slick roads. Although the snow was gone, rain had started as I left the police station and it was now coming down in sheets.

Were they into drugs? "Everybody I know does drugs," Leather had said. Well, powerful cleaning fluids certainly fell into that category. What was Stanley doing? Smuggling industrial paint stripper from the Air Force base? Had Gerty found out about it? Was that why he killed her? Was he into something much more nefarious? Perhaps operating a spy ring, or maybe organizing his own terrorist cell group right under our noses?

Then I felt a shock like lightning ripping through my nervous system. "Why would he kill Bernard then? And why would he use Bertha's gun to do it? Oh, my gosh. Maybe Bertha did kill Bernard, but why? I felt around for my purse, thinking I might pull over at the nearest grocery store to flip through the data I'd collected. Maybe I'd missed an important clue. I felt around, but couldn't find my purse. Then I remembered. Ted had left it at the sisters' house. Then I had a real moment of panic. If the sisters got hold of my data, they knew of my suspicions and all the things I'd learned. This could be really bad. Now I wasn't sure at all who'd done the killing, or why.

But one thing I knew: this night would be the end of the investigation. I was going to find some answers. I glanced fearfully in the rearview mirror, expecting to see some police cars chasing me down. Apparently, Murphy hadn't reported his cruiser missing yet. He knew where I was going; it wouldn't be hard to find me, so perhaps he was covering for me. Sorry, Mikey. I owe ya big time.

I sped south through Harvest and navigated roads until I finally hit the highway doing about seventy, and headed west like my tail was on fire. I ran two red lights, rounded a corner sideways, and accelerated to eighty. Somehow I'd found the windshield wipers and leaned forward to see around the rain and thumping wiper blades. At the rate I was going, there was barely enough time to get my plan together. What would I do when I got to the Poochie Hooch? Who would I find, and did I really know who to worry about? If Bertha had killed Bernard, then she was working together with Stanley. Inez certainly would be a part of whatever they were doing, and the only other person I knew in the trailer court was Jolene. She seemed woefully ignorant of the things going on around her, poor child, so I didn't think I could count on her for any information or help.

I thought about Jolene, then, thinking perhaps she could be of some help, after all. I could use her place as a safe house. Hadn't she said Stanley had been strangely absent for two days? But then, if Stanley had killed Gerty, she probably would know about that. Oh, my. Everything was falling apart. The only things I knew for sure was that there were two dead bodies; Stanley had spent evenings sitting pretty for Gerty in her studio; Gerty had been having a thing with someone, probably Stanley, who worked at the Air Force base and could access the cleaning fluids that killed Gerty; and Bernard had been shot dead from Bertha's gun. A gun, by the way, she'd said disappeared from the inside of her own bedroom dresser.

But who had put Bernard in the trunk of my car? It hadn't been Bertha. I was certain of that. It could have been Stanley. The shadowy figure racing past me in the middle of the night fit the description. That meant one thing.

Stanley and Bertha were in cahoots!

But still, I was lacking one thing. Motive. Even the curator said there was nothing to gain by inheriting the paintings. Was he lying? Was he, too, a part of this ring of thieves, murderers, and miscreants? And what about FETA? Where did they fit in?

I was running fast, burning up the miles. Before I could sort it all out, I was approaching the town of Hunker Hills. The streets were dark and absent of anything living. The rain and cold had pushed everyone indoors. For now, it was clear sailing because the rain had stopped, giving me a chance to look around. I switched off the windshield wipers and leaned over the steering wheel. I was alone, in Mikey's cop car, in enemy territory, and I was terrified.

Suddenly, I felt a little bit sick.

What in the name of all that's holy are you doing, May Bell?

Shut up, Ted. We're playing this one by ear.

I turned off the lights and siren. I even shut down the police radio. I couldn't understand all the squeaking and squawking on it anyway. I slowed way down, and went toward the Poochie Hooch in stealth mode. My teeth were rattling around in my head, my jaws clenched and pulsing. My hands were practically melded to the steering wheel, I was gripping it so tightly. I took deep breaths. *No one could hear her scream.* Shut up, May Bell. Buck up, girl. You have a case to solve. This is your last chance. Stanley may be getting ready to bolt across the country, and Gerty's ashes will be blowing in the wind by Tuesday. It's now or never.

The Poochie Hooch was on my left as I rolled past it. I looked through my window and gave it the once over. There was a light inside. A soft light, like something you'd keep burning for security. No activity that I could see. It was ominously quiet. I looked toward the Peach house. It, too, was quiet and dark. No lights at all. I took the road toward Stanley's house. To my surprise, there was a large moving truck parked in front of his home, and there was a flurry of activity. A large man walked quickly from the house to the truck carrying a large box. He hopped up into the back of the truck, came out empty-handed, and then went back into the house. It was Stanley, and he was moving out.

I wondered if Jolene knew about this. Since I didn't see her, I doubted it. I moved along, hoping Stanley hadn't seen the cruiser. I pulled a safe distance away and parked alongside an abandoned Oldsmobile. I turned the cruiser off and held surveillance. Stanley continued to move from house to truck carrying boxes, heavy-looking barrels—lots of barrels—a chair, a lamp, a

rug, and some bags. He was in a hurry, jogging back and forth.
I reached again for my purse to write down what was happening. Shucks. I'd forgotten again. My purse was in the Peach
sisters' house. My purse, with my life-alert necklace, a new can
of mace, and my data notebook. I might need that.

Carefully I started the cruiser and pulled around the trailer
park, going out the back way. I circled around and parked under
a crop of trees near the Hooch. I watched the Peach sisters'
house for a while but detected no activity at all. Ted said they
weren't home when he left my purse. I watched a little while
longer. Could Bertha and Inez be caught up in something as
horrible as murder? Well, I couldn't take any chances. But just
the same, if they came to the door, I was ready with a story.

Just picking up my purse, just a quick hello and a how-do-
you-do, and I'll be on my way. Would they buy it? But then,
what was I doing here anyway? At that minute I wasn't quite
sure. But there was only one way to find out what was happening at the Hooch. I got out of the car and started walking toward
the Peach sisters' house, slowly moving, walking on rubber legs,
biting my lips, clutching at the place over my racing heart.

I got to the door of the Peach house and didn't bother to
knock. I took the knob in my hands and turned.

"Hello? Bertha? Inez? It's May. Hello?"

No answer. It was dark in the house, the only light coming
through the dusty windows. And it was very quiet. I stepped
inside and closed the door behind me. My purse should have
been nearby, but it wasn't beside the doorway, it wasn't on the
table, and it wasn't on the counter. I looked around, growing
more fearful. I knew Ted had delivered it; why then was it missing? And why was I so worried about my stupid purse?

Because. Because it held all of my secrets, all of my observations and investigation conclusions, and whoever had my purse
knew what I knew. I was in serious danger. It was time to beat

feet out of there.

And so, there I was. An old woman, washed up as a detective because I can't find my purse. A failure.

I turned to go but stopped short when I heard a soft beseeching plea coming from the bedroom.

The voice was spooky. Enough to straighten my dreadlocks and turn my attractive blond highlights gray again.

"Maaaay," said the voice again.

I swallowed a lot of spit and pressed the thumb side of a fist to my mouth. This held back the scream straining behind my lips.

"Maaaay!" The voice whispered like a cry from the dead.

I took my hand away from my mouth and searched the darkness through eyes wide enough to rival those of Inez. "Gerty? Gerty is that you? Are you trying to contact me?"

"May!" Now the voice was clearly audible. It was Bertha, and she was ticked off, I could tell. What to do? Turn and run? Or go to the voice?

"What do you want, Bertha?"

"May, get in here and untie us, you fool!" Bertha was whispering as loudly as she could without turning it into a shout.

"Oh, my gosh!" I raced toward the bedroom and crashed through the door. There in the glow of a Mickey Mouse nightlight, I found Bertha and Inez on a disheveled bed, bound hand and foot. Inez had a hanky stuffed into her mouth; Bertha had a handkerchief, damp and stretched, hanging around her neck.

"Shhhh! He'll hear you!" Bertha admonished. "Quick. Untie us. Don't turn on the lights. Just feel around. Use the night-light."

I hustled to unleash the girls with shaky hands. "Who did this?" I asked, tugging, pulling, and ripping at the ropes around Bertha's wrists.

"That Stanley. He's the one who's been breaking into our place, and he stole my gun. Lucky he lost it, or he'd-a used it on both of us."

"Why would he do this? What does he want?" I got Bertha free and we worked on Inez. We got her hands untied and moved to her ankles.

"I don't know, exactly, but I knew it was him who stole my gun, because I saw his big fat truck tire tracks in the mud out front, and Jolene made me real suspicious when she said he'd been gone. I think he was the one who might have broken into your car, too, May, that's why he's been gone these two days. I knew, too, when I saw that moving van out front of his place. He's getting ready to head out of here. I marched over to his place and asked him if he'd been poking his nose around my place. That's when he grabbed me and hauled me back here and tied both of us up."

"You've got one thing right, Bertha—I'm pretty sure he stole your gun, and I'm sorry to say he shot Bernard with it."

"Bernie?"

"He's dead. And, unless the cops took him out, he's in the trunk of my car."

Inez bit her knuckles. Well, she tried anyway, but she was still gagged. I reached over and pulled the cloth out of her mouth. "He took your purse, May," she said, "and he went through it. I think he found your notebook in there. He got really mad at what he was reading. What was in your notebook?"

"Never mind that now, we need to find out why he killed Gerty and why he shot Bernard, and we've got to get some really good evidence. I'm guessing we're about ready to have a fleet of cops out front any minute and I don't want Stanley to get away. This might be our only chance to catch him."

"No, please, May, let the cops chase him down. I don't want him touching me ever again!" Inez sobbed and blew her nose on the bedsheets.

"She's right, Inez. We've got to put a stop to all this. Stanley's doin' something, and he knocked off our sister and brother-in-law. It's time for war." Bertha stood up and popped her knuckles.

"I'm thinking Stanley was doing something over at the Air Force base. Maybe some illegal smuggling, or a terrorist plot or something, and Gerty found out about it while they were doing their thing in the studio. I'm guessing that's why he killed her, and he used some of the illegally smuggled stuff to do it with. I do know that whatever killed Gerty wasn't your typical artist's cleaning fluid, and we sure know she didn't die of a heart attack. There's no question about what killed Bernard. Poor thing."

"Well, you've got it all figured out, haven't you?" Stanley stood in the doorway.

Inez screamed and crawled under the covers.

Bertha lifted her fists and crouched unsteadily on the bed.

I didn't say a thing. I was trying too hard not to throw up.

Chapter Twenty-Six

"You shouldn't be so nosy," Stanley said.

His voice came to me through the darkness, and I turned to see his shadow. Although it was impossible to identify the face, the smell of him was unmistakable. Thick, cloying, the reek of sweat and sour dirt, in a mix of stench like I'd never experienced before.

Stanley had a gun in his hand. He held it at his waist. "I could always count on the rats to tell me when someone came or went around here."

I was momentarily confused, until I noted the loud barking and general commotion coming from the kennels next door. I hadn't paid attention to the noise before, caught in a moment of severe panic. Now, though, I could see how they were a perfect alarm system. It was apparent, in the way Stanley confidently addressed us, without a hint of apprehension, that he hadn't noticed the police car parked out under the trees. Maybe I could bluff.

"Stanley, you might want to put that away. I've called the cops and they're on their way. In fact, I think I saw a police car pull up outside. Why don't you take a look?"

Stanley paused for a minute, and I thought I heard him smile. "I don't think so," he said. "I disconnected the phone line. Now how would you call the police?"

"Haven't you ever heard of cell phones? Hmm?" I was trying to be brave.

"Hand it over." Stanley made a move toward me.

"My phone?" Oh, great. Me and my big mouth.

"Give it up, lady, or would you like me to frisk ya?"

Inez peeked out from under the covers. "Give it to him, May—you don't want him to frisk you. It's awful, horrible, those big hands—just give it to him."

I gave Stanley my cell phone. Shoot. Dumb me. Just then it rang.

Stanley stuck it in his pocket, muffling the sound.

"Now you've gone and spoiled everything," he said. "A few more minutes and I'd be long gone. Bertha here would be arrested for killing Bernard, and I'd be in the clear. But you really messed everything up."

I wasn't going to let him bully me, even though he had a gun and he had killed twice that I was pretty sure of. "That's stupid, Stanley, don't you think? How were you going to explain the fact that Bertha and Inez were left tied up in their bed? Not to mention, you've left all kinds of forensic evidence everywhere. Fingerprints, footprints, probably some fibers, DNA, all sorts of stuff the police could use."

"Not if I burned the place to the ground."

I laced my fingers to steady the shaking of my hands. "Not a smart move, my friend, because naturally that would qualify as arson, and you'd probably want to use accelerants for that kind of thing, which a good arson investigator could detect if he's worth his salt at all . . ." What was I saying? Burn the place to the ground? Stanley was already collecting the ropes again. Bertha and Inez, and May makes three.

"I hate to use a good traceable bullet when a nice little fire will do," Stanley said. "Now hold out your hands, lady. I'm sure the FETA crowd will give you a good memorial service and might even plant a tree in your honor. That is, if you really work with FETA."

"I think you know I don't." I felt miserable. He'd read all of my data, and my cover was blown.

"No. I didn't think so, since I've been a part of the local group for about two years now."

"Of course," I said.

"Which made me wonder what you were doing asking questions and hanging around here. Jolene told me she'd seen you in here, too. Since Bertha and Inez didn't exactly have a great relationship with their sister, I found that pretty odd."

Stanley stuck his gun in his belt and wrapped the rope around my wrists. He was rough and quick about it.

"Have you told Jolene you're skipping town?" I asked, wincing against the pain. I wanted to stall for time. It looked like we were doomed if Mikey didn't get his partners moving pretty soon. A crispy little fire.

"Ah, I think I'll let her get her beauty rest. Wouldn't want to rock the boat, you know." Bernard finished tying the knots, stood back, and flipped on the light by Bertha's bed. I could see him clearly now, a terrifying vision. He narrowed his eyes, seemed to be thinking of his next move, and scratched his chest hairs. They were poking out of the top of his stained T-shirt. He scratched, round and round, like he'd done before. I could clearly see the ring this time. No doubt about it.

"You're not going to get away with this, Stanley." Bertha's jaws pulsed. Her face was crimson.

"No way, Stanley. I've already told the police what you're up to. They know all about your smuggling business."

Stanley laughed a loud roar. "My what?"

"Don't try to deny it. All those barrels I saw you loading onto your truck. Stuff from the Air Force base. What are you up to, Stanley? Are you a terrorist or something?"

"A terrorist?" Again Stanley laughed hard, ending in a wheezing cough. He pulled a cigarette from his pants pocket and lit up.

"Give me a break, lady." Stanley moved around the bedroom piling up papers, books, clothes, and other burnables. It looked like he was serious about the inferno plans.

"The cops have already done tests on the stuff you used to kill Gerty. Since you just admitted to shooting Bernard, it's not much of a leap to guess you knocked her off, too."

Stanley wadded and smashed paper bags in a corner. Ash from his cigarette drifted down on the tinder. I recoiled, preparing for the whole place to go up in a scorching blaze. The embers cooled and did nothing more than leave an ashy trail on the Peach house floor.

"Well, yes, I did kill Gerty," Stanley said calmly.

Inez peeked out from under the covers again. "Why did you do that, Stanley? Why? I ask ya, why?" She was sniveling and her nose began to run. With her hands tied, all she could do was sniff. She lifted a bony shoulder and wiped her nose on her shirt. "Why did you kill my sister?"

"She was getting in my way."

"I thought you two were an item. It was you she was painting in her studio, wasn't it?" I asked.

Stanley raised his eyebrows and paused. "Pretty good, lady, how'd you figure that one out?"

"You shouldn't wear any incriminating jewelry when getting your portrait painted, buster, especially not when you're planning to kill the artist."

"Good one, May. Real good." Bertha pursed her lips. "Why would you want to kill my sister when you two were having rolls in the hay, Stan? Hmmm?"

"She was just an end to my means." Stanley laughed again at his sick joke. Then he sobered. "Should have taken that painting, but there just wasn't time. But it doesn't really matter now, does it?" Stanley flicked his lighter close to Inez' face. She recoiled, turned pale, and her eyes rolled up into her head. I didn't need her to pass out on us if we were going to make it out of this situation alive. I nudged her strongly and she came around.

"Let me get this straight, Stanley—you two were involved in FETA together. You don't look the type, if you'll pardon me for saying, so what was your gig?"

"Think about it, woman. With FETA behind her, she was going to get this dog place shut down. Now, that wouldn't do at all. Not with the protection it gave me and my little operation over there." Stanley jerked his head in the direction of his trailer. "I kept her distracted for a while, got her painting me when she could have been demonstrating against her sisters here, watched her every move like a hawk. Eventually, she got those papers together and it was time for me to make my move."

"What papers, Stanley? Whatcha talkin' about?" Bertha squirmed. She wrenched her wrists around, struggling against her bindings.

"Shut up. I'm done talkin'." Stanley abruptly stomped out of the bedroom. I could hear him messing things up pretty good in the rest of the Peach house. And after a few minutes, the front door slammed shut. He was gone, probably to get some of those accelerants I so generously suggested to him.

I went into action. "Quickly now, girls. Buddy up. Get these ropes off unless you want to be crispy critters!" We jockeyed around and tugged at the ropes. Stanley had done a good job making our escape appear impossible. Inez kept sniffing and whimpering, but she pulled and tugged for all she was worth. Then she paused, sat up like she'd been struck by lightning, and cried, "Move over! Let me get my teeth at those ropes!"

"Good thinking, Inez!" Bertha cried, and after some maneuvering, she got her wrists up to Inez' mouth. Inez chewed and gnawed, putting those splayed teeth to the test. It was amazing. Her teeth worked like tiny fingers, and within seconds, Bertha was free.

In a feverish pitch, Bertha worked at my ropes, and then together we untied Inez. Stanley had been gone mere minutes, but it felt like hours. He would be back any second, and we had to move fast.

"Quick!" I cried. "I parked a police car out there. We've got to get to the car and radio for help!"

"You stoled a police car?" Inez was incredulous.

"Just borrowed. And I can't understand for the life of me why Officer Murphy hasn't sent backup. Where are they?" I poked my head out the bedroom door, checking to see if the coast was clear.

The front door opened with a loud crash.

Bertha, Inez, and I grabbed each other. "He's back!" Inez whispered.

"Out the window. Quick now." Bertha grabbed Inez by the sleeve and pushed her onto the bed. Together they shoved open a small window over their bed. "We gotta shimmy on through. You first, May Bell, you're most athletic. Then you help Inez through on the other side."

In the other room Stanley was sloshing something around. The metallic clank was that of what I imagined to be a gasoline can striking trinkets, aluminum table, everything the girls possessed. The sound of liquid was followed by a distinct smell. It was gasoline all right.

"Hurry up, May!" Bertha cried, pointing to the window.

What? No trellis? I bounced a couple of times on the bed and vaulted toward the window. I balanced on its sill, resting on my stomach. My top hung out the front while the rest of me stayed behind.

"Rock like a seal, May Bell, rock!" Bertha shoved my

backside, and I rocked, edged out inch by inch, and went over headfirst into a tangle of bushes, leaving a little of my skin on the window ledge. Inez was much more limber and she landed beside me with little effort. Bertha, on the other hand, huffed and puffed, grunted and squirmed, and in the moonlight I saw the agony on her face.

"I think she's stuck!" Inez said. She jumped up and grabbed her sister's hands. I pulled Inez by the belt, and in a rush, Bertha was free. She hurtled down toward us. I'm sorry to say I wasn't as kind as Mr. Fitz, and stepped aside when Bertha made her landing.

"Run girls! Get to the car!" I took the lead and pulled Inez behind me. The trees were about thirty yards away and in the dark we had to lift our feet extra high in order to avoid tripping over things we couldn't see. I glanced back to see Bertha and Inez running as if they were navigating an obstacle course. Knees high, elbows pumping. We were making good time. Luckily, Stanley hadn't frisked me after all, and I still had the cruiser keys in my pocket.

We skidded up to the side of the cruiser and just as I had the key in the lock Bertha grabbed me. "Look! Oh, my gosh, he's going into the Hooch with a gas can! Our doggies!" She spun and ran back to the Hooch with Inez on her heels. I found a burst of energy and tackled both girls in a flying maneuver. We hit the ground and stayed there.

"Don't move. He doesn't know we're gone yet. It looks like he's getting ready to torch the Hooch, too."

Inez took a very long breath, and then began sobbing, her face close to the mud and cold weeds. "He's going to kill our babies!"

"I won't stand for that, May. Now let me go." Bertha was doing a low crawl and I wrapped my hands around her feet to hold her back.

"Wait a minute. He's going back to his house without the can. Probably to get some more gasoline." I shouldn't have said that. Inez wailed.

I was moved by Inez and her distress. "Okay. You're right," I said. "We've got to stop this, and now." I got up on my knees. I'd given up on Mikey—and what in the heck was he doing, anyway? "Quick. While he's in his house. We'll ambush him. I glanced quickly at the cruiser. There was a shot gun in there; it could be useful. But there just wasn't time. Stanley was on the move."

We scrambled to our feet. Bertha moved like a bulldozer. She pumped her beefy arms and chugged her muscled hams, leaving Inez and me behind. She crossed the distance between the police car and Stanley's house in about eight seconds. I guessed the distance to be a good fifty yards, so she was tearing up the turf, not even caring if she tripped or what she stepped on. She got to Stanley's open front door, leapt through, and with a primordial scream, I heard her attack.

Strike that. I think it was Stanley's primordial scream I heard. Bertha was doing something to him, and I wasn't sure I wanted to see firsthand, but, steeling my courage, I bounded up the steps to his house and caught up with her as she put a sleeper hold on big bad Stanley. He was a good six inches taller than the rotund woman, but that didn't deter her. She had him bent backwards, his neck encased in her Tweetie arm, a vice grip of fury.

"You gonna steal my gun, kill my sister, kill Bernie, torch us, and murder my dogs? I don't think so! I'll tear you limb from limb first!" Bertha squeezed. Stanley's mouth opened wide, searching for air. His eyes bulged. He clawed at Bertha's forearms to no avail.

"Hold him, Bertha, hold him!" Inez panted, winded from the sprint, but she had recovered well and now jumped up and down in Stanley's living room. She clapped her hands.

It was clear to see Bertha was losing her strength. Stanley was a big dude, and he writhed around trying to wrest himself free from Bertha's murderous pinion. They danced back and forth across the living room. Bertha squeezed more tightly, but the sweat beading on her upper lip told me she was getting tired. Inez tried to be helpful. She fell to her knees and wrapped her arms around Stanley's ankles. This only caused Stanley to lose his balance and the trio tumbled onto the floor. Quickly, both sisters jumped on Stanley and a wrestling match ensued. I couldn't stand there doing nothing, so I got to the floor as well, and joined the fracas.

"We're losing him, we're losing him!" Bertha screamed out when Stanley bucked Inez off and tossed me aside like a rag doll. I took an elbow to the cheek and watched the sparks fly. Luckily it was Inez' elbow and not Stanley's, so it wasn't too bad. Again we dove onto Stanley's wide back. Inez rode him rodeo-style before being thrown again. She came down hard on her hip. I winced when I heard bone hit floor. Bertha had her mouth open to bite Stanley on the ear when we heard the sirens.

Everything stopped.

I mentally counted the warbles and thought there must be five or six cop cars converging on the Hooch as we tussled there on the floor of Stanley's trailer. The hesitation was all Stanley needed to give a tremendous heave, tossing all of us aside. He jumped to his feet and raced out the door.

Bertha screamed profanities and tried to follow but got tangled in Inez' legs and went down again.

I sat on the floor sucking wind. "Never mind, Bertha. The police are here. Let them get him. We're fine, the Hooch is okay, so we'll be okay."

Stanley's pickup started; I heard him gun the engine, heard tires spin in the mud. He was getting away, but the police would follow him, and all this would be cleared up soon enough. I was just too tired to do anything more than get to my feet, dust myself off, and have a look around Stanley's place.

It was nearly empty, with the exception of a few boxes and some miscellaneous household items. There was one barrel left, something like I'd seen Stanley load onto the moving truck. Whatever was in those barrels were still on his truck. Plenty of evidence for the police. I walked over to the barrel just to take a peek and recoiled.

"Look!" Bertha was at the door. "Stanley's stuck in the mud!" She crowed with laughter. Inez rushed to her side and both sisters screamed in hilarity. "He's stuck in the mud! Look at that, May, the police have him surrounded! He's not getting out of the truck! They've got their guns out and everything. Think we should go help?"

"No. Stay low. We've got enough evidence here to put him away for a very long time. And," I said feeling smug, "I know why Stanley needed to kill Gerty."

CHAPTER TWENTY-SEVEN

Outside the temperature was downright frigid. Rain was swirling in drizzles again, flattening my dreadlocks, adding more dampness to the mud on my clothes. I met Mikey near the truck and led him back to Stanley's trailer.

"Right this way, Mikey. There's something here I'm sure you and your buddies will be interested in.

I ushered Mikey into Stanley's house.

"Look around. If you know your drugs, I'm sure you'll agree with me that Stanley there was running a lucrative little meth-lab business right here in his house." I didn't tell Mikey I'd gleaned my education from his prostitutes. I might need their help again, and I was fairly certain he'd keep us separated if we had the opportunity to be incarcerated together in the future.

I gave Mikey the tour. He'd suspected Stanley was up to something when the fingerprints on the thermos proved to be those of our beefy friend, but Mikey didn't know about the meth.

"What took you so long getting here, anyway?" I narrowed my eyes at Mike, who blushed.

"Sherman gave me a letter of reprimand because you stole my car again. Then we had to process the body. There was a lot of paperwork."

"Sheesh, Mikey, you'd think he had better things to do. Anyway, just look around. Don't mess with anything. It's a crime scene and all."

Mike gave me a look that said, "I know what I'm doing," but I think I might have scored a few points there just the same. Showing him I knew my crime investigation stuff.

While Mikey took the tour, the boys in blue were reading Stanley the riot act. This wasn't an easy thing to do, because the sirens had alerted Jolene, who came out of her bed in flannel shorts and braless T-shirt, and she was reading Stanley a riot act of her own. She kept getting in the way of the shakedown. She wasn't too happy to learn Stanley had planned to run out on her. She kept smacking him on the head until one of the cops grabbed her in an embrace. That calmed her down quite a bit. I think she found a new boyfriend.

A group of other residents came out to see what was happening. Two mulleted guys in cutoff jeans rolled out a keg of beer, three women unfolded plastic webbed chairs, and they all settled in to watch the show.

Back in Stanley's house Mikey came from the back, shaking his head. "I don't know how you did it, Mrs. List . . ."

I couldn't help but smile. "Remember that picture you showed me of the FETA demonstration? The one with Stanley and Gerty? It was the clue I needed to solve this here case," I said with confidence, although it wasn't altogether true. I'd only figured it all out when I noticed Stanley's chemical-lab stuff packed up and ready to go. "Stanley was in cahoots with Gerty."

Mike looked at me quizzically, happy to leave the ranting Jolene and the Stanley arrest to his buddies.

"Why would he get involved with Gerty and her FETA crew?"

"Yeah, May, why would he do that?" Ted echoed. He walked into the trailer and I frowned at him. "You're walking on evidence, Ted. What are you doing here, anyway?"

"I couldn't get you on your cell. Figured something was up the way you tore out of the police station. Sorry I didn't get here sooner but I got a call from the hospital. False alarm, as it were."

"Fine, just don't walk on anything," I huffed, protecting my investigation.

"So, why was Stanley into that FETA stuff?" Mikey asked again.

"Doesn't seem to be pertinent," Ted added.

"Come on, guys, do I have to draw you a map? Bubba wanted to pretend he was interested. He needed to keep an eye on Gerty so he could find out how close she was to getting the Hooch closed. If she succeeded, it would mean curtains for his drug business. He wouldn't have a cover anymore. The stench of the drug business, he blamed on the dogs. They were also perfect as an alarm system if anyone came around. Just before Gerty died, she had filed the final papers. That's when he decided it was time to kill her."

"Amazing," Ted said.

"And, when I was at the Knickers' house, I noticed some hair under the chair in the studio. Gerty didn't have any animals in the house. That same hair I noticed in my purse."

Ted looked confused.

"It's a long story, Ted, but I had the Peach sisters' ferret in my purse a couple of times, and it was the same kind of fur. Same texture, same color, everything. That meant whoever left the fur there had been in the Peach sisters' house."

Ted still looked confused. "You had a ferret in your purse?"

"Just take my word for it."

"Sherman's rat." Mike was getting it.

"Sorry about that, but it's taken care of," I said to Mike. And then to Ted, "You did drop my purse off at the sisters' house like I asked, didn't you?"

"Yeah." Ted's brow was criss-crossed. "They weren't home—I just left it inside their door."

"It wasn't locked?" I sighed. The girls should have been more careful. But then I remembered, they'd been tied up in the back when Ted dropped off the purse. Stanley probably found my purse and read all of my incriminating details. He would have found me eventually, even if I hadn't made it easy for him by showing up unannounced. Stupid me.

"Okay. Here's what I think. Stanley takes home some of the cleaning fluids from the Air Force base. He's cozied up to Gerty; he even visits her for sittings at her house. He's been snooping around in the Peach sisters' place, too, where he stole their gun as a backup, to pin it on them if he had to do any shooting, which, by the way, he did, as you very well know.

"Anyway, he gets some of that fur on his things and leaves it, without even knowing, at Gerty's house when he goes over there for one more late-night sitting. He has the chemicals. Everything is going as planned—they're playing hanky-panky, and he's looking for the right moment. But unexpectedly, Bernard catches them. Stanley takes off in a hurry and Bernard has a fight with Gerty. He locks her in the studio.

"This works great for Stanley. He sneaks back into the house, finds the key to the studio, and opens the chemicals. He holds Gerty down over the degreaser, and in no time she's a goner. Even gets some of that chemical stuff on one of her brushes and puts it up her nose for good measure. He knows Bernard will get nervous. Poor Bern will think he's to blame and won't press for an investigation. So Stanley puts the key back over the door, turns off the ventilation system, and takes off. And he almost got away with it. He figures with Gerty out of the way, the Hooch will stay open a little longer. More time to run his little business."

"But you took the painting home. He needed that painting after you started asking questions, poking around at the curator's and stuff." Ted frowned. "But he couldn't have known you had the painting in the car. You just assumed that. He was busy putting Bernard in your car."

"Right." Then I gasped. "I'll bet he was going to break into our house after that, to get the painting! It's just lucky I stopped that little plan—who knows? We might have been killed!"

"I don't think so, May. If he killed us, there wouldn't be any explanation for Bernard being in the trunk of your car."

"True, true. He had to get Bernard into my car. Scratch the painting idea."

And then I was struck with another thought. "You know what? I went to see the curator, and he left right after in a mighty big hurry. I'm wondering if he wasn't hanging out with Stanley, too, and maybe, just maybe, he hung on to some of those paintings of Gerty's. Do you think they could have been worth more than he thought? Could he have called Stanley to tip him off?"

"We'll look into that for you," Mikey said. "He might not have had anything to do with the murders, but if he's holding back some of Gerty's paintings we can get him for something."

"Grand larceny perhaps?" I asked.

"That might be it." Mikey nodded. "But why would Stanley kill Bernard? Not for the paintings, I wouldn't think."

"I'm guessing Stanley knew I was getting suspicious, and the Peach sisters were getting suspicious, and what better way to get us out of the way than to get all of us locked up for Bernard's murder? Me for having the body in the back of my car, them for having the gun that killed him."

I looked at Mikey. "And with us out of the way he could waltz into my house any old time and make off with the painting. Ted wouldn't have been a problem because he's at work all the time."

Mike nodded. "Even if we couldn't pin it on you, your incarceration would give him some time to get out of town, wouldn't it?"

"Yeah. While the Peach sisters had their Hooch open, there wouldn't be any suspicion about the smell coming from his place. Everyone would just assume it was from the Hooch. Also, he said something about the noise. The dogs would tip him off if anyone was poking around. Perfect cover. He has his own gun, by the way, and wasn't afraid to use it if it came down to that."

"Right," Mike said. He looked anxiously toward his buddies, but they were patting Stanley down. Jolene was subdued; the kegger was in full swing. They'd even brought out a boom box and Metallica was providing the accompaniment.

"May." Ted put his arm around my shoulders. "How do you think Stanley got the trike up to Gerty's?"

"He wasn't riding a trike. He probably parked his car down the road."

"No, May, that's short for trichloroethylene," Murphy explained.

"Oh. Well, I don't know. Also, I don't know how he managed to kill her with it without passing out himself if it's as toxic as you say." I looked at Mikey, who immediately snapped his fingers.

"Remember what you said about the thermos?"

"It all makes sense," I said. "He carries it out of his workplace in his thermos. Perfect. He had to know how to handle the stuff and probably kept some kind of chemical gear with him when he went into the studio."

"I didn't find any of that stuff."

"Not surprising. He would have taken it with him. Look for some of that stuff in the moving van. He missed the thermos, though. Probably didn't think anyone would take a second look."

"Unless someone wanted a cup of coffee," Ted added.

"Now, Mikey, you just get your boys in here and have a look

around. You'll find everything you need to make a solid arrest for murder, drugs, general malfeasance. Just go ahead now." I waved my fingers at Officer Murphy.

"May, I can't do any of that without a search warrant," Murphy, the good cop, said.

"Search what? It's all here! Criminitly, Mikey! What about probable cause or something like that? Can't you use some of your police stuff here?"

"This is true. It's all out in the open here, but don't forget this isn't my jurisdiction. I'm only here with my buddies because you stole my car."

My fists beat against Mike's shoulder. "Well call the Hunker police, for crying out loud! Get them over here! Make the arrests and seize the evidence!"

Murphy smiled. "I'll take care of it. And May?"

"Yes?"

"Ya done good, ma'am. Ya done real good."

"Oh, Mikey, I didn't even think. If we get Hunker PD involved, you won't get credit for the collar!"

"Don't worry about that. I'll provide backup if they need me. We don't want to mess this up. If we do, I can kiss my badge goodbye. Sherman's gunning for me as it is."

I smiled up at Mikey. "So you finally believe me? You believe Gerty was murdered?"

"Of course we believe you!" Ted hollered. "You got the civilian award of the year, didn't you?"

"Remind me to give that back to you when all this is done," Murphy said.

Oh, I just prayed I was right about all of this. If I was wrong, it was more jail time for me. At least I knew my roommates.

CHAPTER TWENTY-EIGHT

When I wandered outside, my hand in Ted's, I saw Sherman with the other cops. I guess he did get out once in awhile, after all. He leaned against the front of Mikey's stolen cruiser, sucking on a fat cigar. When he saw me, his face clouded.

"Pretty good bust, huh Sherm?" I asked, not resisting the urge to jut my chin in his direction ever so slightly. I was quite proud.

"We ain't done here, yet," he said, and intimated there was lots of paperwork to follow. "I think I'll just have a look-see myself. Maybe you missed something."

Sherman pushed away from the cruiser and lumbered toward the Peach sisters' house. The dogs were still raising Cain, but Bertha and Inez had gone to the Hooch to calm them. The drizzle had started again and the mud on my clothes slid down and plopped off in clumps around my shoes. I looked up at Ted, and he touched my face, pushing away a strand of hair.

"What now?" he asked.

Before I could tell him about my desire for a hot bath and a foot massage, a great thundering boom rattled the windshield in Mikey's cruiser.

"What the . . ." Ted looked toward the Peach house.

I looked toward the Peach house in time to see Sherman explode through the door like he'd been launched from a cannon. A blast of air had propelled him, followed by a fireball. He flew head over heels, somersaulted across the lawn, and came up running, and screaming, "I'm concussed! I'm concussed!" Sherman raced around the yard in circles, still screaming out, "I'm concussed! Can I get a hand here?" His clothes were smoldering, and the back of his hair was singed.

"Oh, my gosh," I said. "He was smoking that stogie and set off the accelerants." I shouted toward the group of trailer park partiers. "Hey you! Give Sherman a hand, will ya?" All the rednecks stood and applauded.

I turned to Ted and grabbed his lapels. "We've got to get the sisters out of the Hooch! It's full of gasoline and if that fire moves, they'll be killed!"

Two thunderous booms came in quick succession, knocking Ted and me to our knees. "It's too hot, May! Too risky!" Ted sheltered me with an arm around my shoulders.

The police officers grappled, tripped over one another, and dragged Stanley away from the flames. The kegger group hooted, tossed a beer to Sherman (who, by the way, was still running in a tight circle, but he caught the beer on the fly, popped the top, and kept moving), and dragged their keg back a few feet, after which they settled in again. This was getting to be one hellacious party.

"We've got to get the sisters out of there, Ted! Damn the risk!" I wrestled free from Ted and found a burst of energy. I saw Mikey up ahead—and he saw me. I was moving at full speed, and although he was moving left and right with his arms outstretched, I ran through him like a linebacker. He spun around, fell into a three-point stance, got his balance, and then was up again, racing after me. The smoke and loud pops echoed, dangerously close, but I was on a mission.

The fire had started to move. An explosion blew a couch cushion toward the Hooch and burned with fury. Fingers of accelerant ran up the Hooch steps and the fire followed. I barreled through smoke, felt my eyes sting and my face burn with the heat, but kept moving.

When I got to the Hooch, Bertha and Inez were in a panic, throwing open cages, releasing the hounds. Naked, bald dogs yapped and ran willy-nilly, unsure of what to do with their new-found freedom.

"We've got to get them out of here, May!" Bertha screamed.

"There isn't time! The fire is on your porch and this place is full of gasoline. It's gonna blow!"

"We ain't leaving without our puppies." Inez gave me a hard look.

"Give 'em here, hurry!" I reached toward Inez, who started handing me little squirming doggies. I shoved them down the front of my blouse as quickly as I could.

"The front of the Hooch is on fire!" Inez hollered, her eyes wide as dinner plates. "Get everyone out the back door!"

The fire roiled and expanded, a living, breathing monster. It burned the floors and licked at the pictures of Lucky and Prince and Trixie. It was close, devouring everything in its path. Black smoke curled up to the ceiling, making us cough and gag. The heat threatened to blister my skin. Closer now. Bertha and Inez and I worked in a fury, opening cages and tossing dogs toward the back door.

I could hear Ted and Mikey shouting from the front to get out. It was too hot for them to come through, and I'm sure, now, they probably thought we were doomed.

The dogs were on the run, racing out the back door without any added prompting. We'd have to round them up later, but at least they were safe.

"Let's go!" I screamed. "They're all out! Come on!"

Bertha, Inez, and I barreled out the back way and found a safe place several yards away, just in time to see their house and the Hooch go up in a torch of yellow flame.

Inez leaned her head back and wailed. "Oh, May! Oh,

May, how horrid!"

I patted Inez on the back. "We got all the dogs, and you can rebuild with the insurance. At least you're safe and unharmed. That's what matters." What else do you say in a time like this? And I was serious. They were safe.

"I don't care about our place, that's not it. Horace was in our house! Ahhhh!" Inez let the tears flow.

Sad, indeed. Poor little Horace was a goner. Every time another explosion popped I half expected to see the ferret fly across the parking lot.

The tiny dogs writhed under my shirt. I needed to find a place for them, and what better comfy place than Mikey's cruiser?

I smiled when Ted and Mikey came running, their faces showing both concern and relief that we were okay. I kissed Ted and hugged Mikey. Bertha and Inez ran off to round up their dogs after stopping for a cup of refreshment at the keg.

All emergency units from the Hunker town showed up. Fire trucks, ambulance, police cars; it was a busy time. The ambulance crew was working over Sherman, who kept convulsing. I'd had a little bit of emergency training and joined Ted in what was becoming a group attempt to administer first aid.

"Get away from me!" Sherman roared. "I don't need medical help—I've got this rat up my pant leg. It's chewing on my kneecap!"

"Bertha! Inez!" I yelled for them. Excited to share good news, I told them their ferret was safe and sound in Sherman's pants.

The fire crew poured water on the fire and eventually got it down to a red pile of rubble. The kegger group hustled up with wieners on coat hangers and their party continued. Jolene exchanged her phone number with the cop who'd kept her under control. Most of the Harvest police force left for other crimes, and Mikey turned over the meth-lab investigation to the Hunker detectives, who hauled Stanley off to lockup.

I told the Peach sisters they could stay at my house until they got some insurance money and found a new place to live. They were successful in rounding up the dogs, and had them sequestered in Mikey's cruiser.

Reluctantly, I handed over my litter of puppies. The last one, though, I held onto for a minute.

"Oh, it's looking at me," I said to Inez, who clasped her hands in glee.

"Isn't he sweet, May? He wants you to take him home."

I looked at the puppy, who was, indeed, gazing at me with the most darling expression I've ever seen. I felt my heart grow a couple of sizes. "Do you think I could?" I looked at Ted, who grinned.

"Trixie will hate you."

"So what's new?" I asked.

Inez gently took the puppy from me and I reluctantly let him go. "He'll need a few more weeks, yet, May, and then you can have him. Don't worry about payin'. He's our way of sayin' thanks."

To tell you the truth, I was sad to let him go. I wanted to keep him tucked under my chin all the way home.

"Just a couple of weeks, right? No longer than that."

"He's yours, May."

"Where will you stay? Are you going to come to our house?"

"Nah," Bertha said, stroking the chin of the mom dog. "I think we'll just go on up to Gerty's house. It's ours now, anyway. It was part of her will. It's kinda sad, but she never had time to change it. Would have been nice to tell her thanks."

"I'm happy you have somewhere to go," I said gently, giving Bertha a hug, and then Inez, somewhat relieved, since I hadn't thought about the dogs when I invited them to stay with us.

Trixie might have been able to handle one, but a whole pack would have pushed her right over the edge.

Mikey was off duty and offered to take the sisters and their horde to Gerty's house. Bertha reached down Sherman's pants and grabbed Horace. Sherman was yelling at Mikey about paperwork, but Officer Murphy ignored him and started his car.

"Do your own paperwork. I've got real police business to take care of."

With that, Ted and I waved at the cruiser as it pulled away, the faces of Bertha, Inez, and fifteen little dogs in the windows.

It took a few days, but everything was sorted out. Stanley was accused of a dozen crimes. Bertha and Inez moved into Gerty's house with Horace, and with their insurance money they built a state-of-the-art kennel in an area where the smell and noise bothers no one. Inez got braces put on her teeth, dyed her hair, and bought a new wardrobe. Bertha got a new tattoo.

The curator admitted he had one of Gerty's better paintings and had planned to sell it to Stanley for quite a bit of money. Apparently, it was a portrait of Stanley, much more impressive than the one I had, since he was painted in the buff. The sisters decided not to press charges. The curator and Bertha are now dating. Mr. Bottox is allowed to eat crackers or anything else he wants in bed, but Bertha vows not to share his sheets until she gets a wedding ring.

Sherman has been demoted to dispatch. He now has a nervous twitch, making it too dangerous for him to carry a weapon.

Ted is back delivering babies, and I have a new addition to my family, a tiny little bald dog by the name of Torch. Trixie went on a fast to protest. That lasted two hours.

Jolene is still dating the cop; Gerty was cremated and laid to rest beside Bernard. Mr. Fitz organized a neighborhood watch program. Ted is taking Pilates. Mikey is on special assignment in vice and I've already put in my paperwork to help him on his rounds. He thinks I might make a good decoy. Leather and Spanky are giving me lessons.

Now where did I put that bustier?

ABOUT THE AUTHOR

T. Dawn Richard lives north of Spokane, Washington, with her husband, children, two hairless dogs, and one hairy cat. Years spent in the military, first on active duty as an Army medic and Russian linguist, followed by her marriage to an Air Force pilot, has taken her around the globe. Retirement has now offered Dawn the opportunity to return home to the Northwest, where she is a full-time writer and occasional teacher of creative writing. She participates in the police/civilian ride-along programs, but to this date she has made no citizen's arrests. Visit her website at www.tdawnrichard.com.